Robert Rankin is an unrepentant Luddite, who stubbornly refuses to buy a word processor and still writes his novels longhand, in exercise books. His distrust of computers and all things electronic borders on the manic, and he surrounds himself with Victorian curiosities and a circle of friends only slightly less weird than himself. What his wife has to say about all of this is anyone's guess. His previous novels include The Brentford Trilogy, The Armageddon Quartet, and, his most recent, *The Brentford Chainstore Massacre*. His latest novel, *Apocalypso*, is now available as a Doubleday hardback.

What they say about Robert Rankin:

'One of the rare guys who can always make me laugh'
Terry Pratchett

'To the top-selling ranks of humorists such as Douglas Adams and Terry Pratchett, let us welcome Mr Rankin'
Tom Hutchinson, *The Times*

'A born writer with a taste for the occult. Robert Rankin is to Brentford what William Faulkner was to Yoknaptawpha County'
Time Out

'One of the finest living comic writers . . . a sort of drinking man's H. G. Wells'
Midweek

D0718776

Also by Robert Rankin

ARMAGEDDON: THE MUSICAL

THEY CAME AND ATE US, ARMAGEDDON II: THE B MOVIE

THE SUBURBAN BOOK OF THE DEAD,
ARMAGEDDON III: THE REMAKE

THE ANTIPOPE

THE BRENTFORD TRIANGLE

EAST OF EALING

THE SPROUTS OF WRATH

THE BOOK OF ULTIMATE TRUTHS

RAIDERS OF THE LOST CAR PARK

THE GREATEST SHOW OFF EARTH

THE MOST AMAZING MAN WHO EVER LIVED

THE GARDEN OF UNEARTHLY DELIGHTS

A DOG CALLED DEMOLITION

NOSTRADAMUS ATE MY HAMSTER

SPROUT MASK REPLICA

THE BRENTFORD CHAINSTORE MASSACRE

and published by Corgi Books

THE DANCE OF THE VOODOO HANDBAG

Robert Rankin

CORGI BOOKS

THE DANCE OF THE VOODOO HANDBAG
A CORGI BOOK : 0 552 14580 7

Originally published in Great Britain by Doubleday,
a division of Transworld Publishers Ltd

PRINTING HISTORY
Doubleday edition published 1998
Corgi edition published 1998
Reprinted 1999

Set in 11/13pt Bembo by Kestrel Data, Exeter, Devon.

Corgi Books are published by Transworld Publishers Ltd,
61–63 Uxbridge Road, London W5 5SA,
in Australia by Transworld Publishers (Australia) Pty Ltd,
15–25 Helles Avenue, Moorebank, NSW 2170,
and in New Zealand by Transworld Publishers (NZ) Ltd,
3 William Pickering Drive, Albany, Auckland.

Reproduced, printed and bound in Great Britain by
Clays Ltd, St Ives plc

For my good pals
across the water

Jams, James and Michael

And to celebrate the opening of
The Flying Pig Bookshop

Hip Hip Hoorah.

A Turnip for the Book

'Now that's a turnip for the book,'
The farmer said to the pastry cook.
'That's a rare one, if I ever saw.'
The pastry cook was indisposed,
And both his eyes and ears were closed,
And so he never heard the farmer when the
    farmer swore.

'Here's a strange thing that I see,'
Said the cook of the paste-ter-ee.
'Here's a thing of which I'll later boast.'
The farmer, foaming at the jaw,
Had bolted through the kitchen door,
And was far out in the desert and was making for
    the coast.

The farmer was always far out.

1

Paranoia is a state of heightened awareness.
Most people are persecuted beyond their
wildest delusions.

CLAUDE STEINER

The doctor said that I was a paranoid schizophrenic.

Well, he didn't actually *say* it. But *we* knew he was thinking it.

'Tell me about the butterfly,' the doctor said.

'Which particular butterfly would that be?' I said.

The doctor consulted his case notes. 'The butterfly of chaos theory.'

'Ah, that lad.'

'That lad, yes. Would you care to tell me about it?'

I shrugged. 'It's just a theory. You know the kind of thing. A butterfly in Acapulco flaps its wings and England lose the European Cup.'

The doctor nodded thoughtfully. 'And you believe that, do you?'

I shrugged again. 'I can take it or leave it. I'm not bothered.'

'And yet' – more case note consulting – 'I

understand that you claimed to have such powers yourself.'

'Me? Never!'

'Really?' The doctor raised an eyebrow and also a press cutting. 'But I have here a review of your stage act, "Carlos the Chaos Cockroach".'

'That was just a comedy routine.'

'Really? Yet in a taped interview with me earlier this month you claimed that by moving a biro in your top pocket, or putting paperclips on your ear, you could cause major events to occur' – *more* case note consulting – 'effect fluctuations on the stock market, topple governments, bring about world peace.'

'I might have.'

'You might have.' The doctor adjusted his spectacles. Expensive designer spectacles they were, I'd had a pair like them once. Plain glass in mine, though, an image thing, I don't want to dwell on it.

'But didn't you employ these powers in order to become the President of the United States for a week?'

'That was an error of judgement on my part. I apologized to everyone. I stood down, didn't I?'

'But you *did* have the powers.'

'Yes, all right, I *did*. But I don't have them any more.'

'The tablets are helping, are they?'

'Tablets always help. That's what tablets are for, isn't it?'

The doctor nodded.

'Like God said.'

'God?'

'Like God said to Moses, "Keep taking the tablets." '

'Was that supposed to be a joke?'

'Very possibly. You'd have to ask God.'

'I'm sorry I missed that stage act of yours. It must have been most amusing.' The doctor's tone lacked sincerity.

'Hm,' I said.

The doctor consulted further case notes. He had an awful lot of case notes. A very great many case notes. A considerable wad of case notes. And they were all in a big fat folder with my name on the front. Well, *one* of my names, I use so many.

Sighing just a little, he leaned back in his chair. 'Tell me all about the sprout,' he said.

'Sprout? What sprout?'

'Harry, wasn't it?'

'Harry?'

'No, Barry. The sprout who lived inside your head.'

'He didn't live there. He's not alive.'

'He was a dead sprout.'

'He was a theophany.'

'And what is that, exactly?'

'A manifestation of the deity to man, in a form that, though visible, is not necessarily material.'

'So you could see him?'

'No, I could hear him. He was my Holy Guardian Sprout.'

'As in Holy Guardian Angel?'

'That's right. You see, there are more people in the world than there are angels in heaven, so God has to improvise. He shares out the produce of his garden. You've probably got a radish, or a turnip.'

'Inside my head?'

I nodded. 'It's like the voice of your conscience. Only *you* can hear it.'

'And so Barry spoke to you and only you could hear him?'

'That's how it worked. It got me into a lot of trouble.'

'And is Barry speaking to you now?'

'No, you're speaking to me now.'

'Good. Very good. We are making progress.'

'Does that mean that I can go home soon?'

'We'll see.'

'How about letting me out of this straitjacket?'

'All in good time.'

'Look,' I said, 'I've answered your questions. I've told you about Barry. Barry was a delusion, I understand that now. I'm much better now. I just want to get out of here and get back to work.'

'Ah yes, your work.' The doctor took once more to the consultation of his case notes. 'This would be in your capacity as a private detective, would it?'

'It would, yes.'

'And what exactly does a private detective do?'

'Oh, come off it. Everyone knows what a private detective does.'

'But what exactly did *you* do, when *you* were being one?'

'Well . . .' I had to think about this. It was a tricky question. 'For the most part I just stood around in bars talking a load of old toot.'

'And that's what private detectives do?'

'No, that's what *I* did.'

'And you called yourself' – more bloody case note consultation – 'Lazlo Woodbine, Private Eye.'

'After the new legendary detective in the P. P. Penrose novels. Some called him Laz, you know.'

'Would you like me to call *you* Laz?'

'I'd like you to call me a cab and let me get off about my business.'

'Standing around in bars talking a load of old toot?'

'No, solving my case.'

'And this would be—'

'The case of the voodoo handbag. Please leave your notes alone.'

'Does the consultation of my notes upset you?'

'It's designed to, isn't it?'

'Of course.'

'Then it's working a treat.'

'So, this case of yours, might we go through that again?'

'I'd rather not, if you don't mind.'

'Why?'

'Because I've been through it with you dozens of times, and I'm fed up with telling you about it, and you must be fed up with listening to me telling you about it.'

'I never get fed up,' said the doctor. 'I'm a doctor. We have tablets for that kind of thing.'

'If I tell you about it again, will you take the straitjacket off?'

'We'll see.'

'Who's this *we*?'

'*I'll* see.'

I shrugged once more. A shrug was all I could manage.

'The case was to do with the Law of Obviosity. And before you have to consult your notes again, that's the Hugo Rune Law of Obviosity, which states, "Everything has to be somewhere and nothing can ever be anywhere other than where it is." '

'That sounds logical.'

'It might sound logical, but that doesn't mean it's true.'

'Would you care to explain?'

'OK. Now I'm sure you'll accept that there is a science to detective work. "The science of deduction", as Holmes once put it. Private detective work is mostly to do with finding something that is missing. Something or somebody. So let's say that you have to find something that's supposedly gone missing. Where is the first place you would look?'

The doctor shook his head.

'You'd look in the most obvious place, wouldn't you? But if it's missing, then it won't be there, will it?'

'I would assume not.'

'So then you look in the next most obvious place, and then the next and then the next and so on, until you find it. Because everything has to be somewhere and nothing can ever be anywhere other than where it is.'

'Go on.'

'Right. But in order that you don't involve yourself in an infinite amount of looking, the very best place to start looking would be in the *least* most obvious place.'

'That makes sense.'

'You'd think so. But if the *least* most obvious place is the most obvious place to start looking, then that makes it the *most* obvious place. So therefore it's not the *least* most obvious place any more, because now it's the *most* obvious place and there's no point in looking in the most obvious place for something that's gone missing, is there?'

'Were you any good as a private detective?' the doctor asked.

'The very best. So, having eliminated the *least* most obvious place, because it's the most obvious place to start looking, what you must ask yourself is, where is the least most obvious *least* most obvious place? And ten cent gets you a dollar back on the bottle, that's exactly where it won't be.'

'So where will it be?'

'It will be in the original most obvious place, because that is the least most obvious of all least most obvious places it could possibly be.'

'But if it's in the original most obvious place, then surely it's not missing?'

'Well, if it's not missing, why come bothering me about it in the first place?'

The doctor made a sort of coughing sound in his throat. 'You were searching for a missing handbag, is that right?'

'A missing voodoo handbag, yes.'

'And did you find it?'

'I found *a* handbag, but it wasn't the one I was looking for.'

'Bad luck.'

'Not at all. It was the one I had been looking for

15

on my previous case. And, as the least most obvious *least* most obvious way I was ever going to find that handbag was while looking for a different handbag, I wasn't the least bit surprised when I did find it. It was all so obvious, really.'

'But you didn't find the one you *were* looking for, the voodoo handbag?'

'Well, how could I? You can't find something if it doesn't exist, can you?'

'So the voodoo handbag doesn't exist?'

'The case of the voodoo handbag disproved Rune's Law of Obviosity. I discovered that something *could* be somewhere other than where it is.'

'So the voodoo handbag *does* exist?'

'That's a matter of definition. How *can* a thing exist if it isn't where it is? Surely a thing has to be where it is in order to qualify for existence?'

'So the voodoo handbag *doesn't* exist.'

'Well, if it doesn't exist, why come bothering me about it?'

The doctor made that coughing sound again. 'Is there, or is there not, a voodoo handbag?' he asked.

'That's what I'd like to know. Because if there *isn't*, then I've been looking in all the wrong places. But if there *is*, then I've been looking in all the right places, but I can't find it. Frankly, I'm getting a little confused.'

'You searched for it on the *Internet*, didn't you? Why did you do that?'

'Because you can never find anything you actually want on the Internet. So that was the least obvious place to look, which made it the most obvious place for it to be.'

'But you didn't find it there.'

'No, I found something that I wasn't looking for. Obviously.'

'Obviously. So what did you find?'

'You know what I found, or what I believe I found. And I'm not talking about the other handbag. I'm talking about the other *thing*. The *big* thing. The thing that's got me banged up in here. The thing that no-one believes me about. That makes people think I'm mad – makes *you* think I'm mad.'

'I don't think you're mad.'

'Then let me out of this straitjacket.'

'All in good time. Just tell me calmly and in your own way exactly what it is you believe you found.'

'OK. Calmly and in my own way. You know what virtual reality is, don't you?'

'Of course. It's holographic imagery, generated by computers and accessed by portable headsets and handsets. A synthetic reality modelled by mathematics, creating a hypothetical world commonly referred to as cyberspace.'

'Very precise. But incorrect. There is nothing hypothetical about it. It's a real place, and I've been there.'

Again that coughing sound. 'A real place, and you've been there?'

'For ten long years I was trapped there and it's not an unpopulated region. You see, we didn't invent cyberspace, we only gained access to it. It was there already. It's the same place we visit in our dreams, or when we do hallucinogenic drugs, or have a mystical experience. It's not a physical place, but it's real. It's the *weird space*, the *mundus magicus*. But

17

a company called Necrosoft is messing with it. They're inflicting stuff on it. Messing with its natural laws. Same old game, mankind buggering up the eco-system.'

'And you worry about this?'

'We'd all better worry about it. And we'd better do something about it, before it's too late. Before *they* do something about us.'

'Who are *they*?'

'They, them. The folk who live on the other side of the mirror. I told you, it's not an unpopulated region. They don't like what we're doing, and if we don't stop it they'll stop us.'

'And they told you this, did they? They chose you to pass on this message to mankind?'

'What?'

'Or perhaps it was Barry, your Holy Guardian Sprout, perhaps he told you all about it.'

'*What?*'

'Calmly now. Tell me about these folk. The ones on the other side of the mirror. Who are they?'

'They're us. Or they're a reflection of us, or we're a reflection of them. Or a bit of both. But what does it matter, you don't believe a word I'm saying. And the only way I'm ever going to get out of here is if I stop believing it too.'

'And do you think you can stop believing it?'

'Sure. I've stopped. Look at me. I've stopped and I'm all better now, so can I go home, please?'

'Early days yet,' said the doctor.

'Early days? I've been here for months.'

'These things take time.'

'But we're running out of time. If I can't sort things out, then—'

'Then what?'

'Then . . . er . . . nothing. I just have some things to sort out at home. Plants to water, aunties to visit. Normal sane things.'

'I don't think you're being one hundred per cent truthful with me, are you?'

'Look, can't we be reasonable about this? Say I did believe everything I've just told you, which I don't, of course. But say I did. Where's the harm in it? The world is full of harmless loons with wacky ideas. You don't bang them all up in mental institutions, the streets would be empty if you did that.'

'You do have a point.' The doctor gave his chin a bit of a stroke. 'Eccentricity is not in itself a criminal offence.'

'Of course it isn't. So, what do you say?'

'Well . . .'

'I'm harmless, aren't I?'

'Well . . .'

'So I hear voices in my head. So did Joan of Arc.'

'Well . . .'

'And I'm a technophobe, I've got a thing about computers. So what?'

'Well . . .'

'And I suffer from delusions that only I can save the world. That's no big deal, is it?'

'Well . . .'

'And I stir up a bit of insurrection, talk about blowing up a few computer companies. And assassinating Billy Barnes, the World Leader. History would thank me for it anyway.'

19

'. . .'

'Er, you didn't say "Well . . ." that time.'

'Nurse,' said the doctor, pushing a little button on his desk. 'Nurse.'

'Hang about, I was only joking about the insurrection and the blowing up and assassinating. You didn't think I really meant it, did you?'

'Nurse.'

'Look, we've been getting along so well. Let's not spoil it by calling the nurse. Let's talk about something else. Who's your favourite Spice Girl? I like the vicious-looking one with the big tits, I bet she really—'

'Nurse!'

The doctor's door swung open, and a large male nurse loomed in the doorway.

'Ah, Cecil,' said the doctor. 'Would you please escort Mr Woodbine back to his room?'

'With pleasure, sir.'

'No,' I said, struggling to rise. 'I don't want to go back to my room. I have to get out of here. I really do. Everything depends upon it.'

'Would you care for me to administer Mr Woodbine's medication, sir?'

The doctor nodded. 'Use the big syringe,' he said.

'No, no, not the big syringe.' I fought to free myself. But I was onto a loser. Male nurse Cecil caught me firmly by the scruff of the straitjacket. 'Shall I use the *very* big syringe?' he asked.

'The great big one,' said the doctor. 'With the extra long needle.'

'No, let me go. You're making a terrible mistake. You have to let me go, I'm the only one who knows the truth.' As with the farmer in the poem, I began to foam somewhat about the jaw regions. I kicked out at Nurse Cecil, but I only had my hospital slippers on and he had his big shin guards. And his big boots. He stamped on my foot and he smiled as he did it.

'Ouch!' I screamed. 'Set me free, you don't know what you're doing. I'm not mad. I'm not. I'm not!'

'Come along now, Mr Woodbine,' said Cecil. 'There's a good gentleman.'

'It's a conspiracy. You're all in it together. You're all in the pay of Billy Barnes.'

'Come along now, please.'

I was hauled, still kicking and screaming, out of the doctor's office and along the corridor. Fellow loons, who had the run of the place, turned their faces away as I passed them by, and whistled nonchalantly.

'You're all in it!' I screamed. 'All of you! The lot of you!'

'Quietly now, please, Mr Woodbine. Don't go upsetting the other patients.'

'You'll get yours, you bastard.'

Back in the privacy of my room, I got mine.

Nurse Cecil performed certain unspeakable acts upon my helpless person, gave me a sound kicking, and then employed the great big syringe with the extra long needle.

'Good night, sweet prince,' he said, as he closed the padded door upon me.

I lay strapped to my bunk, effing and blinding and

hurting and bleeding and waiting for the medication to kick in and plunge me once more into oblivion.

But just before it did, I heard a little voice calling me. Calling me from inside my head. It was the voice of Barry, my Holy Guardian Sprout. Offering me solace and comfort.

'That might have gone a little better, chief,' it said.

Adding later, 'You twat!'

Tall Tales
and
Jumping Beans

'Drat,' said the old enamel vicar,
Kept for purposes of pleasure,
Kept in the tiny sainted box,
Handed down through generations,
Spoken of by rising nations,
Blessed at festive celebrations,
And I use for my socks.

Twang, went the Mexican jumping bean,
Brought home from my travels,
Carried over distant seas,
Made venerable by Rose's mother,
Saying, not like any other,
Teaching, thou shalt love each other,
Which seems OK to me.

'Bye,' went Doc, as he boarded the plane,
Bound for the Amazon Basin,
Bound for the pygmies and tsetse fly,
Off in search of the Holy Grail,
Lost in the belly of Jonah's whale,
Personally, I think he'll fail,
But some say I'm a cynic.

2

The theory of Space and Time is a
cultural artefact made possible by
the invention of graph paper.
JACQUES VALLEE

In the year 2002 my Uncle Brian brought down the British book publishing industry. He had nothing personal against it; he had no axe to grind, no cross to bear, no chicken to stuff. But he did have an awful lot of right-handed rubber gloves.

You see, my Uncle Brian had bought a consignment of rubber gloves for thirty-five quid from a bloke in a pub. Thirty-five thousand pairs. It seemed like the deal of a lifetime. One thousand pairs for a pound; you just couldn't fail to make money on a deal like that. But what my uncle didn't discover until some time later was that he had been done. He had seventy thousand rubber gloves all right, but that was the trouble, they were *all right*. All right-handers.

And the method he chose to sell on these seemingly useless articles at a handsome profit brought down the British book publishing industry.

Of course you will find no record of this on any

database, and you can scan the pages of the *History of the 20th Century* on your home terminal until your eyes grow dim; Uncle Brian has no mention there. In fact the only place where you can learn of my Uncle Brian's part in changing the course of history is right here and right now.

And as *all* books will be destroyed in the great Health Purge of 2001 you must read here while you are able.

Uncle Brian was a tall-story-teller (I speak of him in the past tense as he is now long dead, cruelly cut down in his prime in a mysterious incident involving a grassy knoll and a high-powered rifle). I come from a long and distinguished line of tall-story-tellers, and I would like to make it very clear from the outset that tall-story-telling is in no way to be confused with lying.

Lying is a wicked, shameless, ignominious thing, indulged in by crude evil folk, to the detriment of others and to the benefit of themselves. Tall-story-telling is, on the other hand, a noble art, performed by selfless individuals, designed to enrich our cultural heritage and add a little colour to an otherwise lacklustre world.

So there.

My father was a tall-story-teller, as my earliest memory of him set down now before you will confirm.

It was my first year at infant school, and the teacher had asked us to paint a picture of what our fathers did for a living. I painted mine and it so impressed the teacher that she stuck it up in the school hall (a big honour, that). And when open day

25

came around a week later, she hastened over to my father to engage him in conversation.

'Mr Rankin,' she said. 'I wonder if you might consider coming into the school and giving a talk to the children about your occupation?'

My dad, a carpenter by trade, asked why.

'Because,' said the teacher, 'you are the first father we've ever had at this school who's a whaler.'

You see, several weeks prior to this my dad had given me a whale's tooth as a present, and had told me a marvellous tale about having prised it from the jaw of the slain creature during one of his many whaling voyages. He had never actually been to sea in his life; he was simply entertaining his young son with a tall tale well told.

Now any 'normal' father, upon being faced with this teacher's question, might simply have owned up to the truth and laughed off the whole affair. But not my dad. He had a duty to his calling. He agreed, without a moment's hesitation, went home, fashioned for himself a makeshift harpoon to illustrate throwing techniques, and returned to school the following week to give his talk.

I was quite a hero throughout my second term at infant school.

And so it continued throughout my father's life. He rose, at length, to the not-so-giddy heights of general foreman, but wherever he went he spread wonder. And never more so, nor with greater panache, than when many years later he finally went to his grave.

His apotheosis as a tall-story-teller came at his funeral where he was paid a posthumous tribute to his supreme mastery of the craft. No-one really expects to leave their father's funeral with tears of laughter in their eyes. But I did. My dad had the last laugh, and he let us share it.

A slightly surreal incident at the start of the proceedings set the tone for what was to come. One of the pall bearers had a cold and pulled from his pocket an oversized red gingham handkerchief. Such an item wouldn't have meant much to anyone else, but it meant a lot to me.

The last time I had seen a handkerchief like that was nearly forty years before. My Aunty Edna, my dad's sister, always carried one in her handbag. It was scented with lavender and I loved the smell so much that whenever she came to visit I would pretend to have a cold so she would let me blow my nose on it. I would bury my face in that hanky and draw in the marvellous perfume.

The sight of the pall bearer's hanky stirred some long-forgotten childhood memories. But it wasn't just the handkerchief.

It was the Polo mint.

As he pulled out the handkerchief, a Polo mint popped from his pocket. It flew through the air and fell to the church floor, spiralling slowly forward until it came to rest beneath my dad's coffin.

And there it remained throughout the service.

But the curious incident of the oversized red gingham handkerchief and the Polo mint was nothing, *nothing* in the face of what was to come.

The vicar was one of those young, earnest, eager fellows, with the shining face of a freshly bathed infant. Why do they scrub their faces up like that? Is it the 'cleanliness is next to godliness' angle? I don't know, but, all aglow and full of beans, he climbed into the pulpit, gathered his robes about him and began a discourse upon my dad.

'I have only been in this parish for nine months,' said the vicar, 'and so I only knew Mr Rankin during the final stages of his long illness. But it became clear to me, through my many talks with him, that Mr Rankin was no ordinary man. He had lived the kind of life that most of us only read about. He had walked alone across the Kalahari Desert, sailed alone around Cape Horn, conquered some of the world's highest peaks, and been decorated twice for deeds of outstanding valour during the Second World War.'

My gaze, which had become fixed upon the Polo mint, rose rapidly upon hearing all this, and a look of horror must certainly have appeared upon my face. My immediate thoughts were that the vicar was talking about the wrong man. It was bloody typical, wasn't it, one old dying man looking just the same as another to a new vicar with his mind on other things, young housewives of the parish, probably! I was almost on the point of rising from my pew to take issue with the erring cleric when I heard the first titters of laughter.

The church was packed, my dad had a great many friends, and the laughter came in little muffled outbursts from his old cronies. And as the vicar continued with tales of my father's daring escapades, world wanderings and uncanny knack for always being in the right place at the right time when history was being made, the laughter spread.

But never so far as the pulpit.

My father had spent the last nine months of his life priming up the vicar.

As I say, I left the church with tears in my eyes. But the best was yet to come, and it was almost as if my dad had planned it. In fact, looking back, I feel certain that he did.

'Would you care to come back to the house for a cup of tea?' I asked the vicar. 'Evidently you were very close to my dad at the end, and I'd like, at the very least, for us to have a chat.'

The vicar agreed and we returned to my dad's place.

And we hadn't been there for ten minutes when it came.

The vicar pointed to the large swordfish saw that hung above the fireplace. 'Now, that can tell a tale or two, can't it?' he said to me.

I glanced up at it. As far as I knew the thing had been utterly mute ever since my dad had purchased it in a Hastings antique market. But then it might have confided a tale or two to him in private, I couldn't be certain.

'Would you like to refresh my memory?'

'Indeed,' said the man of the cloth, sipping tea. 'Your father told me about the time he was fishing for sailfish alone off the Florida Keys, and a sudden storm blew his boat far out to sea. He lost all contact with land and during this storm, which was, according to your father, nothing less than the infamous Hurricane Flora of 1966, his oars were blown overboard.

'Your father thought that his time had surely

come and, being the pious man he was, he offered himself to God's tender mercy. There was a flash of lightning and at that very moment a swordfish burst its saw – that very one hanging there – up through the bottom of the boat. Using the skills he had learned while working as a circus strongman, your father snapped off the saw, thrust his foot into the hole and, using the saw for a paddle, rowed back to land.'

To say that I was speechless would be to say, well, I *was* speechless.

After the vicar left, my mum took me quietly to one side. 'I think it would probably be for the best if none of this was ever spoken of again, don't you, dear?' she said.

I nodded thoughtfully. 'Trust me, Mum,' I told her. 'I won't mention it to another living soul.'

And I have, of course, remained true to my promise.

My Uncle Brian, my dad's younger brother, was not a carpenter or a general foreman. He was a fox farmer. I never even knew that fox farms existed before he told me about them. Apparently, without fox farms the entire British economy would have ground to a halt a long time before it actually did in the year 2002, with the fall of the British book publishing industry and pretty much everything else. But during the 1980s and 1990s, fox farming at secret government establishments kept it buoyant. You see, there weren't enough foxes to hunt and so fox farms had to breed even more.

Allow me to explain.

As most folk will know, blood sports have, in recent times, become something of an issue and one which has deepened the divide between the rural and the urban communities.

There has always been a divide, but this is to be expected. Country folk have long considered themselves to be a cut above the simple townie. Country folk feel themselves to be closer to nature, more in tune with its natural rhythms and custodians of the land for generations yet to come. Townies, in their opinion, are a bunch of glue-sniffing football hooligans, packed like lab rats into high-rise blocks, stunted both mentally and physically by a diet of McDonald's burgers and traffic fumes. Gross, perverted and not nice to know.

Townies, however, lean to a different opinion. They consider themselves a cut above the simple bumpkin. Townies feel themselves to be better educated and more sophisticated, having greater access to the arts and information technology. They look upon country folk as a bunch of ignorant, inbred sheep-shaggers who get off on cruelty and blood-letting. Gross, perverted and not nice to know.

Both sides are, of course, way off the mark, although it could be argued that sheep-shagging is an almost exclusively rural recreation.

So it comes as little surprise to find that the countryman and the townie disagree over the matter of blood sports.

In the summer of 1997 almost half a million concerned country folk marched peacefully upon London to heighten the awareness of the public at large regarding the threat to rural England posed by a proposed Bill to abolish the blood sport of fox-hunting.

What the dim-witted townie failed to understand, the country folk patiently explained, was that without foxhunting there would be no English countryside. Consider, they said, all those people whose livelihoods depend directly upon foxhunting. The saddlers, the grooms, the ostlers, the stable lads and lasses. The riding instructors, the vets, the manufacturers of horse pills and tackle and donkey nuts and stirrup cups. The blacksmiths and the blacksmiths' apprentices, the horse-breeders, the makers of horse boxes and those who worked in the factories that produce those stickers you see in the rear windows of Range Rovers that say 'I ♥ greys'.

And that was only the horses. What about the dogs? What about those packs of beautiful cuddly foxhounds? They'd all have to be destroyed. Destroyed! Dogs destroyed! A national shame! And with their destruction would go the livelihoods of the Masters of Foxhounds, their apprentices and assistants, the whippers-in, the manufacturers of dog collars and dog biscuits and dog food, more vets and so on and so forth.

Thousands upon thousands upon thousands of hard-working honest country folk would be doomed to lives of dole-queue misery only previously reserved for town-dwellers.

Catastrophe!

And worse, far worse, what about the land itself? England depended upon its farmland. Its farmland

and its produce. The land! Dear Lord, the land!

To put it plainly, there would be no more land. Without the efforts of the gallant foxhunters to keep the evil vermin that was the fox at bay, the English countryside would be no more. The fox, that hellish chimera of wolf, jackal, tiger and ghoul/demon/ werewolf, would multiply, growing in unstoppable numbers, forming mighty packs and wreaking havoc across the land. Snatching infants from their cots, devouring entire herds of sheep and cattle in a hideous feeding frenzy, before moving on to destroy the towns and cities.

To ban foxhunting was to do little less than herald in the End Times and welcome the arrival of the Anti-Christ.

Blimey!

This all came as a bit of a revelation to the townie. For one thing, the townie had always believed that the greatest threat to a farmer's crops came not from the meat-eating fox but from the strictly vegetarian rabbit, which was, by a curious coincidence, the all-but-staple diet of the fox. And surely only one and a half per cent of the British populace actually lived in the country, and the countryside only contributed three per cent to the Gross National Product. And surely most farmers had guns? After all they were always pointing them at townies who inadvertently picnicked upon their land. Couldn't they simply shoot the foxes?

It was indeed a bit of a revelation, and one that served to pave over that aforementioned divide which had for so long, er, divided the rural community from its urban brother. Foxhunting provided full employment for the country folk, and spared the town-dweller from the rabid attentions of the demonic fox pack.

Harmony.

So where did the fox farms come into this? Well, as I thought I'd explained, there weren't enough foxes to hunt.

It was the town-dwellers' fault. Their love of motor cars and motorways. You see, ten times as many foxes are killed by motor cars than are killed by foxhunts, which explains why country folk always protest so much about new motorways.

It's all so simple when it's explained, isn't it?

So my Uncle Brian worked on a fox farm. It was one of the new ones. A fox factory farm. My uncle was employed as a genetic engineer. The aim was to breed the super-fox. A vegetarian fox that was a really slow runner, as so many foxhunters are old and fat, just like their hounds.

My Uncle Brian enjoyed the work. Playing God and tampering with the laws of nature had always appealed to him. But he became unemployed in 1997 with the change of government, and this in turn led him to lose the thirty-five quid which in its turn came to bring down the British book publishing industry.

Allow me to explain.

What happened was this. The new Labour government was very keen to save money. Having the nation's interests ever at heart they decided to cut back on government spending, and one way they found of achieving this was by amalgamating certain top secret departments and restructuring them so that they would run at a profit. Lumping them all together, as it were, sharing jobs. Fox farming, which was *Very* Top Secret, got amalgamated with UFO back-engineering, which was *Above* Top Secret. UFO back-engineering is when a government acquires a grounded flying saucer and then takes it apart in order to see what makes it run. This has not as yet been successfully achieved, which explains why we do not at present swish around in flying saucers and commute between the planets. But we're trying.

So UFO back-engineering got amalgamated with fox farm genetic engineering, and a chap called Hartly was put in charge with the remit to make the enterprise run at a profit.

Hartly was a bright young spark and almost immediately he saw a financial opportunity. Fox pelts. As townies were now convinced of the good of foxhunting and the evil of foxes, surely they would be prepared to purchase fox fur coats just like the good old days? Hartly set about the genetic engineering of the angora fox. It was a brilliant idea, but where he slipped up was in using genetic material taken from a UFO.

As all those who have access to Above Top Secret information will know, UFOs are mostly organic. Which explains why they don't show up on radar. The UFO genetic material used for the creation of the angora fox did not result in the creation of the angora fox. It resulted in the creation of the *stealth fox*.

Now, whereas the Stealth Bomber does not show up on radar, the stealth fox didn't show up anywhere. It could blend in with its surroundings to a degree that made it virtually invisible. It was there all right, if you took the trouble to look hard enough for it (after all *everything has to be somewhere and nothing can ever be anywhere other than where it is*), but escaping notice was what the stealth fox did best.

That and escaping from secret government research establishments. Naturally.

Using the cunning for which it is famed, this new order of fox sought out its old adversary – the foxhound. It began to blend in with the packs, and in fact so convincingly did it do this that the pack took it for one of its own. In no time the stealth fox was cross-breeding with the foxhounds, producing a stealth fox/dog hybrid indistinguishable from the ordinary foxhound. Within a couple of years many packs of foxhounds consisted of nothing but stealth fox/dog hybrids.

This cross-breeding produced a larger, more powerful strain of stealth fox, roughly the size of a Great Dane (or small horse). The next step was inevitable.

The large stealth fox/dog hybrids began to blend in with the horses in the hunt, and soon the first stealth fox/dog/horse hybrid appeared.

Now the next step up the evolutionary ladder taken by the stealth fox may well be considered by those of a prudish disposition to be too distasteful to chronicle. But in the noble quest for truth, it must be told.

Those of you who have ever viewed the now legendary porno vid *Down on the Farm* will recall the episode of the lusty stable lass and the frisky stallion.

Enough said.

The stealth fox/dog/horse/human hybrid was born.

And it was one of these very stealth fox/dog/horse/ human hybrids who, several years later in the guise of a bloke in a bar, did my uncle out of thirty-five quid, which in turn led my uncle to bring down the British book publishing industry.

And how this came about, and what it all has to do with a voodoo handbag, a Holy Guardian Sprout and a threat to mankind from the denizens of cyber-space, will soon become blindingly obvious.

Although not, perhaps, in the *most* obvious way.

The Laird of Dunoon

The Laird of Dunoon
Leans back in his chair,
Trousers rolled up to the knee.
Easing his braces
With courteous graces
He sips at his Newcastle B.

The Laird of Dunoon
In the newspaper bonnet
Smiles as he looks out to sea.
Taking a drag
From a finely rolled fag,
He sips at his Newcastle B.

The Laird of Dunoon
In the Fair Isle pullover
Whistles 'The Rose of Tralee'.
He swivels his hips
As he purses his lips,
And sips at his Newcastle B.

The Laird of Dunoon
Glances down at his Rolex
And sees that it's time for his tea.

He slips on his socks,
Puts his specs in a box
And finishes his Newcastle B.

Ah, if only all of life could be as this.
But regretfully, it cannot!

3

Smart from books ain't so smart.
CAROL BAKER

The ambition of every tall-story-teller is to create an
urban myth. One of those 'it happened to a friend
of a friend of mine' stories that enters the collective
consciousness and takes on a life of its own.

You hear them all the time: at work, in the pub, at
a party. Told to you by folk who'll swear they're
true. And the thing about a really good one is it can
make you feel that even if it isn't true somehow it
ought to be.

For instance, does anyone remember Johnny
Quinn? Yes, no, maybe. Well, about a year ago I was
in the Jolly Gardeners drinking Death by Cider
and chatting with my good friend Sean O'Reilly.
William Burroughs had just died and Sean was
saying that Old Bill had been one of his favourites. I
said that he had been one of my favourites too, and
although I never really understood what he was on
about most of the time, it didn't seem to matter,
because I just loved the *way* he was on about it.

And then Sean asked me whether I'd ever read
anything by Johnny Quinn, who had apparently

been a mate of Burroughs and was somewhat easier to understand. I said I was sure that I had, but I couldn't remember what. And then I said, yes I could, and wasn't it Johnny Quinn who wrote *The Million Dollar Dream*? And Sean said he thought it was, and also *Sailing to Babylon*, and something about tears.

'*Tomorrow's Tears*,' I said. 'I've got that book somewhere.' And we talked a bit about what we could remember of Johnny Quinn, which didn't seem to be much, and his books, which seemed to be even less. And at the end of the evening Sean said that he'd really like to read *Tomorrow's Tears* again and I said, 'Let's go back to my place and I'll see if I can find it.'

And we did. But I couldn't.

We searched through all my paperbacks, but *Tomorrow's Tears* was nowhere to be found. 'Never mind,' I said. 'I'm going into Brighton tomorrow, I'll see if I can pick up a copy at Waterstone's.' Sean said to get whatever Johnny Quinn books they had in stock and he'd pay me for them next time he saw me. And we both got quite excited about the prospect of reading some Johnny Quinn again.

Which turned out to be a pity, really.

The chap at Waterstone's was very helpful. I asked him if he had any Johnny Quinn books in stock and he said the name rang a bell and he'd have a look. He had a look and said that no, sadly, they didn't. So I asked him if I could order some and he said he didn't see any reason why not and cranked up his computer. But he couldn't find a mention of Johnny Quinn. 'Are you sure it's *Johnny* Quinn?' he asked. And I said I was sure that it was, and he said he felt sure that it was too. But we couldn't find him although there were several books with similar sounding titles to the ones I was looking for.

'They must all be out of print,' said the very helpful chap. 'Perhaps you should try the library.'

The lady at the library was also very helpful and she employed *her* computer. But she couldn't find any Johnny Quinn books either. 'That's odd,' she said, 'because I'm sure I remember reading one of his books when I was at school.' But she couldn't find him and eventually she got tired of looking and suggested I try one of the specialist bookshops in the area.

So I did. In fact I went to each and every one of them. The chaps who ran these shops were also very helpful and although they all felt certain they could remember old Johnny and had enjoyed reading his books, none of them had a single one in stock.

I must confess that by mid afternoon I was beginning to feel a little stressed.

At the very last shop I visited, the proprietor, a very helpful chap, grew quite lyrical over the recollection of Mr Quinn. He'd once had a girlfriend, he said, who had named her cat Toothbrush, after a character in one of his novels.

Toothbrush? I didn't remember any character called Toothbrush!

'Are you still in touch with this old girlfriend?' I asked.

'No,' said the proprietor with a sigh. 'She died.' And his face became sad, and he said he was going to close up early and he hustled me out of his shop. And I too became sad and went home.

But by now the search for a Johnny Quinn novel was becoming something of a crusade. I was determined that I would lay my hands upon one, come what may. By fair means or foul.

I decided to try the fair means first.

So that evening I went through my personal telephone book and called everyone that was listed in it. I called all my friends, and old friends too, some of whom I hadn't spoken to for years. And I called business acquaintances and even the doctor and the dentist, as I had their numbers. Some of them felt sure that they had read Johnny Quinn, and I waited anxiously while they looked through their bookshelves before returning to the phone with the reply I was coming to dread.

Gilly, an old friend from college days, rather put the wind up me when I spoke to her. She said that she'd had a Johnny Quinn book but she'd lent it to a friend and never got it back. Apparently this friend had lent Gilly's book to another friend and never got it back from her.

A friend-of-a-friend that would be then, wouldn't it!

By midnight I had run up a very large phone bill and worn out my friendship with quite a few people, but I was absolutely no nearer to finding what was now acquiring the status of a literary Holy Grail.

I went off to bed in a very bad mood!

But I was up bright and early the next morning.

Because I'd had an idea.

I'd remembered that there are companies in London that specialize in finding books for collectors. That's what they do. You pay them a finder's fee and they seek out the book. Mind you, I'd heard that this can take years, but I felt it was certainly worth a try.

Directory Enquiries put me on to the most famous one. I'm not allowed to mention their name here, but you've probably heard of them, they do posh auctions, too.

The chap I spoke to first was very helpful, and very posh. 'Was it Jonathan Quinn?' he asked. 'The contemporary of Beau Brummel and the Prince Regent?'

'No,' I said. 'Just plain Johnny, mucker of Billy Burroughs back in the Swinging Sixties.'

'Ah,' said the chap, 'then you will need to speak to our Mr Hiemes, who specializes in books from the 1960s. He's our resident expert on the period.'

'Splendid,' I said.

He put me through to their Mr Hiemes and I told their Mr Hiemes that I was looking for *any* book by Johnny Quinn.

'Johnny *who*?' asked their Mr Hiemes.

'Quinn,' I said, 'surely you've heard of him?'

Their Mr Hiemes said no, he hadn't.

I said to their Mr Hiemes that I'd been told he was the resident expert on the period.

'I am,' said their Mr Hiemes, 'and I've never heard of Johnny Quinn.'

'You have to be joking!'

But he wasn't.

And nor were any of the other experts I spoke to

that morning. None of them had ever heard of Johnny Quinn. None of them.

'But that's absurd,' I told the last in a dismal line. 'I spent yesterday afternoon going around Brighton and just about everyone I spoke to remembered Johnny Quinn. And you blokes are supposed to be experts on the literature of the Sixties, and none of you have ever heard of him. You're all a bunch of tosspots.'

And the chap put the phone down on me.

Absurd!

But then it got beyond absurd.

I went through the *Yellow Pages* and started phoning bookshops. Any bookshop. All bookshops. High street chains, collector's bookshops, independents, weirdos, every kind of bookshop. And though I spoke to some very helpful people, not a single one of them had ever heard of Johnny Quinn.

I was truly rattled. How could it be that yesterday nearly everyone had heard of him, and today nobody had?

I decided to retrace my footsteps. I went back to Waterstone's. The chap behind the counter remembered me from the day before. But when I told him that I had drawn a complete blank on Johnny Quinn, he told me that he wasn't in the least surprised.

'*What?*' I said.

'Well,' he said, 'after you'd gone I got to thinking, and the more I thought about Johnny Quinn the less I seemed to remember. And eventually I got to thinking that probably I didn't remember Johnny Quinn at all, I only thought I did.'

'Absurd!' I said.

'Not really,' he said. 'You see, it happens all the time in this business. Someone will come into the shop asking for a book that doesn't exist, saying that a friend of a friend of theirs read it and thought it was wonderful. They know, or think they know, all kinds of details about the book and its author. But the book doesn't exist. Even though it seems as if it should. It's like an urban myth, someone starts it off in a bar or something and it takes on a life of its own. I've developed a mystical theory about it. I think that the book exists in some kind of parallel universe and it's trying to exist in this one too. Like your Johnny Quinn, perhaps he's trying to exist here. And if enough people believed in him, maybe he would. Maybe if enough people believe in anything strongly enough, it will actually happen. And perhaps Johnny Quinn did exist here yesterday, sort of. But he won't exist today. He had his moment, when your belief spread to others, but that moment's passed. Not enough people believed hard enough. Johnny didn't make it into this reality. Sorry.'

'What a load of old toot!' I said.

But he might have been right. About some of it anyway. Because all the other chaps in all the other shops I went back to said pretty much the same thing. They'd all thought they'd remembered Johnny Quinn yesterday, but the more they thought about it . . .

The chap who'd had the girlfriend with the cat called Toothbrush was not at all pleased to see me. He said I'd stirred up a lot of unhappy memories and he'd probably have to go back into therapy. And, for my information, his girlfriend's cat had actually been called Steerpike and I should bugger off.

So I buggered off.

I didn't see Sean again for a couple of weeks, and when I did bump into him at the Jolly Gardeners I thought I'd wait until he asked me about the Johnny Quinn books before I told him about what had happened. But Sean never did ask me. Sean seemed to have forgotten all about Johnny Quinn. In fact Sean never mentioned the name of Johnny Quinn ever again.

'Do you remember a painter called Karl Bok?' Sean asked me.

And that might well have been it for old Johnny Quinn, the author who never was, had it not been for something decidedly odd that happened to me the next month.

It happened in the Jolly Gardeners on a Tuesday evening. Andy, the landlord, goes off somewhere on Tuesday evenings, and Paul the part-timer takes over. Tuesday evenings are always slow and Paul is good at slow. He generally spends the evening doing the *Times* crossword or reading a book. On this particular Tuesday evening he was reading a book.

I went in, hung up my hat and cloak and placed my silver-topped cane upon the counter. 'A pint of Death by Cider, please, Paul,' I said.

Paul hastened without haste to oblige me.

'What are you reading?' I asked, spying the open book on the counter.

'Book,' said Paul, viewing the rows of identical pint glasses upon the shelf and waiting for one to take his fancy.

'Does it have a title?' I asked.

'Yes,' said Paul, still waiting.

'Might I ask what it is?'

'You might.'

I turned the book towards me and closed it. It was a publisher's proof copy. It had a white card cover. The title of the book was *Snuff Fiction*, the author was Johnny Quinn.

'Bugger me,' I said.

'No thanks,' said Paul.

'But it's a Johnny Quinn novel. You've got a Johnny Quinn novel.'

'No I haven't,' said Paul.

'Yes you have, I'm holding it in my hands.'

'I haven't,' said Paul. 'It's not mine. It belongs to a friend. A friend of a friend, actually.'

'But you've got it. It exists. Johnny Quinn exists.'

'He doesn't,' said Paul, who had finally found a glass he liked the look of.

'He bloody does,' I said. 'This book proves it.'

'He doesn't,' said Paul, slowly filling the glass from the wrong pump. 'Because he's dead. Committed suicide.'

'Blimey,' I said. 'Poor old Johnny. He really did exist and now he's topped himself. He probably got fed up with people not believing in him.'

'What?' asked Paul, presenting me with my pint.

'Nothing,' I said. 'What's this supposed to be?'

'Search me,' said Paul.

I held the book very tightly. 'I want to buy this book,' I said. 'I'll give you ten quid for it.'

'It's not mine. I can't sell it.'

'Twenty quid, then, and that's my final offer.'

'It will be out in the shops next week for a fiver.'

'What?'

'They're republishing all his stuff. *The Million Dollar Dream*, *Sailing to Babylon*. There's been a big revival since he croaked. And *Snuff Fiction* is the last one he wrote before he blew his brains out. It's never been published before. It'll probably go straight into the bestseller list. You'll be able to buy it at a discount.'

'I don't get this,' I said. 'When I asked at the bookshops a while back, they couldn't trace any of his books.'

'That's because they were all private editions, printed in the States. His books were never published in this country. People used to say they'd read him in order to seem hip and well informed.'

'Hm!' I said, giving my chin a scratch.

'But that's what you blokes from the Sixties were all about, wasn't it?' said Paul. 'Always saying you'd done the Hippy Trail and been to Woodstock and watched the Stones in the Park and gone to college with Freddie Mercury and taken every drug there was to take and all the rest of it. A bunch of bull-shitters, the lot of you. Did *you* ever read any Johnny Quinn novels, then?'

'Not me,' I said, and paid for whatever it was I'd just bought, and sat down in a corner and drank it.

★

And what Paul said made a lot of sense, really. I'd obviously heard of Johnny Quinn, but I'd never actually read him. But I must have told people that I'd read him in order to seem hip and well informed. And as the years had gone by, I'd come to believe that I'd really read him. That had to be it. And it was probably it with all the other people who'd told me they'd read Johnny Quinn. They were all just a bunch of Sixties bull-shitters, like me. A lot of tall-story-tellers.

Tall-story-tellers!

That made me think. That made me think about my dad. I swallowed hard upon my ale. What if my dad hadn't considered himself a tall-story-teller at all? What if he'd actually believed all those tales he'd told to the vicar? Thought he'd really done all those things? It was all too much to think about. I finished up whatever it was I was drinking and went home.

I went back to the Jolly Gardeners the following Tuesday evening. I wanted Paul to lend me that copy of *Snuff Fiction*. All right, it would be out in the shops the next day. But I wanted *his* copy. Because I wanted to be able to say to people, '*Snuff Fiction*? Oh yes, I read that *before* it came out.'

But Paul wasn't there.

Andy was behind the pump.

'Where's Paul?' I asked Andy.

'Not turned in,' Andy said. 'I've telephoned, but there's no answer. I can't think what's happened. This isn't like Paul at all.'

'Damn!' I said. 'Do you have Paul's address?'

'No,' said Andy. 'Do you?'

Wednesday morning found me back at Waterstone's, and there behind the counter was the chap I'd spoken to before.

'Remember me?' I asked him.

'No,' he said.

'Come on now, you do, you know.'

'I don't, you know.'

'Well, never mind. I've come to buy a book.'

He looked at me. Questioningly.

'It's a Johnny Quinn book,' I said. 'The *new* Johnny Quinn book. And it comes out today. Although I don't see it anywhere on your shelves.'

'That's because there's no such book,' he said.

'Oh yes there is. I've seen a copy. It's called *Snuff Fi*—'

But I didn't get the second word out, because he lunged at me and clamped his hand across my face. And then he shinned over the counter, forced my arm up my back and sort of frog-marched me away to the store room.

'What the fuck do you think you're doing?' I shouted, once I'd got myself free.

'Keep your voice down,' he said, in a menacing tone. 'Who sent you, anyway?'

'Nobody sent me. What are you talking about?'

'How do you know about that book?'

'Because I've seen a copy.'

'Nonsense. You wouldn't be here if you had.'

'What?'

'Just go away,' he told me. 'Forget all about it.'

'I certainly won't. I'm not leaving here without a

copy of *Snuff Fic*—', and his hand was all over my face again.

'Stop doing that,' I said, once I had prised it free.

'Stop saying that title, then.'

'What, *Snuff Fic*— Get your hands off me!'

'Then don't say the title again.'

'Then sell me a copy.'

'I can't. We don't have any.'

'I don't believe you. I want a copy and I want it now.'

'You can't have one.'

'But you do admit there's such a book.'

'Of course I do. But I'll only admit it in here. With you. As you've actually seen a copy.'

'Tell me what's going on,' I said, 'or I will go out into the shop and shout very loudly. I will shout "Give me *Snuff Fic*—"'

'All right. All right. I'll tell you. But you have to promise. Promise that you'll never pass on what I tell you here.'

'All right,' I said. 'I promise.'

'Really truly, cross your heart and hope to die.'

'Cross my heart and hope to die.'

'It's a nightmare,' he said. 'It's Quinn's revenge.'

'What?'

'It seems that he was famous in the Sixties but the world forgot about him. His books went out of print and he became more of a myth than a living person. He blamed the publishers and the book-sellers and the public. He blamed everyone. He was a paranoid schizophrenic, voices in the head, the whole bit. And he vowed to take his revenge on everyone. So he wrote his final novel, *Snuff Fiction*.

51

And he paid for it to be printed and published himself. Millions and millions of copies, to be distributed to booksellers all over the world. He ran up debts of millions of dollars, then he committed suicide.'

'I'm not getting this,' I said. 'So he publishes his own book, runs up millions of dollars of debt and commits suicide. But that's a big story. That alone should make the book a bestseller.'

'That's exactly what he planned, yes.'

'So what's the big deal? Why aren't you selling the book?'

'Because it's snuff fiction.' He whispered the words. 'It really *is* snuff fiction.'

'I don't understand what you mean.'

'You know what a snuff movie is?'

'Of course. Although it seems to be an urban myth. Nobody you meet has ever seen one themselves, but they've all got a friend whose friend has seen one.'

'Well, this is the real thing. If you read this book, you die.'

'What, someone comes round and kills you?'

'The book kills you.'

'How can a book kill you? I've read a few that have put me to sleep. But how can a book kill you?'

'The pages are impregnated with poison. It comes off on your fingers while you're reading the book. Enters your bloodstream and kills you.'

'I don't believe it. There's no such poison.'

'There is. It comes from the Amazon.'

'Who told you that?'

'A friend.'

'And who told your friend? A friend?'

'Look, it's true. There have already been deaths. Book reviewers, people like that. The books have all been pulped now, so it's OK. But the whole thing is a nightmare.'

'I've never read anything about this in the papers.'

'And you won't. It's all being hushed up. Can you imagine the implications of a thing like this? If people thought that books could kill them—?'

But I was way ahead of him there. A thing like that could bring down the whole British book publishing industry.

And I could imagine quite clearly how it might start.

Rumours on the conspiracy pages of the Internet. A big publisher was pulping books under mysterious circumstances. A mention of the word *virus*. Which is always a great word to start a panic with. And then the tall stories told in the pub. A friend of a friend's mum had been found dead in her armchair with a paperback book clutched in her hands. Another friend of a friend's dad had gone likewise, but he had been reading the *Sunday Sport*. And blokes in radiation suits had bagged up his body and torched his house.

It was the eco-warriors, some said, out to save the rain forests. Or that Japanese bunch who had put the chemical warfare bombs in the Tokyo Underground. Or it was the Discordians, or the Church of Euthanasia, or J. Bob Dodds. Or it was the evil French or the New Age Travellers.

And the rumours would spread and the panic would grow and newspapers would deny it. Then one newspaper would come out in a cling film wrapper, demanding that government health warnings be put on rival newspapers. And people would freak out and say that it wasn't safe to read any book or newspaper unless you were wearing rubber gloves. And there would be a lunatic rush to buy up rubber gloves, at any price.

I left Waterstone's that day with my head spinning. The implications were indeed terrible, and it was a very good thing that all the Johnny Quinn books had been pulped and the matter could be laid to rest. The chap at Waterstone's made me take a solemn vow that I would never reveal a word of anything he'd told me.

'Trust me,' I told him. 'I won't mention it to another living soul.'

And I have of course remained true to my promise.

Well, apart from mentioning it to my Uncle Brian.

Just in passing.

The Spurs of the Cockerel

Boy racers pass in large numbers
Waking priests from their reverent slumbers,
Vanish in clouds of blue gasoline
Leaving dark marks where their tyres have been.
Engines that move by the power of ten horses
Occupants altered in shape by G-forces.

Boy racers pass in their white GTs,
With the spurs of the cockerel behind them.

Climbers on peaks in the Andes
Dream of the life of the dandies,
Slim cigarettes held in holders of jade
Drag boys who stroll on the glass esplanade,
Cool Coca-Cola in blue-tinted glasses,
Silver decanters and late dinner passes.

Climbers on peaks sit and wonder,
With the spurs of the cockerel behind them.

Crass Latin waiters hold trays up
In clubs where the night person stays up,
News-reading ladies in glittery togs,
Paid baby-sitters look after their dogs,
Cherries that toast in a sea-fire of brandy,
Debutantes sipping their apricot shandy.

Crass Latin waiters swear under their breath,
With the spurs of the cockerel behind them.
Brown paper clerics read masses
To herds of the best-tailored Fascists,
Fast people's custom-made Rolles and Mercs,
White hands that ill disguise tailor-made smirks.
Silk-lined cravats and velvet pray-dos,
Never a glimpse of the old tennis shoes.

Brown paper clerics are playing it safe,
With the spurs of the cockerel above them.

Not that I'm bitter.

4

Times don't last, tough people do
MACHO MAN RANDY SAVAGE

'Cock-a-doodle-do, chief. Up and at it.'

I opened up my eyelids and almost managed to focus on the ceiling. Almost.

'Come on, chief, it's a glorious day. What shall we do first, breakfast at Tiffany's, or hit the big surf on Bondi?'

'Get out of my head, you little shit.'

'Come on now, chief, that's no way to speak to your Holy Guardian.'

'Demonic tormentor, more like.' I re-opened my eyelids the merest crack and squinted bitterly at the ceiling. It was the same ceiling, the same *padded* ceiling, that I'd been waking up to for almost three months now.

'I have to get out of here,' I told Barry. 'I have to. I do.'

'I know, chief. I'm on your side, after all. But if you want to get out of here you're gonna have to sharpen up your interview technique.'

'Yeah, right. But what can I do? If I lie, he says

I'm "in denial", and if I tell the truth, he thinks I'm a stone bonker.'

'Difficult times for you, chief.'

'Thanks for your warm support.'

'That's what I'm here for.'

'Huh!' I flexed my aching limbs as best I could in the straitjacket. I sorely needed the toilet. 'Couldn't you put a word in for me with the doctor's Holy Guardian?' I asked Barry.

'Vic the Spud? Wish I could, chief, but it's against the rules. Have you thought any more about my suggestion as to how we might get you out of here?'

'Now which particular suggestion would that be? The slimming-right-down-until-I-can-squeeze-through-the-bars suggestion? The digging-my-way-out-with-a-hypodermic-needle suggestion? The gluing-pillow-feathers-together-to-build-a-pair-of-wings suggestion? The—'

'I was thinking more of my persuading-someone-in-authority-from-the-outside-world-to-sign-your-release-form suggestion, actually, chief.'

'Ah, this would be the suggestion-you've-never-suggested-before suggestion.'

'I've suggested it loads of times, chief. It's just that you never listen.'

'I hang on your every God-given word, Barry. Should I fax the Pope, do you think? Do you have his private number?'

'I was thinking more of your Uncle Brian, chief. He's something secret in the government, isn't he?'

'He was going to be my second choice, naturally.'

'Naturally, chief. So when it's your turn to use the telephone in the recreation room again, perhaps you might give him a bell, rather than Sexy Sandra's Spanking Hot Line.'

The door of my padded cell swung open and male nurse Cecil loomed largely.

'Good morning, dreamboat,' he said. 'And who are we today?'

'Shouldn't it be *how* are we?'

'No, *who*. Are we Carlos the Chaos Cockroach, or Lazlo Woodbine the Private Eye, or Barking Barry the Talking Sprout, or—'

'Just plain old Mr Rankin today,' I said. 'And I'd like to use the toilet, have my breakfast and then make a telephone call, if that's all right with you.'

'A bit early in the day for Sexy Sandra, isn't it?'

'It's never too early for— What? You bastard! You listen in on my phone calls!'

'Hospital policy. You'd be surprised how many patients try to persuade someone in authority from the outside world to come in and sign their release forms.'

'Better pass on breakfast if you're gonna squeeze through those bars then, chief.'

Male nurse Cecil released me from the strait-jacket and marched me off up the hospital corridor. I had a poo, which I rather enjoyed, and a cold hose down in the showers, which I didn't. And then I was allowed to dry and dress myself before being marched off to breakfast.

I took a regulation steel tray and queued for my tucker.

'What do you want?' asked the big fat ugly-looking son-of-a-bitch behind the counter, when my turn came at last.

'Lightly poached quail's eggs, olive bread with honey topping. Kedgeree and black coffee. I'll try the Colombian roast today, if I may.'

The big fat ugly one ladled a helping of cold porridge onto a chipped enamel plate and thrust it in my direction. 'Twat,' he said. I fished a spoon from the counter bucket and took my breakfast to a vacant table.

As I sat, manfully munching, it occurred to me that there had never ever been a Golden Age of Loonies.

Every other walk of life had enjoyed its golden age. Racketeers spoke of the Twenties, big band leaders the Thirties, fighter pilots the Forties, Rock 'n' Rollers the Fifties, hippies the Sixties, someone-or-others the Seventies and yuppies the Eighties. But there had never been a good time to be a banged-up basket case. From manacles and cold water baths to electric shock treatment and experimental surgery, the going had always been grim, grim, grim.

'Anyone sitting here?' An inmate indicated the vacant chair next to me. In the outside world such a question would be easy to answer. But not here.

'You tell me,' I said.

'No, it's vacant.'

'Splendid.'

The inmate sat himself down. He was your standard issue inmate. Young, thin, pinched-faced, glassy-eyed, greasy-haired, pimply, bad-breathed, evil-smelling—

'Hey, let up,' said the inmate. 'I've got a lovely smile.' He showed me his lovely smile.

Black-toothed, yellow-tongued—

'Give it a rest.'

'Sorry,' I said. 'I was only thinking out loud.'

'You want to watch that, they'll put you in the nut house.'

'Ha ha ha,' I said, as I hadn't lost my sense of humour.

'I'm glad you haven't lost your sense of humour,' said the inmate, tucking into his porridge. 'I'm Dan, by the way.'

'Pleased to meet you, Dan.'

'No, it's Dan-by-the-way,' said Dan by the way. 'I'm only Dan to my friends.'

'And do you have many of those?'

'Well, none, actually.'

'Then don't let me spoil a perfect record.'

'Oh, what the heck, you can call me Dan, if you like.'

'Cheers, Dan.'

'No, I said Dan-if-you-like. Are you taking the piss, or what?'

'I'm just trying to eat my breakfast.'

'Yeah, well, let's have no trouble then.'

'Fine.' I picked what appeared to be a toenail from my teeth and cast it aside.

'What are you in for?' asked Dan.

'Multiple murder, cannibalism and necrophilia,' I said, as this often proved an efficient method of subtly discouraging further conversation. 'Do you have a problem with that?'

'Absolutely not.' Dan tucked further into his porridge. 'That's what I'm in here for.'

'Let's eat up and piss off, shall we, chief?'

'Absolutely.'

'Absolutely,' said Dan.

A little later Dan said, 'Actually I'm not in for multiple murder. Well, I am, a bit. But it's not the real reason I'm in here. I'm in here because I know things *they* don't want the outside world to know.'

'*They?*'

'*They*, them. The powers that be.'

'Always the same old *they*,' I said. 'Been having trouble with them myself.'

'I uncovered this terrible secret,' said Dan. 'You see, every man, woman and child in the entire world has an invisible alien sitting on their shoulders manipulating their thoughts.'

'Bummer.'

'Yes, isn't it? And no-one will believe me. Because the aliens manipulate their thoughts and tell them not to.'

'Tricky situation.'

'And I know about the Jesus conspiracy.'

'Is that like the JFK conspiracy?'

'Only in that it's a conspiracy.'

'So it's not like Jesus wasn't really crucified, he was shot with an arrow from the grassy knoll, or anything like that?'

'No, it's about the second coming.'

'Oh yeah? What, you know the date or something?'

'July the twenty-seventh.'

'This year?'

'No, not this year, don't be stupid.'

'Sorry.'

'July the twenty-seventh, nineteen sixty-seven.'

'How about a stroll around the exercise yard, chief?'

'In a minute, Barry, I don't want to miss this one.'

'Barry?' said Dan.

'Never mind about Barry. July the twenty-seventh, nineteen sixty-seven, you say? I wonder how that slipped by me.'

'Perhaps you were doing the Hippy Trail, or at Woodstock, or reading a Johnny Quinn novel, or something.'

'That must have been it.'

'Of course it wasn't it.' Dan banged his spoon on the table. 'It was never in the newspapers. It's a conspiracy. Didn't you ever wonder about the Summer of Love? Why nineteen sixty-seven was different from any other year? It's because it was the year Jesus was reborn. He was reborn in San Francisco. The CIA knew it was going to happen, they had copies of the missing pages from the Bible that were suppressed by the Pope prior to the English translation being done for King James. The date of the second coming was in there. The CIA took Jesus into protective custody, he's being brought up on a farm in Wisconsin. He was born in nineteen sixty-seven, so he will be thirty-three, his age at his former death, when the millennium comes around.'

'Something for us all to look forward to there, then.'

'Twat,' said Dan.

'And I thought we were getting along so well.'

'Take the piss if you want. But when Jesus comes down in glory from the clouds, in a helicopter would be my guess, you and all the other un-believers are going to look pretty silly.'

'Don't get me wrong,' I said. 'I'm no unbeliever. But let me put this to you. The Bible Belt of America called the Summer of Love an abomination unto the Lord. They said that all free love was the Devil's doing. You don't suppose your CIA friends have got the wrong fellow by any chance? Perhaps it isn't Jesus at all. Perhaps it's the Anti-Christ.'

Dan had a bit of a think. 'Let me get back to you on that,' he said. 'So, do you want to tell me what you're *really* in here for?'

'Propagation of conspiracy theory, same as you. This is the Conspiracy Theorists' Correctional Facility, isn't it? We're all in here for the same reason: "Oral dissemination of rumour and hearsay, liable to ellicit independent thought and cause a breach of the status quo" – Clause 23 of the new Suppression of Misinformation Act. I'm a tall-story-teller by profession. All I was doing was plying my trade, chatting to a bloke in a bar. Trouble was, the bloke in the bar turned out to be an off-duty clerk from the Ministry of Serendipity. Six o'clock the next morning, bang goes my front door, in storm the men in grey, and I'm dragged off here for a spell of corrective therapy.'

'And are the tablets helping?'

'Tablets always help. That's what tablets are for, isn't it?'

'Have you thought about planning an escape?'

'Novel idea.'

'Oh, are you writing a novel?'

'Certainly not! How dare you!'

'Sorry. But I'm planning to escape.' Dan drew me closer, but I wasn't keen. Not with the BO and the bad breath and everything. 'I'm building wings,' whispered Dan. 'From pillow feathers. I'm going to fly out of here.'

'Well, give my regards to Jesus when you see him.' I rose to take some exercise in the yard.

'Or I might just go out through the tunnel tonight with everyone else.'

I sat back down again. 'What did you say?' I asked.

'Chief,' said Barry, as I jogged around the exercise yard. 'Chief, I really don't think you should put too much faith in young Danny boy.'

'Oh really, Barry, and why not?'

'Because he's two eggs short of an omelette, chief. He's cooking without the gas on.'

'He said the tablets were helping.'

'Tablets always help, chief. But he's still a wacko. You can't trust him. It will end in tears.'

'No it won't, Barry. Because I have no intention of following Dan down any tunnel.'

'You don't, chief?'

'I don't, Barry. But the idea set me thinking. I've been going about all this in entirely the wrong way. Tunnels and feathered wings and squeezing through bars. Those are all *obvious* ways of escaping. What I should be doing is applying Rune's Law of Obviosity. I should be thinking of the least most obvious way of getting out of here.'

'Shouldn't that be the least most obvious, least most obvious way, chief, because the *least* most obvious way would be the most obvious way to choose, which would make it the *most* obvious way and—'

'Shut up, Barry.'

'Sorry, chief.'

'The least most obvious way of escaping would be simply to walk out of here in broad daylight.'

'I do foresee a problem or two there, chief.'

'Good.'

'Good, chief?'

'Good, Barry. Because the more problems there are, the more impossible the task becomes. And the more impossible it becomes, the more it proves itself to be the least most obvious way of getting out.'

'It's all so simple, once you explain it, chief.'

'Isn't it always?'

I walked back to my room. This I considered a very good start, as normally I would have been marched back to my room. But male nurse Cecil was busily engaged striking Dan with a truncheon and shouting something about a tunnel. So he didn't notice me as I strolled past.

I packed my suitcase, put on my street clothes, and stepped from my room into the corridor. An orderly wandered by, tripped, fell, struggled to his feet and continued his wanderings. I picked up the keys he'd dropped and unlocked the door that divided the Conspiracy Theorists' Correctional Facility from the rest of the hospital beyond.

Here I met a nurse who mistook me for a visitor.

'Would you like me to call you a cab?' she asked.

'Yes, please,' I told her.

'Well I'm not going to, because it's a really crap old joke.'

'Fair enough.'

'But I'll give you a lift if you want. I'm just going off my shift.'

I looked the nurse up and down. She was a very pretty nurse. Gorgeous blond hair, really sexy brown eyes, fabulous mouth, marvellous tits—

'Do you mind?' asked the nurse.

'Sorry,' I said. 'I was just thinking out loud.'

'You want to watch that, they'll put you in the nut house.'

'Ha ha ha,' I went.

'So do you want a lift or not?'

'I do, yes please.'

I followed the nurse to her car. It was one of those new solar-powered electric jobbies. Very smart, very high-tech. I drive a 1958 Cadillac Eldorado myself, electric blue, big tail fins, the whole caboodle. It's an image thing, I don't want to dwell on it.

I sat down next to the nurse.

'So,' she said, 'where do you want to go?'

I gave this some thought. The most obvious place would be my office. But when Cecil and co found I was missing, that would be the most obvious place they'd choose to come looking. So where would be the least most obvious place for me to go? I had to get back on my case. Track down that voodoo handbag. Save the world the way only I could save it. But not in the most obvious way. Obviously.

'Why don't you come back to my place?' asked the nurse.

'An obvious choice,' said I.

'But I'll have to ask you a favour,' she said.

'Go ahead,' said I.

'I need some help moving a bit of junk out of my attic. Would you object to giving me a hand?'

'I certainly wouldn't. What kind of junk do you have in mind?'

'Just junk,' she said. 'Stuff that belonged to my aunt. Old clothes, pictures, umbrellas, a voodoo handbag—'

I smiled a lot as she drove me back to her place. And I blessed the name of Hugo Rune. When we got to her place I was pleased by the way it looked. A big place it was, a mansion, no less. Georgian, very up-market. Hardly the most obvious place you'd expect to find a nurse living.

Splendid.

She drove up the sweeping gravel drive and parked in the double garage next to the Rolls Royce.

'Come on,' she said, and I followed her across to the big front door. It was open.

'That's odd,' she said. 'I'm sure I locked it when I came out.'

'Leave this to me, lady,' I told her. 'I'm a professional.'

Now you probably didn't notice that, but I slipped the word *lady* in there. 'Leave it to me, *lady*,' I said, rather than just 'Leave it to me.' I might have said, 'Leave it to me, *sweetheart*,' or 'Leave it to me, *luv*,' but I didn't, I said, 'Leave it to me, *lady*.' And the reason I did this was because I was moving into genre. A most specific genre, that of the American Private Eye circa 1958 (same year as my Cadillac Eldorado and no coincidence).

Back in those days your American Private Eye was a hard-nosed, lantern-jawed, snap-brim-fedora'd, belted-up-trench-coated, Bourbon-swilling, fag-smoking, lone-walking, pistol-toting, mean-fighting, smart-talking, broad-humping, tricky-case-solving son-of-a-gun.

And none more so than Lazlo Woodbine.

Woodbine, described by Sir Arthur Conan Doyle as 'the detective's detective', was the creation of the English writer P. P. Penrose. Woodbine was the classic 1950s American Private Eye. He worked just the four locations: his office where clients came, a bar where he talked a load of old toot, an alleyway where he got involved in sticky situations, and a rooftop, where he had his final confrontation with the villain. And he always ended the very first chapter by being struck on the head from behind and tumbling down into a deep dark whirling pit of oblivion. In one hundred and fifty-eight thrilling adventures, Woodbine never deviated from this award-winning format.

Woodbine was *the man*.

He wasn't cheap, but he was thorough and he got the job done. With Woodbine you could expect a lot of gratuitous sex and violence, a trail of corpses, and a final rooftop showdown. No spin offs, no loose ends, and all strictly in the first person. And the literary style, the language, the description, the nuances, the running gags. Magical stuff.

And I had him off to a T.

So let's take it from 'Leave it to me, lady'. You'll soon get the picture.

'Leave it to me, lady,' I said. 'I'm a professional.'

The dame took a step to one side and I cast my steely gaze over the door lock. It was a *Dovestone-Wilberforce* triple-lever mortice deadlock. Five rotational tumblers, multi-facet optional reverse-action interior facility. I knew this lock, every good detective did. In this game, knowing your locks can mean the difference between cutting a dash and splitting the beaver. If you know what I mean, and I'm sure that you do.

'Does anyone else have a key to this door?' I asked.

She copped me a glance like she was polishing fish knives and shook her beautiful bonce.

'Then you'd better let me take a look inside. Wait here.'

I put my foot to the door and kicked it fully open. Then I leapt into the hall, rolled over a couple of times, and prepared to come up firing.

And then I was struck on the head from behind, and found myself tumbling down into a deep dark whirling pit of oblivion.

So I'd got off to a pretty good start.

Stokers, Luggers and Jumping Jacks

The stoker called Tom
From Newcastle,
The lugger called Tim
From Dundee,
The old jumping Jacks
In their ill-fitting macs,
Are more than the whole world to me.

The stoker called Pig
With his whistle,
The lugger called Pan
With his flute,
The old jumping Jacks
With their harps on their backs,
And Nick in his best Sunday suit.

The stoker called Jack
With his rabbits,
The lugger called Nick
With his hair,
The old jumping Jims
And Alastair Sims,
And Jock with his sanitary wear.

At about this time the party began to get a bit
    boisterous,
So I made my excuses and left.

5

*My dear boy, forget about the
motivation. Just say the lines
and don't trip over the furniture.*
NOEL COWARD

There was Tom and there was Tim and there was
Nick and there was Billy. A stoker, a lugger, a
hairdresser and Billy. Billy Barnes. Billy didn't
come to the party because Billy had business elsewhere. Billy always had business elsewhere. Nobody knew quite where elsewhere was, but Billy
did, and he always had business there. There was
something different about Billy, it was hard to say
quite what, but it was there. He was very clever, I
remember that. Too clever, really. I used to sit next
to him in junior school, and once in a while his
cleverness would burst to the surface and splash all
over the rest of us.

I recall one Friday afternoon our teacher, Miss
Moon, posed a question to the class. It was: 'How
far can a man walk into the desert?' We chewed
upon our pencils; the question was surely un-
answerable. Who was this man? How old was he?
How strong was he? How much food and water did

72

he have? How large was the desert? Billy put his hand up straight away.

'Yes, Billy?' said Miss Moon.

'I have the answer, miss,' said Billy.

'Go on then, tell us what it is.'

'It's half way, miss. Because after he's gone half way, he'll be walking out of the desert again.'

Billy was quite right, of course. His answer was correct. But this didn't seem to please Miss Moon. She had evidently hoped that her question would keep the class occupied for the rest of the afternoon. Billy wasn't at all popular with the rest of the class either, for a while.

Because no-one likes a smart-arse.

At the age of twenty-three Billy went missing. He went for a walk and he never came back. Those of us who remembered him from junior school wondered whether he had gone for a walk in the desert. One story was that he had hitch-hiked to Brighton, fallen off the pier and been carried out to sea.

But nobody knew for sure, and the mystery of Billy's disappearance has never been satisfactorily laid to rest. Years later, when I was living near Brighton, I met a bloke in a bar who told me a tale that might well have explained what happened to Billy.

I relate it here for two reasons. Firstly, because if it hadn't been for Billy's disappearance I would never have got involved in the case of the voodoo handbag. And secondly, because I consider there is a strong possibility that the tale is true.

The tale was told to me by a travelling salesman, but as this in itself may raise doubts regarding its reliability, I have taken the liberty of changing the tale-teller's trade.

To that of wandering mendicant.

The village I live in is called Bramfield. It lies about ten miles north of Brighton, just off the A23, which is the main London to Brighton road. It's a pretty enough village and the folk who live there are happy, being mostly engaged in occupations connected with foxhunting. They keep themselves to themselves and do not encourage tourists. Small boys pelt visiting cyclists with stones and farmers run off walkers at the point of a gun. Travelling salesmen are often to be seen, however, but rarely a wandering mendicant.

The one who wandered into the Jolly Gardeners one Wednesday lunchtime was a mendicant in the grand tradition. He was short and shoeless, rough and ragged, wild of eye and long of beard. He walked with the aid of a knobbly staff and he called for a pint of best bitter.

Andy took one look at the wandering mendicant and ordered him straight out of the bar. I considered this a bit harsh and I said so.

'I consider that a bit harsh,' I said to Andy.

'Dress code,' said the landlord. 'He can't drink here looking like that.'

I viewed the mendicant's apparel. He wore the traditional brown sacking robe, secured at the waist by a length of knotted string. It was a fetid robe, frayed about the hems and gone to buggeration at the elbows.

'So what's the problem?' I asked Andy.

'Tie,' said the landlord. 'He isn't wearing a tie.'

74

Now I am renowned as a charitable fellow, in fact the term *living saint* has more than once been used to describe me. And I took pity upon this thirsty traveller and led him outside to my car, in the hope that I might have something that would serve as a tie. I had a good old rummage in the glove box and under the seats, but all I could come up with was a pair of jump leads in the boot. I knotted these about the mendicant's neck and we returned to the bar.

'All right now?' I asked Andy.

Andy scrutinized the jump leads. 'All right,' he said to the mendicant. 'You can come in, but *don't start anything*.'

Oh how we laughed.

'I'll have a pint of best bitter, please,' said the mendicant. 'Before you turn nasty.'

'Why should I turn nasty?' Andy asked.

'Because I don't have any money to pay you with.'

'I'll pay,' I said. And I did.

I sat down in my favourite corner and the mendicant sat down with me. He sipped at his bitter and then he said, 'You're a Telstar, aren't you?'

'I'm a *what*?'

'A Telstar. Born under the sign of Telstar. I'm an astrologer. I know these things.'

'But Telstar was a satellite,' I said, 'put up in the 1950s.'

'It's a heavenly body and astrology is all to do with the influence of heavenly bodies.'

'Stars and planets, yes, but not telecommunication satellites.'

The mendicant drank deeply of his pint. 'Well,

that's where you're wrong,' he said, wiping froth from his beard. 'It's all to do with proximity. Everything in space influences everything else. And we are influenced by everything in space. The stars and galaxies exert influence, but they are thousands of light years away, man-made satellites are a whole lot closer. They exert a far stronger influence.'

'I find that difficult to believe.'

'Well you would, you're a Telstar. Consider the youth of today. All into name brand sportswear and name brand trainers and burger chain dinners and manufactured pop music. Why do you think that is?'

'Search me,' I said.

'They all have the Sky TV satellite in their birth charts.'

'Bugger me.'

'No thanks. And I'll tell you something more.'

'What's that?'

'I've finished my pint and I'd care for another.'

'Incredible!'

I purchased another pint of best bitter for the mendicant and a Death by Cider for myself.

'A strange thing happened to me on my way to this pub,' said the mendicant. 'Would you like me to tell you about it?'

'That would be nice.'

'No it wouldn't, but I'll tell you anyway. How old would you say I am?'

I viewed his grizzled visage. 'Sixty maybe, sixty-five.'

'I'm sixty-six.'

'Well, you don't look it.'

76

'I keep myself fit, that's why. I walk twenty-five miles a day on average. Have done for the last thirty years. I did the Hippy Trail in the Sixties and went to Woodstock and—'

'Would you mind just telling me about this strange thing that happened to you, because I have to go in a minute. I've got an appointment to see the doctor.'

'Are you ill?'

'No, I have to get some sleeping pills for my wife.'

'Why?'

'Because she's woken up again.'

Oh how we laughed.

'All right,' said the mendicant. 'I'll tell you my tale, but it's an odd one, and you must make of it what you will.'

'Go ahead then.'

'All right. Now, as I say, I get about a bit. I wander the world, and I sleep rough, the stars above and Mother Earth below and that kind of stuff. Well, the other week I was camped out in the middle of the big roundabout just outside Brighton.'

'The one on the A23?'

'The very same. Hitch-hikers always stand there thumbing lifts to London, you've probably seen them.'

I nodded. I had.

'Well, I'm sitting there and I see this young bloke with his bit of cardboard with London scrawled on it, standing there thumbing, and I see this old yellow and cream VW Camper pull up to give him a lift. And I hear the driver say "London?" and the hitch-hiker say "Yes, please." And then they go off together.'

'So?' I said. 'What's unusual about that? I've seen that happen loads of times.'

'Me too. But not an hour later the van is back. Same van. And it picks up another hitch-hiker. "London?" says the driver. "Yes, please," says the hitch-hiker and off they go.'

'An hour later?' I said.

'An hour later. And an hour after that the van is back once more.'

'And picks up another hitch-hiker?'

'Another one. I watched all day. Eight hitch-hikers, he took.'

'But he couldn't have taken them to London and been back to Brighton in an hour. Perhaps he only took them as far as the motorway.'

'Perhaps. Well, I'm quite comfortable on the roundabout and I think maybe I'll stick around for another day. And I do, and bright and early the next morning, the old VW Camper is back, and he's picked up another London-bound hitch-hiker.'

'Perhaps it's some kind of community bus service or something.'

'Or something! Well, I sit there all day and count another six hitch-hikers going away in the VW and then I have to move off the roundabout because a bloke from the council arrives to cut the grass. I mention to him about the VW, and he says that he'd noticed it picking up hitch-hikers and it had been doing so for the last five years.'

'Definitely some community bus service, or something, then.'

'Or something. Well, you hear strange tales when you're on the road and you see strange sights and I didn't quite know what to make of this, but as I was heading in the direction of London myself, I thought I'd get a piece of cardboard, scrawl the city's name on it, stick out my thumb and see if I could cop a lift from the VW the next time around.'

'And did you?'

'Oh yes, I did.'

'And did he take you to London?'

'Oh no, he didn't.'

'Go on then, tell me what happened.'

'Well, I see him coming and I stick out my thumb and hold up my piece of cardboard. He stops and calls, "London?" through the open window. "Yes," I say. "Hop in," he says. And off we go. The VW Camper is pretty knackered up inside and the driver doesn't say much, he's very gaunt and pale and he doesn't smell too good. "Can you take me all the way to London?" I ask. "Certainly," he says. "That's where I'm going. Go up there every day at this time." I ask what line of business he's in and he says "recycling".

' "Recycling what?" I ask.

' "Waste," he says.

'And we're about twenty minutes into our journey when he says, "I have to make a slight detour here to drop something off. You don't mind, do you?" And I say "No, I don't mind, what do you have to drop off?" And he says "Just a letter." And I

79

notice, in the back, he has a big carton of sealed envelopes. He takes a turning off the A23 and we go along some country lanes, then he turns up this farm track and we drive into this broken down old farmyard. He pulls up, reaches over his shoulder and takes one of the envelopes. "Do me a favour," he says. "Take this to the farmhouse. Knock at the door, and if no-one answers, put it inside on the hall table." I say, "No problem." I take the envelope and off I go.

'The farmhouse is about thirty yards away, and I glance back over my shoulder a couple of times and notice that the driver is watching me very intently. I knock at the door and I wait. Then I hear this dog barking and look back and see a great big dog snapping at the VW. The driver is momentarily distracted, so I duck down behind some old corrugated iron and wait to see what will happen next. The driver shouts at the dog, and the dog ambles off. The driver looks back in my direction. He can't see me, smiles, turns the VW around and drives away.'

'This is all bloody odd,' I said.

'Bloody odd,' said the mendicant. 'And bloody suspicious. So I decide to take a look around. No-one has answered my knock at the front door and the place seems deserted so I slip round to the back of the house to see what might be seen. And the first thing I see is the first mountain.'

'The first mountain?'

'About ten feet high. Hundreds of pieces of mouldy cardboard, thousands in fact. The ones at the bottom of the mound look ancient, the ones at the top a lot newer. These have all got something written on them. The same something. A single word. *London*.'

'London?'

'And then I see the second mountain. A mountain of rucksacks and sleeping bags.'

'Good God,' I said.

'Good God is right. I go back to the front of the house and I'm wondering what to do. I figure I'll push open the front door a couple of inches and take a careful peep inside. And I'm just doing this when the big dog attacks me. It comes rushing up out of nowhere and it leaps at my throat. I duck out of the way and the dog hits the front door, knocking it wide open. As I roll over I see the dog land in the hall, and as its feet hit the floor the floor tilts like a trap door and there's this terrible sound of whirling machinery. And I just catch a glimpse of the dog as it vanishes into all these thrashing blades, howling hideously, before the floor swings back up into place, the front door closes and all goes very quiet indeed.'

'Holy shit!' I said.

The mendicant finished his second pint. ' "Re-cycling",' he said, 'that's what the driver called it. "Recycling waste". I told you I'd heard strange tales and I'd heard this one before. I'd heard tell that there are vans like that all over England. That's why you see so many of those old VW Campers. They clean up the streets, recycle the dispossessed. It's all the government's doing, and the minced-up meat goes to feed animals in secret research establishments.'

'But someone should do something. Where is this farm?'

'Not far from here. But it won't do you any good. The strange thing that happened to me on the way here was this: I went back there. Back to the farm today. But it wasn't there. The place had been razed to the ground and concreted over. I figure they had secret security cameras and they saw me escape. So they destroyed the evidence. They're cunning, you see, cunning as—'

'Foxes,' I said.

And that was the mendicant's story. Well, the travelling salesman's story. But the mendicant told it better. I can't say whether it's really true, of course, and it certainly wouldn't have been true if it had been told to me by a travelling salesman, because *he* wouldn't have been hitch-hiking, would he? But if it is true, then it could have explained what happened to Billy. Although, as I would later learn, what happened to Billy Barnes was something far more sinister.

The reason Billy's disappearance led me to become involved in the case of the voodoo handbag was this:

Billy's mum was a friend of my mum and so, shortly after Billy went missing, Billy's mum came round to tea with my mum, and my mum suggested that Billy's mum should have a word with me.

I had just opened my first private detective agency, nothing swanky, just a table and chair in the shed, but I was hungry to take on something big. A missing person case was right up my alley, and so when Mrs Barnes came right up my alley and knocked on the shed door, I was more than pleased.

I ushered her in and sat her down on the half-bag of solid cement that served as 'client chair'.

'So,' I said to Mrs Barnes, 'how might I help you?'

'It's my Billy,' said the distraught lady. 'He's gone missing.'

'Yes, I read about it in the newspapers. Do you want me to see if I can find him?'

'No thanks,' said Mrs Barnes.

'No thanks?'

Mrs Barnes shook her hair-net. 'I'm quite pleased to see the back of him, really. It's the handbag I want returned.'

'Billy took your handbag?'

'Oh no. Billy vanished a couple of weeks earlier. But it was only a matter of time before the handbag went too.'

'I don't quite understand,' I said.

'It's a voodoo handbag,' said Mrs Barnes. 'Belonged to my mum.'

'And what, exactly, is a voodoo handbag?'

'It's an object of veneration.'

'Like a saint's relic, or something?'

'Very much like that, yes. In voodoo there is a pantheon of gods. Papa Legba, most benevolent of all, he is the guardian of the gates. Damballo Oueddo, the wisest and most powerful, whose symbol is the serpent. Agoué, god of the sea. Loco, god of the forest, Ogoun Badagris, the dreadful and bloody one, and Maîtresse Ezilée, an incarnation of the Blessed Virgin Mary.'

'And the handbag was hers originally?'

'Maîtresse Ezilée's, yes. From her bag the good receive favours, the bad something else entirely.'

'And your mum had this very bag?'

'Not the real one, no. A copy, cast in plaster.'

'And is it valuable?'

'Only to those who know how to use it.'

'I see,' I said. But I didn't.

'It is a *transitus tessera*, literally a ticket of passage. He who carries the bag and understands its ways can travel from one place to another.'

'And you're quite certain Billy didn't take it when he went off on his travels?'

'Quite certain.'

'What does it look like, this voodoo handbag?'

'About twenty inches high, handbag-shaped, covered in skulls. You'll know it when you see it.'

'And it's important that you get it back?'

'More important than anything else in the world. You see, the bag holds power, great power. When I said that you can use it to travel from one place to another, I didn't mean ordinary places. The bag allows you to travel between the worlds of the living and the dead. To enter the spirit world and return safely.'

'Hm,' I said.

'Don't "Hm" me, you little shit.'

'Did I say Hm? I meant, of course, *Yeah, right!*'

'The bag has been held in safe keeping by my family for four generations. We are its guardians.'

'But I thought you said it was only a copy.'

'Look, it's the *only* copy, all right! Just look upon it as something precious that's been lost.'

'Stolen, surely?' I said. 'I mean you didn't just mislay this precious object, did you?'

'It's gone missing, that's all. A policeman called Inspector Kirby came to see me about Billy's disappearance, and he got involved with the handbag and then the handbag went missing.'

'The policeman nicked it?'

'No, he didn't. It's just gone missing, OK?'

'If you say so, but I really don't understand any of this.'

Mrs Barnes made little sighing sounds. 'All right,' she said. 'I'll tell you everything. But it's a tale of terror. Of gruesome deeds and eldritch horror. Once you know the full story you will understand why the handbag must be returned to my family. And you will know things that few living men know and fewer still wish to know.'

'I'm all ears,' I said.

'Then I must whisper.'

And she whispered.

And I listened.

And then she whispered some more.

And I listened some more.

And then she did a bit more whispering.

And I threw up all over the floor.

'That's a nasty bit, isn't it?' she said.

And I agreed that it was.

And then she whispered a whole lot more.

And then she finished.

'And that's it,' she said.

'And I'm very glad to hear it,' I replied.

And then she made me solemnly swear that I would not mention a word of anything she'd told me to anyone else.

'Trust me,' I said. 'I won't mention it to another living soul.'

And I have, of course, remained true to my promise.

Maladroit Mal

Down the busy shopping street,
Tripping over two large feet,
Frightening babies in the pram,
Sneering at the traffic jam.
Maladroit Mal,
Nobody's pal,
Taking a chance in the open.

Over local village green,
Geeing up the beauty queen,
Yelling great and profane oaths,
Making bakers soil their loafs.
Maladroit Mal,
Nobody's pal,
Taking a chance in the open.

Up the cut and down the dells,
Followed by unsavoury smells,
Ambling,
Shambling,
Crawling and
Gambolling.

Strolling,
Rolling,
Tripping,
Bowling.

Stumbling,
Bumbling,
Twitching,
Tumbling.

Maladróit Mal,
Nobody's pal,
Taking a chance in the open.

6

The quality of weirdness has always been high.
BOB RICKARD

A True History of Billy Barnes

The child that is truly different rarely ever looks that way. It has always been instinctive in the herd to drive off the 'different one', no doubt to ensure the purity of the species. This is definitely the case with mankind. Children learn early to mock the fatty, or the thin kid, or the one with the ginger hair, but they're not taught to, it's instinctive, they can't help themselves. They just do it. But the child that is truly different, the individual who will one day grow up and change society, alter the direction of the herd, this child often has a defensive camouflage. This child looks like all the rest.

But he's not.

Billy Barnes looked like all the rest. He looked a bit like Dave Rodway, with those dark eyebrows. And a bit like Norman Crook, with that snubby nose. And he had Peter Lord's shoulders, and Neil Christian's knees and Peter Grey's feet and so on and so forth. In fact he looked pretty much like everybody other than himself.

Which made him quite hard to describe, really.

But he *was* different.

And the difference was all on the inside.

Billy Barnes was a regular boffin. He was, quite simply, the brightest kid in the class. In the school, probably. But he kept it mostly to himself. Once in a while it bubbled right up, as in the notorious 'man walks into the desert' affair, which earned him considerable contempt and cut him right out from the herd for a while. But he was soon back, strictly low-profile, blending in with the rest and not looking out of place.

He was a subtle manipulator, Billy. Always up to something, but no-one knew quite what.

He was different, you see.

And he always had 'business elsewhere'.

There are now well over one hundred Billy Barnes web sites. These range from the official World Leader corporate pages that list Billy's business interests as resource management, social engineering and off-world development, to the Unofficial Conspiracy pages that have Billy down as the sole cause of all the world's ills.

Today the face of Billy Barnes is the best-known face on the planet, but you'd still find it hard to pick it out from an identity parade.

Exactly how Billy rose to his exalted position of ultimate controller has never been satisfactorily explained or fully chronicled before. Rumour has it that an unofficial biography, exposing Billy as an arch criminal, depraved pornographer and all-round bad egg, was withdrawn before publication and destroyed in the great Health Purge of 2001, along with all other books, newspapers and printed material. But that is only a rumour and the man who spread it is long dead, cut down cruelly in a freak accident involving handcuffs and an electric drill.

So what do we *really* know about Billy?

Well, not a lot.

We do know that at the age of twenty-three he went missing and that ten years later, at the age of thirty-three (which may or may not be a significant age), he reappeared and swiftly took control of just about everything.

But there's an awful lot of unanswered questions.

It is interesting that those who knew him at school remember him only as the boy who answered the 'man walks into the desert' question and for very little else. It is to be noted that all the great prophets have their missing years, and that each of them walked into a desert. Entering as a man, but returning as a son of God.

So what went on with Billy?

Well, let's go back and see.

If you enter the village of Bramfield from the end where the common is, turn right at the mini-roundabout that everyone drives straight across, pass the restaurant that is always changing hands, the off-licence run by the fat bloke with the earring, and the newsagent's where they sell the dreary greetings cards, you will come to the war memorial.

It's only a very small war memorial, because it was built by public subscription and the public weren't too giving, but it's there all right if you're prepared to look hard enough. And if you do look hard enough and you take the left where you find it, you'll find yourself in the lane where Billy lived.

There is no road sign on this lane. The elders of Bramfield felt that the name of this lane was not in the best possible taste, so they had the road sign taken down. The name of this lane is Colin Regis Lane.

As you may know, the word Regis is tacked onto the name of a town to signify that some old king or queen of times past slept there and liked it very much, as in Lyme Regis or Bognor Regis. Exactly who Colin was is now anyone's guess, but he was obviously someone who caught the royal fancy.

Moving along this lane you will pass several fine-looking Georgian houses on the right. There is Lugger's View, where Tim lives. Stoker's Folly, where Tom lives. Barnet Villa, where Nick resides. And Colin's End, which is presently unoccupied.

Moving further along you will come to the allotments, and presently, the yucky pond. The yucky pond is actually called Tinker's Pond, but it is locally known as the yucky pond due to the excess of yuckiness that floats upon its surface.

The yucky pond is maintained by public subscription.

Opposite the yucky pond there stands a fine big house. All on its own with a high wall around it. This house is built in the Tudor style and its name is Houmfort House.

And Houmfort House was Billy's house.

Billy lived in Houmfort House with his mum

and his granny. Billy's dad did not live there. Billy's dad had business elsewhere and only came home every once in a while to hand out presents and tell Billy tales of the places he'd seen. Billy and his dad were not 'close'. But then Billy wasn't really 'close' to anyone.

Billy was different.

And 'different' is hard to be close to.

Billy's mum was *not* different. Billy's mum was the same. Very much the same. The same as she had always been, as long as Billy had known her. Billy liked her that way, although sometimes he felt that he could do with a change.

Like today, for instance.

Today being Tuesday.

Billy always took Tuesday's breakfast on the veranda at the back of the house. Whatever the weather, or the time of year. It was a tradition in the Barnes household. A tradition, or an old charter or something.

Billy feasted this particular Tuesday morning upon roll-mop herrings and bitter-sweet tea. His mum had her usual, which was the usual, same as ever.

Billy always kept very still while he ate. Only his jaw moved, slowly and rhythmically. Twenty-three times a minute. Billy's mum, on the other hand, was a flamboyant eater, given to sweeping gestures and guttural utterances. Belching and flatulence. Food-flinging and the banging down of cutlery. They complemented one another, as is right between a mother and her son.

'It says here,' said Billy's mum, reading aloud

from the *Daily Sketch*, 'that he engaged in certain practices which gave him the kind of moustache you can only get off with turps.'

Billy swallowed a well-masticated segment of herring and turned his eyes in the direction of his mother. She was a fine woman. A fine *big* woman. Generously formed. Of ample proportions. Why, a starving man could feast upon such a woman for a good two months. Assuming that he had a large enough freezer to keep the bits fresh in.

'Ah no,' said Billy's mum. 'I must have misread it. The ventriloquist's name was Turps. The dummy didn't have a moustache.'

Billy moved his head ever so slightly, just enough to take the drinking straw between his lips. He sipped up bitter-sweet tea, but he didn't swallow.

'That's Africa for you,' said Billy's mum. 'The white man's grave and the black man's dingle-dongler. Which reminds me, have you fed your granny today, Billy?'

Billy nodded with his eyes. Of course he had fed his granny. He aways fed his granny. It was his job to feed his granny. And he enjoyed it very much. After all, he loved his granny.

Billy kept his granny in a suitcase.

It was a large suitcase and it had holes bored in the lid, so it wasn't cruel, or anything. And it saved space. Billy's granny used to take up quite a lot of space. Her bed was the biggest in the house and the most comfortable. Billy now shared this bed with his mum.

Granny lived under the bed. In the suitcase.

Billy took Granny out at weekends and gave her a

wash and a change of clothes. Not every boy was as good to his granny as Billy was.

But then not every boy had a granny quite like Billy's.

In her youth she had danced the candle mambo with Fred Astaire, trodden the boards with Sarah Bernhardt, glittered at society functions, and cast her exaggerated shadow in fashionable places.

But now she was old and weak and withered. Bereft of speech and movement and much gone with the moth. Deaf and blind and dotty and gnawed away by rats.

But Billy still found time for her. Although he wasn't 'close'.

'Apparently,' said Billy's mum, tapping at her tabloid, 'the Welsh have no concept of Velcro. I went to North Wales once with your father. He was very tall in those days and the Welsh are very short. Midgets, most of them, positively dwarf-like. They were quite in awe of your father. The Mayor of Harlech presented him with a pair of braces that glowed in the dark. Something to do with the mines, I believe.'

Billy swallowed his bitter-sweet tea, his Adam's apple rising to the occasion.

'You'd like Wales, Billy,' said his mum. 'Plenty of room to move furniture around and no Velcro getting under your feet.'

Billy smiled with his eyes.

The front door bell rang in the hall.

'That will be the postman,' said Billy's mum. 'He's always doing that.' She poured herself a noisy cup of coffee, sloshed in the milk and stirred vigorously. *Slap*, *slap*, *slap* went her big fat feet upon the tiled veranda floor. But she didn't get up. She leaned back in her chair and farted loudly.

The door bell rang again, and then again, and then no more. At length the postman made his entrance through the garden door.

'I've a package here for a Mr William Barnes,' said the postman. 'And it has to be signed for.'

Billy eyed his mum. The big woman shifted uneasily in her wicker chair. She never took kindly to tradespeople as a rule, especially, as now, when she was naked. But she always had time for a postman, or a porter, as long as their fingernails were clean.

Billy's mum spread her *Daily Sketch* modestly across her knees and beckoned to the bearer of the Queen's mail.

The bearer of the Queen's mail seemed strangely reticent. 'It's for your son,' he said. '*He* has to sign for it.'

Billy turned his head by twenty-three degrees and spoke his first words of the day. 'From whom?' he asked.

The postman examined the parcel. 'From *Necrosoft Industries*,' he said. 'Of Brentford, Middlesex.'

Billy nodded thoughtfully and then sprang to his feet. He vaulted over the veranda rail, performed a handspring and a cartwheel and came to rest before the postman.

'Pen,' said Billy, extending a hand.

The postman handed Billy the parcel, fumbled with his clipboard and pen. 'Your mother shouldn't be allowed,' he whispered.

Billy signed upon the dotted line and returned both pen and clipboard to the postman. 'Fuck off,' he told him. And the postman took his leave.

Billy returned to his chair on the veranda and sat down upon it. Birdies gossiped on the garden walls, bumblies toiled amongst the roses, and the sun beamed down its blessings over all.

Upstairs in the suitcase underneath the bed, Billy's granny sucked upon her sunken gums and dreamed of Fred Astaire.

'Have you thought any more about getting a job?' asked Billy's mum, over lunch, which was taken, as of Tuesday, in the greenhouse.

Billy sucked soup through a straw. He had *not* thought any more about getting a job.

'You're so very qualified, dear,' said his mum, herself now prettified in a floral frock. 'You have all your school certificates and your university degree and here you are at the age of twenty-three, a virtual recluse. You never go out anywhere and you never have any lady friends round to call. You were always such a popular boy at school. You used to fit in so nicely. Could you not find a job you could fit nicely into?'

Billy raised an eyebrow. The subject of 'a job' always came up on a Tuesday. Which was why Billy always felt that he could do with a change of mum on a Tuesday.

'Well, dear?' asked Billy's mum.

'No,' said Billy. 'I have important matters that must be dealt with.'

'More of this "business elsewhere"?'

'Just so.'

'But if you have "business elsewhere", how come you're never elsewhere getting on with it?'

Billy tapped at his right temple with a skinny digit. 'Elsewhere can be closer than you think,' he said.

Over tea, which being Tuesday they took in the cupboard underneath the stairs, Billy's mum asked, 'What was that package that arrived for you this morning?'

'I don't know,' said Billy. 'I haven't opened it yet.'

Billy and his mum never dined together on Tuesday evenings. Billy's mum always put on her best tweed suit and went out somewhere. Billy wasn't altogether certain where this somewhere was. But he suspected that it was the same somewhere that Andy the landlord of the Jolly Gardeners always went to.

Although he had no idea as to where *this* somewhere was, either.

But as Billy didn't care, it didn't matter.

Billy now sat all alone at the kitchen table and opened up his package. The brown paper fell away to reveal a bright plastic something of no obvious purpose and some sheets of printed paper.

Billy put the bright plastic something carefully aside and read from the top sheet of paper.

Surfing the web?
Anyone can do that! Why not
Try something *really* radical?

*A*ccess the dearly departed by body-boarding the
*N*ecronet.

*N*ever has it been more
*E*asy. All you have to do is
*E*nter the Soul
*D*atabase, by taking a left-hand turn off the
Information *S*uperhighway and

*Y*ou're there. In the Land
*O*f the Virtual Dead.
U know it makes sense.

Billy laid this sheet of paper aside and read from the
next one.

Dear Mr Barnes.

We at NECROSOFT would like to make you an
offer you will not wish to refuse. NECROSOFT is a
rapidly expanding organization on the cutting
edge of computer technology. Our goals are
high, but our aim is true.

It is the intention of NECROSOFT to bring about
a new world order. Not in the political sense, but
by creating a situation where the individual can
live in peace and harmony and happiness.

Our intention is to totally eradicate death
within the next five years.

An impossible dream?

Not a bit of it.

Through the use of our advanced neural-
network scanners we are now able to download
the memory and personality of an individual
into the NECRONET.

The NECRONET is a virtual world, computer-simulated, fully accessible and of boundless dimension. Nothing short of a heaven on earth, in fact. Those downloaded into it will become immortal, capable of being accessed by their children, grandchildren and so on endlessly.

An opportunity of a lifetime?

No, the opportunity of many lifetimes yet to come.

And all this could be yours.

For a small fee.

Billy screwed the paper into a ball and flung it onto the floor. One sheet remained and he idly perused it.

EARN BIG £££ate

read this one:

Do you have an elderly or infirm person living with you? One whom you dearly love, and whose needs you minister to daily? How about sending them on the journey of a lifetime? With all expenses paid and a big cash bonus for you? Like the sound of it? Phone this number for further details:

Billy sat awhile and stared into space. His fingers found themselves toying around with the bright plastic something. It was warm to the touch and it gave at the edges. There was something pleasurable about it. Billy bounced the something gently on the table. He had been expecting this. This or something like it. A package in the post, an offer on the phone. The chance of a lifetime in one form or another. But he hadn't been expecting it today.

Which made it perfect, really.

Billy had taken no employment, although much had been offered him. He had waited patiently for The Opportunity to present itself. He had followed Hugo Rune's Law, that the greatest opportunity must present itself in the least most obvious way. And the least most obvious way of finding employment was to stay at home and avoid looking for it.

Billy smiled. There would be a job for him at Necrosoft. And a big cash bonus when he handed Granny over. Billy was perfectly capable of reading between the lines. Necrosoft were obviously looking for some old and infirm types, that no-one cared much about, to experiment with in order to perfect their neural-network scanning techniques. It was the way he would have gone about things if he'd been running the show.

'And I soon will be running the show,' said Billy, picking up the telephone.

The Secret of Eastern Moguls

Swanky stretch-limos from faraway states
With Arabic symbols on gold licence plates,
Driven by sheikhs, you can see by their smiles
Own gardens the size of the whole British
    Isles,

And more fine women than our dog's had
    fleas,
And thousands of acres of valuable trees,
And Turkish Delight that they order by
    phone,
And barrels and barrels of Eau de Cologne.

I once met the son of a rich potentate,
Who taught me the way to fish peas from
    your plate.
When you've nothing at all but your fingers
    to eat 'em,
I tried it myself and quiet frankly was beaten.

7

God must really love the working class,
I mean, he made so many of them.
ANTON LAVEY

I awoke with a terrible pain in my head.

'How are you feeling, chief?' Barry asked.

'Like shit. What hit me?'

'Danny hit you, chief.'

'Danny?' I rubbed at my head and I looked all around me. I was lying in an alleyway. It was the real McCoy all right. Bar back door with a neon sign above, fire escape with retractable bottom section, lots of scrunched-up paper and cardboard cartons. I cocked an ear.

'He's gone for his lunch,' said Barry.

'Who has? Danny?'

'The saxophone player, chief. The one you were listening for. The solitary sax player who always sits at an open window playing mournfully to add that extra bit of atmosphere to an alleyway like this.'

'Fine, so where's—'

'I'm here,' said Danny, looming in my direction.

'Don't breathe on me,' I told him, 'and don't loom so close.'

'Some thanks,' said Danny.

'For knocking me out?'

'For saving your life.'

'Are you kidding, or what?'

'He's not kidding, chief, listen to what he has to say.'

'I saved your life,' said Danny.

'Are you kidding, or what?'

'Put a sock in it, chief.'

'Oh, do excuse *me*.'

'I followed you,' said Danny, looming a little further away. 'I got fed up with being walloped by male nurse Cecil so I upped and awayed.'

'Feathered wings?' I enquired.

'Nah. I tried to figure out what was the least most obvious way of escaping, but then I figured that if I *could* figure out the least most obvious way, then it couldn't really be the *least* most obvious, because I'd obviously—'

'Frankly, I don't care,' I said. 'So why did you hit me?'

'To save your life, I told you.'

'Are you kidding, or what?'

'Chief, the humour of that line frankly evades me.'

'So sorry, Barry. Please continue, Danny, but keep down wind.'

'A while back,' said Danny, 'I met this mendicant in a pub and he told me a story about hitch-hikers. You see there is a fleet of old VW Campers and they—'

'Heard it,' I said.

'About how they recycle dispossessed people?'

'Heard it.'

'Have you heard the similar one about the woman who pretends to be a nurse and hangs around in mental hospitals waiting for patients who are hoping to escape?'

'Er, no.'

'Well, she takes them in her car off to this house in the middle of nowhere and they go inside and—'

'I don't wish to know. Thanks very much for getting me out of there.'

'No sweat,' said Danny. 'You'd have done the same for me.'

'That's not altogether true.'

'Well you're best out of there, that's for sure.'

'Too right.'

'I mean, how much could you have taken?'

'Of plunging to my death in a mincing machine? Not too much, I should think.'

'I'm not talking about a mincing machine. I mean the other thing, her thing.'

'Her thing? You mean it's an even worse thing?'

'Damn right. According to the story I heard, this woman keeps her victims there for months.'

'Months?'

'And does it to them again and again and again.'

'Does what?'

'Screws them. Like sex slaves, makes them have sex with her morning, noon and night.'

'Don't hit him, chief.'

'You're too late, Barry.' I caught Danny a fine right-hander and sent him into the cartons. 'You stupid bastard!' I told him.

'Look on the bright side, chief.'

'*What* bright side?'

'Well, if you'd spent months as a sex slave, you'd never get your case solved, would you?'

'No, I reckon you're right.' I climbed wearily to my feet, went over to Danny and gave him a good kicking.

'Got that out of your system, chief?'

'Yes, Barry. I have.'

'Jolly good. So where to next?'

I pointed to the neon sign. 'What does that say to you?' I asked.

'It says EXIT, chief. But then what do I know?'

'Wake up, Barry. I'm in Lazlo Woodbine mode here. Knocked on the head at the end of the first chapter. Wake up in an alleyway. Woodbine only worked the four locations, didn't he, so what's next on the list?'

'A bar, chief, where you stand around talking a load of old toot. Something you excel at.'

'I shall ignore that remark. But a bar it is. And would you care to hazard a guess as to the name of this bar?'

'Might it be Fangio's Bar, chief?'

'Isn't it always?'

And it always is. Or, at least, was in the Lazlo Woodbine thrillers. Woodbine's best buddy was Fangio the barman. Woodbine always went into Fangio's, talked a lot of toot and met up with a dame in trouble. The significance of this dame's trouble would not be immediately obvious, but it would cleverly dove-tail in with whatever case Woodbine was working on. The dame would inevitably do Laz

106

wrong, but then dames always do, but he'd get her in the end, and she'd help him solve the case. That's the way Woodbine did business, here or there, or elsewhere.

'Come on then,' said Barry. 'Let's get it over with.'

I pushed open the exit door, stepped along a dingy hallway and out into a bar of equal dinginess.

I say 'of equal dinginess', but this doesn't quite paint the poodle. This bar was drab. Which is to say, it was lacklustre. Here was a cheerless bar, uncomforting and uncongenial. A dismal bar, lugubrious, funereal and dull. A bar that was gloomy and sombre, long-faced and woebegone. A bilious bar. A tearful tap-room. A doleful dive. A pulch—

'Turn it in,' said Fangio. 'I've just had the place decorated.'

I copped a glance at the fat boy. There he stood behind the counter, large as lard and smiling like a dead cat on the road to Hell. Fangio was girthsome, which is to say—

'I said, turn it in.'

'I'm sorry, Fange,' I said. 'I was just thinking out loud.'

'Well if it's a running gag, then it's a shitter.'

Oh how we laughed.

Although I don't remember why.

Fangio called me over to the bar and I sat right down before it. 'New stools,' I said, as I comfied myself.

'I bought them in a job lot,' said the fat boy.

And we laughed again.

And then we stopped.

'The humour of that is quite lost on me,' said Fangio.

I took off my fedora and twiddled with the brim. 'I think it's word association and toilet humour,' I explained. 'You said "shitter", I said "stools", you said "job", as in "jobbie", and then we both laughed again.'

'What a pair of characters we are,' said Fangio.

And this was true. We were.

'So,' said Fangio, once we'd both stopped laughing and he'd served me with a shot of Bourbon and a plate of Twiglets. 'Now we've put the stools behind us, as it were, let's turn our attention to the chairs; what do you think?'

I viewed Fangio's chairs. 'Disproportionately large,' I said. 'Where did you buy them?'

'At Big Chairs R Us.'

'And these were the biggest they had?'

'These were the smallest.'

'I see,' I said. But I didn't.

'I can see you see,' said Fange. But I don't think he did.

We laughed again, just to be on the safe side, and I tucked into my Twiglets.

'So,' said the fat boy, 'any luck with the case?'

'It's not a case,' I told him. 'It's a handbag.'

'A handbag?' Fange whistled. 'All I hear today is "a handbag", "a handbag".'

'Do you?'

'Yes, indeed I do. Take this morning, for instance. I'm standing here behind the bar minding my own business when this bloke walks in. Ordinary bloke, smart suit and tie, polished shoes, but something odd about his head.'

'His head?'

'Tiny,' said Fange. 'He's got a tiny head, about the size of an orange.'

'You're making this up.'

'I swear I'm not. Well, the bloke orders a beer, but he can see I'm staring at him and he says "Go on, ask me, then," and I say "Ask what?" and he says "About my head." And I say, "I had no intention of asking you." And he says, "Well, I'll tell you anyway," and he does.

' "I wasn't always like this," says the bloke, pointing to his tiny head. "Once I was chief petty officer on *The Mary Grey*, a pleasure cruiser out of San Francisco. I've always been one for the women, you see, and a job like that was right up my street. Smart uniform and plenty of unattached females looking for love. I was at it morning, noon and night, it was marvellous." '

'Bastard,' I said.

'Quite so,' said Fangio. ' "Well," the bloke continued, "we were several days out of Frisco on this particular voyage and I was enjoying the attentions of a particularly well-endowed young woman who liked to get it on in the lifeboat. And one night we were bonking away and she kicked out unexpectedly and I got tipped over the side. The ship went on without me and I was left all alone drifting in the sea. I thought I was a goner, I can tell you, but I kept afloat somehow. I drifted in and out of consciousness and then I saw a bloke go rowing by using a swordfish saw for a paddle, but he didn't hear my

109

cries for help. After what seemed like days I was finally washed up on a desert island.

' "There was food enough to eat: I caught fish, and ate fruit and survived. But I was mad from loneliness and lack of female company. I was dying for a shag. And then one day, as I'm walking along the beach, I come upon this handbag." '

'*A handbag?*' I said.

'A voodoo handbag,' said Fangio. 'But let's let the bloke tell it. "I recognized it at once," says the bloke, "because we'd docked a while back in Haiti and I'd been to one of the voodoo temples to see the black girls dancing with their kit off. And on one of the altars I'd seen one of these handbags. All covered in skulls. Real weird shit. So I pick up this handbag from the beach and I open it up. And out comes this beautiful woman. A genie like, she materializes right before me." '

'Get away,' I said.

'Shut up,' said Fangio. ' " "You have freed me from the voodoo handbag,' says the genie, 'where I have been held captive for a thousand years. In order to reward you I will grant you a wish.' Well, I should have said, 'Get me off the island,' but I didn't. All I could see was this beautiful woman and I was gagging for it. 'I want to make love to you,' I said. But the beautiful genie shook her head. 'Genies don't have those parts,' she said, pointing to her groin regions. And I was desperate, so I said—" '

'*What about giving me a little head, then?*'

'Correct,' said Fangio. 'However did you guess?'

'Because it's a crap old joke and I've heard it before.'

'I haven't,' said the fat boy. 'So you think he was making it up?'

'I think *you* made it up.'

'Oh yeah?' Fangio reached beneath the counter and brought out what appeared to be a tiny Homburg. 'So what do you make of this then, sucker? He left his hat behind.'

I examined said hat. 'This,' I said to Fange, 'is the hat of a glove puppet. The hat of a Norris the Boil glove puppet, to be precise. Norris was the creation of an illustrator called Albert Tupper back in the 1950s. Albert wrote a whole series of books based on Norris' adventures. Norris was a boil on the back of a nightclub owner's neck and he got into all kinds of humorous scrapes. Sadly, however, the world was not ready for books about buboes and Albert died, the tragic victim of a freak accident involving rubber bands and a bathing cap.'

Fangio whistled. 'You sure know your spin-off products,' he said.

'Buddy,' I told him, 'in my business, knowing your spin-off products can mean the difference between crawling the kerb and fouling the footpath, if you know what I mean, and I'm sure that you do.'

'Excuse me, chief,' said Barry, 'and I do hate like damn to break in on you like this. But much as I know that talking a lot of old toot in bars is an important part of the Lazlo Woodbine methodology, I can't help feeling we're losing the plot here.'

'Patience, Barry. It will all become clear.'

'Yeah, right.'

111

'So,' said Fangio, 'I'm sorry you don't believe me about the man with the little head. Perhaps if I showed you the handbag.'

'He left the handbag here? The voodoo handbag?'

'Said he felt embarrassed carrying it around. Said it made people stare at him.'

'Show me this handbag and show it to me now.'

'Sure,' said Fange, reaching down. 'No, wait just a moment, I have to serve this customer.'

I turned to look at the customer in question, and frankly confess that I liked what I saw. She was beautiful. A goddess. A Helen of Troy. An Aphrodite. A Venus. She was graceful and majestic, leonine and lovely, radiant and ravishing, cute and curvaceous—

'I like the way you think,' she said, and she grinned through a gap in her teeth.

'Let me get this for the lady,' I said to Fange, who was pulling her a pint of mild.

'What a gentleman you are.' She grinned again and swung round in my direction.

'The name's Woodbine,' I said. 'Lazlo Woodbine. Some call me Laz.'

'Pleased to meet you, Chas.'

'Er, *Laz*,' I said. 'Laz is my name.'

'Oh, excuse me.' She turned her head on one side and bashed her right ear with her fist. 'Got a bit of carrot stuck in my left ear,' she explained. 'You know how it is, as much as you can eat for a fiver, so you get your head right down into that old salad bowl.'

I concurred. (Well, you would!)

112

'Stuff it in while you can, I always say,' she grinned, gappily.

'I do so agree.'

'Well, you would.'

Fange served the lady with her pint. 'Another for yourself, sir?' he asked.

'Just a look at that handbag,' I said.

'Oh yes, handbag, handbag, now what did I do with that handbag?'

While he was looking I thought I'd engage the dame in conversation. Chat her up a bit and see where it led. Dazzle her with the old sparkling repartee. Mould her like putty, then play her like a violin.

'You don't sweat much for a fat lass,' I said.

'Smooth talker,' she replied, giving me a slap across the jaw that loosened several fillings. 'And don't think I don't know your game.'

I smiled, charmingly. 'Haven't I seen you in movies?' I continued.

'Perhaps.' She swallowed her ale and wiped froth from her chin.

'I know I have,' I said. 'I'll get it in a moment.'

She turned her face in profile and pointed to her nose.

'I've got it,' I said. 'You're Jabba the Hutt.'

She smacked me right in the gob. 'Casanova,' she giggled, 'you'll be the death of me.'

I clicked my jaw. It didn't seem to be broken. 'You've got a good right hand there,' I said, in the voice of one who knows these things. 'Try this one for size,' and I kicked her in the stomach.

She doubled right over, but came up fast. 'You really know how to treat a lady,' she said as she head-butted me in the face.

I fell hard on my neck, but I knew I was winning her round. I got to my feet and I hit her with a stool. 'Your place or mine?' I asked her.

'Mine,' she said, pulling a knife.

'I hate to interrupt you two love birds,' said Fange. 'But I've found the handbag.'

I kicked the dame's knife from her mitt and laid her out with a blow to the skull. 'I'll be right back, honey,' I told her.

Fangio placed the handbag on the bar counter. 'So what do you think?' he asked.

I cast a professional eye over the handbag. 'My goddess,' I said. 'I think this is it.'

The bag was about twenty inches high, handbag-shaped, covered in skulls and cast in plaster. Billy's mum had said that I'd know it when I saw it, and now that I'd seen it I knew it.

I didn't know what to say. I'd been searching for this handbag for ten long years. The search for this handbag had taken me from Bramfield to Brentford. And into another dimension. I'd crossed trackless deserts, wandered in the hinterlands, plundered the tundra, hitch-hiked and mountain-biked, staggered and swaggered, sallied forth and headed north, looked in high places and vast empty spaces, abseiled down—

'Put a sock in it,' said Fangio.

'I'm speechless,' I said

'No kidding?'

'I *am* speechless. I'm lost for words. Struck dumb,

114

choked for utterance. Made mute. Put to silence. Robbed of all—'

'The secret, chief,' said Barry, 'is in knowing when to stop.'

'You're right, Barry. But we've done it. Pulled off the big one. Solved the case. Got things sorted.'

'That we have, chief.'

'Swept aside all obstacles. Stemmed the current. Weathered the storm. Come home safe to port—'

'Hand over the handbag, shithead!'

I turned in some confusion.

Danny stood in the doorway to the dingy hall. He had a pistol in his hand.

'Danny,' I said. 'This is a surprise. I thought we'd said our fond farewells in the alley.'

'Just slide the bag along the bar counter. Slowly now, don't make any sudden moves.'

'Why are you doing this, Danny?' I did as I was bid.

'Because I know the truth, and I know what must be done with the handbag.' Danny reached out his hand.

'Don't touch it, kid!'

I glanced around. Fangio had pulled his Colt Peacemaker out from beneath the bar. He was pointing it at Danny.

'Put down the pistol, kid,' said Fangio, and Danny put down the pistol.

'Nice one, Fange,' I said.

'But not nice enough!'

I glanced around once more. The dame was back on her feet. She was holding a Derringer and pointing it at Fangio. 'Drop the gun,' she said. 'The handbag comes with me.'

Fangio laid his gun upon the counter.

'Nice one, dame,' I said. 'No, hang about. The handbag comes with me? That can't be right.'

'Only I know the *real* truth,' said the dame.

'I'd have said that I knew the *real* truth,' said Fange. 'But you didn't give me a chance.'

'Only *I* know the real truth,' said someone else. Which gave me the opportunity to have another good glance around.

A man stood in the main doorway. He was a well-dressed man, nice tie, polished shoes. But there was something odd about his head. It was tiny. About the size of an orange.

'Drop the Derringer,' he told the dame. And the dame dropped the Derringer.

'Drop *your* gun!' said Danny, who had snatched his up again.

'Drop *yours*!' said Fange, who had done likewise.

'And *yours*!' said the dame, who had done likewise, likewise.

And I stood right there in the middle. It was the now legendary Mexican stand-off. Fangio pointed his gun at Danny. Danny pointed his gun at Orange head. Orange head pointed his gun at the dame. And the dame pointed her gun at Fangio.

And as no-one was pointing anything at me, I picked up the handbag and buggered off.

Mills on Wheels

Mr Mills of twenty-three
Said, 'Look at this and envy me.'
He'd kitted himself out with trolley wheels.
I said, 'Yes, well, very nice.'
I'd seen that trick done once or twice
But cared not for it either time, preferring
   house-trained seals.

House trained,
House trained,
Rat and mouse trained,
In and out,
And roundabout trained.

Mr Mills of twenty-three
Was given out the OBE,
For services to pe-des-tri-an-ism as a whole,
I said, 'Yes, well very nice.'
I'd seen that trick done once or twice
But cared not for it either time, preferring the
   house-trained vole.

House trained,
House trained,
Rat and mouse trained,
Up the spout,
And all about trained.

Mr Mills of twenty-three
Became a big celebrity,
And opened up the Summer fête for three
    years in a row.
I said, 'Yes, well, very nice.'
I'd seen that trick done once or twice
But cared not for it either time, preferring
    Jean Cocteau.

But then I went to art school, so what else
    would you expect?

8

Information wants to be free.
CYBERPUNK MAXIM

Billy took two suitcases to the station. One contained his clothes. The other, his granny. It was now Wednesday morning, and as on Wednesday mornings Billy's mother always took breakfast in a high tree at the end of the garden, Billy had taken the opportunity to slip away through the front door.

The telephone conversation of the previous evening had not been to Billy's liking. The man at Necrosoft was vague and evasive. He did not answer Billy's questions to Billy's satisfaction. He offered Billy fifty quid for his granny, 'and no more questions asked' and then put down the phone when Billy asked more questions. Billy called back, but there'd been no reply.

So Billy set out for Brentford.

He would take the offices of Necrosoft by storm.

But it would be a gentle storm. More of a light shower, really. A bit of a breeze that would waft Billy gently into employment. Once the management of Necrosoft met Billy they would be instantly impressed by his eminent suitability. Billy would be just the chap they needed. He would fit in perfectly. After all, he looked like all the rest.

Only he knew he was *different*.

And how *very* different he was.

Billy caught the London mail train at Bramfield Halt. He did not have the exact address of Necrosoft. The package had said only Brentford, Middlesex, and the unhelpful chap Billy had spoken to on the phone refused to give out the address. But this presented no problem for Billy.

Once Billy had found himself an empty carriage, he placed the suitcase containing his granny on the luggage rack and opened the other on his knees. From this he took out a brightly coloured parcel. It was addressed simply to NECROSOFT INDUSTRIES. BRENTFORD. MIDDLESEX. Billy closed his suitcase and placed this on the other luggage rack. Then he slipped along the train to the guard's van and when the guard was distracted he slipped the parcel into the mail sack marked Brentford.

And then Billy went off to the buffet car and had a cup of tea.

Now, for most travellers, entering Brentford for the first time is an unforgettable experience. The sky seems bluer here, the grass more green, the trees more tall, the river much more rivery. And see, the mellow London brick, the grey slate roofs, the terracotta chimneys. And view the women, fair of face, the happy children singing hymns, the trades-men plying their trades. And smell the honeysuckle and the dog rose and the sweet wild—

Billy checked his suitcases into the left-luggage office, then stood upon a corner of the street smoking a cigarette and gently squeezing the bright plastic something he'd received in the post.

Presently a van came to pick up the mail sacks. Billy followed it the two streets to the sorting office. Outside he smoked two more cigarettes and gave the something further squeezings. And then he followed the postman who came out pushing a bicycle.

On the front of the bicycle was a rack and in the rack were several drab brown paper parcels and one that was brightly coloured.

Billy kept his eyes on this.

The postman set off upon his round. He was a very small postman. Positively dwarf-like. Billy wondered whether, perhaps, he was Welsh.

The small postman went about his business in a quite unhurried fashion. He dillied and dallied and dawdled. He looked into shop windows and picked flowers in the park. He did take a short cut across the allotments, but only so he could steal some sprouts from one of the plots. It was nearly three in the afternoon before he parked his bicycle next to a boarded-up shop front and took Billy's parcel from its rack.

Billy hastened forward. He squeezed himself between the postman and the shop door.

'Something for Necrosoft?' he said. 'I'll take it, I'm just going in.'

The small postman looked up at him. 'There's three bob to pay,' he said.

'There bloody isn't,' said Billy, who knew he had put on sufficient stamps.

'And how would you know?'

Billy smiled. How would he indeed? 'Three bob, you say?' And he fished out the coinage and gave it to the postman.

'Have a nice day,' said the postman, passing him the parcel.

Billy watched the postman as he dilly-dallied and dawdled away. And then he took stock of the shop front. This was *not* what he had expected. He had expected some big corporation building, all mirror glass and Bauhaus furniture. Why would Necrosoft Industries, 'The cutting edge of computer technology', be holed up in a dump like this?

Billy pushed upon the door, which opened groaning on its hinges. He stuck in his head and sniffed. The air smelt stale. He stepped into the shop. It had evidently once been a draper's. Most of the old fixtures and fittings remained, hung with cobwebs and downy with dust. Wan light fell through the unwashed windows, illuminating here, a tailor's dummy standing like an impaled torso, and there, some mouldy balls of wool that looked like shrunken heads. These were not sights to inspire confidence in Billy.

The lad glanced down at the floor. There were the signs of many footprints, leading from the shop door to—

Where?

To a stairway at the rear.

Billy crossed the shop floor and felt his way up the unlit stairs. At the top a door, and Billy pushed it open.

'Come in,' said a voice. 'You're late.'

Billy found himself in a dull little room. Lit by a single dangling bulb and containing nothing but a table and two chairs. Behind the table on one of the chairs sat a young man. He was pale and hollow-eyed, stubble-chinned and shabby. 'Sit down,' he said. And Billy sat.

'Right then,' said the young man. 'I was just going to ask how you did it, but I see your parcel. Very enterprising.'

'Thank you,' said Billy.

'And polite with it,' said the young man.

'I do my best to please.'

'I'll bet you do.'

'Is this the office of Necrosoft?' Billy asked.

The young man nodded, spilling specks of dandruff. 'You were expecting something far more flashy, I'll bet.'

'You can't always tell a book by its cover,' said Billy with care.

'You can if it's written by Johnny Quinn,' said the young man. 'So, let's have a look at you. Stand up.'

And Billy stood up.

'Sit down.'

And Billy sat down again.

'Stand up.'

And Billy stood up once more.

'And stay.'

And Billy stayed.

'It's impressive, isn't it?' said the young man.

'What is?'

'The way you do exactly what you're told.'

'If you say so.'

'I do. And I'll prove it. Whip your willy out.'

'What?' said Billy.

'Your willy. Whip it out. Let me have a look at it.'

Billy slowly unzipped his trousers and exposed himself to the young man.

'Mine's bigger than that,' said the young man. 'Now tuck it away and sit down.'

Billy did so in considerable confusion.

'Wondering how it's done? Why you did what I told you?'

Billy nodded.

'Get out your little plastic something.'

Billy took it from his pocket.

'Put it on the table.'

Billy tried to, but he couldn't.

'Don't want to part with it, eh? They never do.'

'I don't understand.'

'Of course you don't. But I'll explain: the plastic something is impregnated with a special chemical. It's addictive and it makes you subservient.'

'There's no such chemical,' said Billy.

'Oh yes there is. It comes from the Amazon. Johnny Quinn discovered it.'

'And who's this Johnny Quinn?'

'You've never heard of him?'

'Never.'

'That's because you're different, you see. You're like me, I'm different too. In a few years from now things are going to be very different from the way they are today. And that's when folk like us will really come into our own. We're the vanguard of the new movement, we are.'

'Are we now?'

'Yes we are. The world's full of greedy bastards

who'll happily sell their old grannies. But we're not looking for them, well, we are of course, but not quite yet. For now we're looking for the *different* greedy bastards. The special ones. The ones special enough to use their initiative and find their way here.'

'It didn't take that much initiative,' said Billy. 'It was pretty straightforward.'

'Don't be modest.'

'OK,' said Billy. 'I won't.'

'That's right, you won't. Not if I say you won't. In fact you'll do whatever I say. *Whatever* I say. I can make you do anything I want, just by asking. So you'd better be polite to me, if you know what's good for you.'

Billy nodded, thoughtfully. 'Do you have one of these little plastic impregnated somethings yourself?' he asked.

'Of course I do.'

'Please show it to me.'

The young man took his from his pocket and held it tightly. 'I won't give it to you,' he said. 'So don't waste your time asking.'

'Oh, I had no intention of doing that. But surely your one is bigger than mine.'

'Like my willy,' said the young man.

'Indeed,' said Billy. 'But I bet mine weighs more.'

'Don't be absurd,' said the young man.

'I'll bet it does. Here.' He extended his hand. 'Take it and feel the two together. Tell me I'm not wrong.'

'Okey doke.' The young man reached across the table and took the bright plastic something from

Billy's outstretched hand. Billy felt a sense of terrible loss as it left his possession. As if the most precious item he had ever owned was being torn from his grasp. He bit at his lip and gripped the edge of the table. Sweat broke out on his brow and his breath came in strangled gasps.

'Here take it back,' said the young man. 'It's exactly the same as mine really.'

'No,' said Billy, through gritted teeth. 'You keep it.'

'Oh, thanks very much.' The young man grinned hugely and tucked Billy's treasure into his trouser pocket.

Billy took several very deep breaths and then he too grinned hugely. 'Now,' he said slowly, 'show me your willy.'

The police fished the young man's body from the canal a week later. The coroner's report stated that he had been the victim of a violent sexual assault. But this was not the cause of his death. Death was due to asphyxiation, a small bright plastic something being lodged in his windpipe.

Vanguard of the New Movement

Behind his polished cedar desk,
Surrounded by his phones,
Sits Blazer Dyke (the yachting type),
The vanguard of the clones.
The archetype,
The number one,
The vanguard of the clones.

Crossing over busy streets,
Where noisy traffic drones,
Walks Blazer Dyke (without a bike),
The vanguard of the clones.
The autocrat,
The ectomorph,
The vanguard of the clones.

He strides across the cobbled yard,
Where pawn shops offer loans,
That Blazer Dyke (whom I dislike),
The vanguard of the clones.
The cannibal,
The parasite,
The vanguard of the clones.

He passes through the wicket gate,
To churchyards full of bones,
That Blazer Dyke (on a midnight hike),
The vanguard of the clones.
The necrophile,

The narcissist,
The coprophage,
The sybarite,
The telepath,
The Anti-Christ,
The vanguard of the clones.

9

Life is a Joke

J. PENNY II

(Scrawled upon his school blackboard in 1977 shortly
before he took his own life, aged seventeen.)

'I'm impressed,' said Blazer Dyke. 'In fact I'm very
impressed.' He sat at his cedar desk in an airy office
with an open window that overlooked the church-
yard of St Joan's Church in Brentford.

'Remarkable,' he continued. 'You would definitely appear to have the *right stuff*, as they say.'

The object of this praise sat on the other side of
the cedar desk. The object's name was Billy Barnes.

'My actions were calculated to impress,' said the
object. 'The young man answered all my questions
about your organization before he met his tragic
end. "Necrosoft writes its own rule book on matters
of morality," was a phrase he used.'

'And one I'm particularly proud of,' said Blazer
Dyke. 'Would you care for a cup of tea?'

'Absolutely not. And I'll keep my rubber gloves
on if you don't mind.'

'Priceless. You'll go far in this organization.'

'I intend to,' said Billy.

Blazer Dyke leaned back in his chair and gazed at the young man before him. It was remarkable just how unremarkable he was. How perfectly average he was. How absolutely ordinary. But *right*. He was right. He looked right just sitting there, as if that was where he should be sitting. He fitted.

Blazer Dyke rose from his chair. 'Indulge me,' he said. 'Sit here for a moment.'

Billy got up, went around the desk and sat down in Blazer's chair. Blazer looked him up and down and gently shook his head. 'Quite remarkable. You look as if you belong there. Quite remarkable indeed.'

Billy smiled. 'I'm so glad you approve,' said he.

'Oh, I don't approve. But I understand you, Billy. We understand each other, I believe.'

'In that we are *different*, yes.'

'Different.' Blazer Dyke shooed Billy from his chair and plonked himself back into it. 'Your gift is for fitting in. Mine is for organization. Together we will make a good team. But know this, Billy. Although I do not disapprove of what you did to the young man, neither do I condone it. I am simply aloof to it. You exposed a weakness in the structure of our organization which has now been rectified. But there will be no more "tragic accidents" to my personnel. Do you understand me?'

'Perfectly, yes.'

'Also you must view the experience as part of the learning process.'

'How so?'

'To take greater care.'

'In what way?'

'The room was under close-circuit video surveillance. Cutting-edge stuff, naturally. All your actions were observed and recorded.'

'I see,' said Billy. 'Then I shall take greater care in the future. Thank you for drawing this to my attention.'

'My pleasure, my boy. Now I'm sure you have questions you'd like to ask.'

'Many,' said Billy. 'I know the young man told me what he believed to be the truth. But—'

'But,' said Blazer Dyke, 'you do not believe that he knew the truth.'

'Precisely.'

'And of course he didn't. Although fiction can sometimes be truer than fact. So what should I tell you? Of how this company came to be, perhaps? Of its goals? Of its plans for the future?'

'All,' said Billy.

'Then all it shall be. Necrosoft is a private company specializing in the development of advanced micro-processing computer technology. EW and AT: Electromagnetic Weaponry and Artificial Telepathy. Lumped under the heading of NLWT: Non-Lethal Weapons Technology.'

'Who funds this organization?' asked Billy.

'The American government. They fund many such privately owned companies in order to side-step the Freedom of Information Act. It comes loosely under the heading of covert operations, but you will only find it listed as Research Technology. As there is no longer a cold war between East and West, America has no immediate enemies. Except of course the now legendary "enemy within".'

131

'Its own people,' said Billy.

'Exactly. Terrorists, activists, anarchists, cultists. Agitators in general. Dissidents, if you like. Those who won't toe the Party line. Those who act up. And so military weapons technology is no longer aimed at foreign powers, it is now being developed for urban pacification. To keep the unruly in their place. With the grand view of creating a peaceful, stable society.'

'Absolutely,' said Billy.

'Absolutely. We don't want to shoot our own, we just want to pacify them.'

'Keep them under control,' said Billy.

'Not an expression we like to use here. But in essence, yes. Now, Electromagnetic Weaponry has been in development since the Second World War. The Nazis were at work on sound weapons that could disable vehicles and as you may know, many of their top scientists escaped the war trials and were quietly spirited over to America to work for the government there. Work progressed and with the development of micro-chip technology, it came on in leaps and bounds.'

'Go on,' said Billy.

'I will,' said Blazer. 'Electromagetic Weaponry, zapping the engines of tanks and such like was all very well, but tanks can be shielded and systems over-ridden. It is far easier to disable a person than a tank. And so EW led eventually to AT: Artificial Telepathy. Which is what we specialize in here.'

'Please explain this to me.'

'Certainly. With Artificial Telepathy, a computer relays a radio communication directly into a human brain without the need of an electronic receiver. A microwave carrier delivers an analogue of words known as an *audiogram*. The big bonus, indeed the whole point of this, is that the recipient of the message is unaware that it is being broadcast. He or she thinks that it is their own thoughts.'

'You are saying that you can put voices into people's heads?'

'Voices. Words. That's crude, but it can be effective sometimes. The old "God told me to shoot the president," you know the kind of stuff. But we're talking *concepts* here. Implanting a concept to change a subject's mode of thinking. Let us say that you were to implant the concept of "guilt at wrong doing" – you wouldn't stop all the wrong doing, but you'd make a lot of people think twice and that would make a difference.'

'And you'd have your urban pacification.'

'Subtle concepts don't work on mob mentality. You need to be a little more robust. Terror is an effective concept, but the terrified man will act irrationally. The most effective we've found so far, and the most amusing, is to beam the concept of a pressing need to use the toilet.'

'Very humorous,' said Billy.

'Indeed, but in the future it should not be necessary. We are currently engaged in other forms of experimental research. The pleaser, for instance.'

'The pleaser?'

'You experienced its efficacy yourself. The bright plastic something you so liked to squeeze.'

'Impregnated with the mysterious drug from the Amazon?'

'Yes, well, that was not altogether true. It has more to do with resonance and frequency. But, tell me this, why do you think that the young are the way they are today? Obsessed with name brand designer clothes and trainers, McDonald's burgers and manufactured pop music?'

'Because they all have the Sky TV satellite in their birth charts?'

'That's probably part of it,' said Blazer Dyke.

'Really?'

'No! Of course not really! EW technology. Just like your pleaser, all geared towards urban pacification. Once you have your young all dressing the same, eating the same, listening to the same music and thinking the same, they are very easy to control.'

'This is very sensitive information you are giving me,' said Billy.

'Well, you're not going to spread it around, are you?'

'Absolutely not.'

'Because we'd have to kill you, if you did.'

'Quite so.'

'And moving right along, we come to the Necronet itself. The latest port of call on our electromagnetic voyage. We have in place the EW technology, the computer is capable of despatching the microwave carrier which creates the audiogram in the recipient's head. What is the next logical development?'

Billy put up his hand, as he had done so long ago in the junior school. 'To programme the computer to *receive* as well as to *send*.'

'Exactly, and then?'

'And then you can effectively read people's thoughts.'

'Precisely, and not just their thoughts. Access their memories also. And thoughts plus memories equal *personality*. Equal in fact the *mind* of the subject. The computer downloads the subject's mind and stores it.'

'To what purpose?'

'At present for espionage. Subject one is downloaded, subject two has his memory blanked, the concept of amnesia is implanted. Then subject one's downloaded mind, complete with all previous thought and memory, is beamed into subject two. Mentally subject two is now subject one.'

'And subject one?'

'Into the canal with subject one.'

'I see. But where does the Necronet concept come into this? "Access the dear departed" et cetera?'

'By happy accident, really. We downloaded a number of subjects. Disposed of their bodies, but kept the downloaded minds stored in the computer for access.'

'Who were these subjects?'

'Rivals in the field. Computer scientists. Our way of beating the opposition. Absorb it.'

'So you have their downloaded minds, their memories and thoughts stored in your computer banks, what then?'

'Then we noticed something extraordinary. They were communicating with one another. Exchanging information. One of our technicians likened them to being souls in limbo. Souls in cyberspace, if you will. And so we created a virtual world for them in there. All the comforts they might require, virtual food, virtual sex, whatever. They're very happy in there. And *very* cooperative.'

'I see,' said Billy. 'So what do you need the grannies for?'

'Historical reference. A granny is a walking history book of the twentieth century. She might have forgotten much of what she experienced. But only in the conscious mind. It's all there in the subconscious, ready to be downloaded and stored.'

'And so the virtual granny in cyberspace has a digital memory. She can remember everything.'

'That's right, and all these memories can be accessed by us. You see the beauty of this. We are slowly building a world database. And it leads to an interesting spiritual question. If you download a person before they die, when they do die, do they *really* die? Their personalities, complete with all thoughts and memories, are inside the virtual world of the Necronet. They are alive in there. So is the person actually dead? The body, yes. The mind, no. Interesting, isn't it?'

'Fascinating,' said Billy. 'But where is it all leading to?'

'Control,' said Blazer Dyke. 'Control is what everything leads to. There is the herd and there is the herd leader. The herd leader is the individual, the *different* one. The herd is just the herd. Control the herd and you control the game. There are those who do the accessing and those who are there to be accessed. I know which of these I am. And you know too, don't you?'

'Born to access,' said Billy. 'And I accept the position.'

'Which position is this?'

'Whichever position you offer me. I assume that I will not be offered a choice.'

'You are correct. But why do you assume this?'

'Because you have me under your control. You have the incriminating video tape and you hold the power of life and death. Should I refuse to do what you ask, you can always download me. I am sure your virtual world is a wonderful place, but I would prefer to live here for the time being.'

'Well put. The job in question is that of "information gatherer".'

'Which is a euphemism for what?'

'Assassin. Your particular gift, Billy, is for blending in. You are a regular stealth fox.'

'A what?'

'An unfortunate by-product of our rural pacification programme. Nothing to concern yourself about. But it is your ability to fit in, to look just right wherever you are, which makes you valuable to us. We need someone who can *get in close*. EW technology is not as yet long-range. The microwave carrier is only effective over a few metres. We will issue you with a list of subjects. Folk whose personalities we would like added to our database. You will *get in close*, download these people and dispose of their bodies.'

Billy nodded thoughtfully. 'Sounds most

challenging,' he said. 'Are there prospects for promotion?'

'For a lad like you. Oh yes, indeed.'

'Then we have a deal.'

'Shall we shake upon it? Perhaps you will take off your gloves.'

'I think not,' said Billy. 'But we have a deal.'

'Splendid.'

'Just one or two small details. Accommodation?'

'Pick out a place you like in the area. The company will cover the costs.'

'Transportation?'

'You acquired the young man's car, I believe.'

'It will do for now, I suppose.'

'Splendid. We'll have all the documentation altered to your name.'

'And my granny,' said Billy.

'Ah yes, your granny.'

'I'd like her downloaded straight away, if that's all right.'

'That's perfectly all right. Just bring her in whenever you want and I'll take care of it myself.'

'Thank you,' said Billy. 'I have her with me now, actually. She's downstairs in the car.'

'I didn't notice any passenger when you drove into the car park.'

'Well, you wouldn't have,' said Billy. 'She's in the boot.'

Legs Kirby

'Here, what's this?' says Kirby,
Kirby with those legs he wears,
Kirby with his books and prayers,
Kirby living under stairs,
Stupid bow-legs Kirby.

'So, who's there?' says Kirby,
Kirby with his Fifties suit,
Kirby with his iron book,
Kirby with his pheasant shoot,
Stupid bow-legs Kirby.

'Well, why's this?' says Kirby,
Kirby with his kipper tie,
Kirby with his lazy eye,
Kirby with his tasty fry,
Stupid bow-legs Kirby.

'Yes, I see!' says Kirby,
Kirby with his winning ways,
Kirby with his love of praise,
Kirby with his open days,
Stupid bow-legs, greaseball, over-fed, toffee-
    nosed, know-it-all, no-good-son-of-a-pig
    who wouldn't let me in his gang—
Stupid bow-legs fat-head!

10

I never deal with the common man.
The common man has no spirituality.
The common man thinks that
Ganesha is Dennis the Menace's dog.
HUGO RUNE

Mrs Barnes gave it two weeks and then reported Billy's absence to the police. They sent round Inspector Kirby who had done courses in bereavement counselling and community relations. He had also done courses in stress management, positive thinking, actualization of the self, releasing the spirit within, neoistic post-modernism and macramé. He held a degree in Humanities and was qualified to teach hang-gliding and white water rafting. Exactly what he was doing in the police force was a mystery to both him and his mother.

Inspector Kirby rang the doorbell, but receiving no reply took himself round to the side of the house.

Mrs Barnes sat upon the veranda in her wicker chair. As it was a Thursday she was cross-dressed. Evening suit, dickie bow, patent pumps and a rather fetching Clark Gable moustache sketched in felt-tip pen beneath her nose.

140

'Madam?' said Inspector Kirby.

'How dare you!' said Billy's mum. 'Does this look like a brothel?'

'No, madam. This looks like a mock-Tudor house. Circa 1933 and the work of the architect Klaus Bok, brother of the painter, Karl. Bok favoured the use of traditional materials, but was not averse to modern innovation, as can be seen in the window catches and guttering.' Inspector Kirby had also done 'Architectural Styles of the Twentieth Century' in an Open University course.

'My husband was a great friend of Bok,' said Mrs Barnes. 'Which was curious considering the disparity in their heights. My husband was very tall and Bok was positively dwarf-like.'

'Was he Welsh?'

'If he was, he kept it to himself. They could put you in prison for that, back in those days.'

'For being *Welsh*?'

'Oh, Welsh? I thought you said "raving homosexual".' Mrs Barnes put her head on one side and pounded her right ear with her fist. 'I've a bit of carrot stuck in my left ear, you know how it is.'

Inspector Kirby nodded. 'As much as you can eat for a fiver. So you get your head right into the salad bowl.'

'No,' said Mrs Barnes. 'It's vomit.'

Inspector Kirby scratched at his knees.

'Your legs are extremely bowed,' Mrs Barnes observed. 'Do you have your trousers specially tailored?'

'Only the ones I wear when I'm on duty.'

'And when you're off duty?'

'I normally wear a kilt.'

'Well, it's legal nowadays. Although it's still frowned upon in the armed services.'

Inspector Kirby shook his head and gave his knees another scratch.

'That's why my husband left the country,' said Mrs Barnes. 'Because of homosexuality. "Mavis," he said to me, "two hundred years ago they hanged you for it, one hundred years ago they jailed you for it, thirty years ago they legalized it and I'm getting out before they make it compulsory." '

'It's regarding your son, Billy,' said Inspector Kirby.

'I wouldn't have thought he was your type.'

'He's not my type.'

'So what type do you prefer then?'

'I don't prefer any type. I'm not gay.'

'Don't knock it if you haven't tried it.'

'I wasn't knocking it.'

'Then you *have* tried it.'

'No, well, er, that is neither here nor there. I am here regarding your son's disappearance.'

'Come and sit down over here,' said Billy's mum. 'Your legs are distracting me. It's like looking through a porthole.'

Inspector Kirby joined Mrs Barnes on the veranda. 'When did you last see your son?' he asked, as he sat himself down.

'The Wednesday before the Wednesday before last.'

'And he said nothing to you about where he might be going.'

'He might have mentioned business elsewhere.

But I can't be certain. We've never been close, you see.'

'Does he miss his father, do you think?'

'He's never mentioned him.'

'Probably in denial,' said Inspector Kirby. 'An inability to express outwardly feelings of loss and abandonment can often result in deep-seated psychological trauma. Introversion, bed-wetting, masturbation, voyeurism—'

'Homosexuality?' asked Mrs Barnes.

'No,' said Inspector Kirby. 'I wasn't going to say homosexuality.'

'Well, you should say it. After all it's homosexuality that has raised us above the animals.'

'I don't think I quite follow that.'

'Well, you just think about it. What is it that elevates mankind? Makes it superior to the animal kingdom?'

'A more sophisticated brain, opposing thumbs, the ability to communicate through language—'

'At first, yes. But think about culture. Think about the arts. Think what homosexuals have contributed to the arts. How many artists, poets, writers, singers, musicians, composers, filmmakers, dancers, actors, clothes designers, setdressers and hairdressers are homosexuals?'

'A very great many,' said Inspector Kirby.

'Exactly,' said Mrs Barnes. 'They may not breed. But breeding is for the herd. The homosexual is one apart. He's different. An individual. The homosexual contributes to the quality of life.'

'You're quite right,' said Inspector Kirby. 'I'd never thought about it like that before.'

'Everything in the gene pool is there for a purpose. And homosexuality is not an evolutionary hiccup or blind alley. It serves its purpose. Through the culture of the arts we are all ennobled. I always cross-dress on Thursdays as a personal tribute to homosexuals for all the joy they have brought to mankind.'

'Bravo,' said Inspector Kirby, clapping his hands. 'It makes me proud to be gay.'

'Bravo!' agreed Mrs Barnes. 'As so you should be. But tell me this.'

'What's that?'

'How come they let a shirt-lifter like you into the police force?'

Inspector Kirby stayed for lunch. As it was a Thursday they took lunch in the trophy room surrounded by the many curious artefacts Mr Barnes had brought back from his world wanderings.

'That's a whale's tooth,' said Mrs Barnes, in answer to the Inspector's question. 'My husband pulled it from the jaw of the slain creature while on one of his many whaling voyages.'

'How very interesting,' the Inspector said.

They dined upon mince and slices of quince, which they ate with plastic forks, as the runcible spoons were away being cleaned.

'What are the chances of finding my Billy?' asked his mum, munching loudly and rattling her plate about.

'Very good,' said the Inspector, examining his uncooked mince. 'After all, we have yet to establish whether he is actually missing. You say he took a

144

packed suitcase. It is most likely that he has just gone off for a while and will contact you shortly.'

'He's never gone off before.'

'He's twenty-three years of age, Mrs Barnes, perhaps he just wanted to get a bit of space. Spread his wings. Expand his horizons.'

'So you don't think he's in any danger, then?'

'Let us not be pessimistic without due cause.'

'Fine,' said Mrs Barnes. 'Then let's forget all about him. If he turns up dead in a canal or something you can always give me a call, can't you?'

'Well yes, but I— Listen, do you . . . I mean, are you all alone here now?'

'My mum lives with me. She's an invalid, she's upstairs.'

Now this was a lie and a deliberate one. Mrs Barnes had no intention of mentioning her mum's disappearance. Mrs Barnes collected her mum's pension every week and she needed the money for her Tuesday evening activities.

'I'd like to meet your mother,' said Inspector Kirby.

'She's asleep. Perhaps another time.'

'That would be nice. This really is a fascinating room, Mrs Barnes. A regular museum. That carved cabinet on the mantelpiece, where did that come from?'

'Haiti. My grandfather was the governor there at the turn of the century. The cabinet is a reliquary, it holds the family's most precious possession.'

'Absolutely fascinating. And what is that, exactly?'

'A plaster cast of a voodoo handbag. The handbag

of Maîtresse Ezilée, the Haitian incarnation of the Blessed Virgin Mary.'

'Incredible. I did a night school course on the occult a couple of years ago and we studied the voodoo pantheon. Papa Legba, Agoué, Loco and the rest. Isn't the handbag supposed to possess certain powers? Act as an oracle, or something?'

'They say it speaks, although I've never heard it. Billy said it used to speak to him, tell him stories.'

'What kind of stories?'

'Tall ones, I think.'

'Fascinating,' said the Inspector. 'Do you think I might see it?'

'Absolutely not!' Mrs Barnes bashed her big fists down upon the table. 'Far too dangerous. The handbag is a *transitus tessera*. It can take you from the world of the living to the world of the angry dead.'

'You mean I might die if I saw it?'

'If you were to touch it you would die.'

'I see. Is it then impregnated with some poison from the Amazon?'

'Possibly. But trust me, if you opened that cabinet and touched the voodoo handbag you'd die.'

'Incredible,' said Inspector Kirby. 'Absolutely incredible.'

'I suppose so.' Mrs Barnes shrugged noisily. 'But you get used to things, don't you? And you learn by your mistakes.'

'Indeed.'

The telephone began to ring.

'That might be your Billy,' said Inspector Kirby.

'No, that's not his ring.' Mrs Barnes forked up some quince and gobbled it down.

'Aren't you going to answer it?'

'It will stop ringing eventually, it always does.'

'It might be for me.'

'Oh, all right!' Mrs Barnes flung her fork aside, rose rowdily and stomped out of the room, slamming the door behind her.

'What a very loud woman,' said Inspector Kirby, pushing his plate aside. 'A voodoo handbag, eh?' His gaze wandered over to the cabinet on the mantelpiece. 'How very fascinating.'

He sat awhile and pondered. Great shouts came from the hall. Mrs Barnes was in heated discussion on the telephone, but with whom it wasn't clear.

'I might just have a little peep,' said the Inspector, quietly to himself. 'It couldn't do any harm, just a little peep.' He rose from the ottoman and glanced towards the hall door. More shouting. Inspector Kirby crept over to the mantelpiece.

Beside the cabinet lay a key. It was a brass key with a skull on it. A luggage label was attached to this key.

Inspector Kirby picked up the key and examined the label.

DO NOT USE THIS KEY TO UNLOCK RELIQUARY, he read. AWAKEN NOT THE ANGRY DEAD. Inspector Kirby whistled, then cocked an anxious ear. Further shouting came from the hall. Inspector Kirby dithered, but not a ditherer by persuasion he then thrust the key into the reliquary's key hole and turned it sharply to the left.

A click and the door swung ajar.

Inspector Kirby dithered anew. This was not a good idea. Why was he doing it? He was a policeman, he couldn't just go opening up people's private cabinets. Well, of course, actually, he could. That was one of the benefits of being a policeman, being able to pry into people's private belongings. But what about all that stuff about dying if you touched the handbag? Superstition surely? Voodoo wasn't real. It was the power of suggestion. Like an Aborigine pointing the bone at you. You didn't die if you didn't believe. Awaken not the angry dead, indeed!

A quick peep, then lock the cabinet up again. What harm could that possibly do?

Inspector Kirby swung open the door.

And then took a swift step backwards.

Something moved. Inside the cabinet. Something white. It had jerked as he opened the door, and now it was moving. Squirming.

Inspector Kirby gaped at it, fascinated.

It *was* a handbag. White, plaster cast or carved. But it *was* moving. There were skulls on it, many skulls. A large one in the middle, clearly human, but other smaller ones around and about that were anything but. And these were . . . moving. They clicked their tiny jaw bones as if taking in the air. Yawning, breathing, and now snapping angrily.

Inspector Kirby didn't like the look of them one little bit. He stepped smartly forward to slam the door shut.

But as he did so he slipped upon the fireside rug and fell towards the grate. In a desperate attempt to save himself he snatched at the mantelpiece.

But missed.

And his right hand plunged into the cabinet.

★

Inspector Kirby awoke with a start to find Billy's mum smiling down at him.

'Don't try to move,' she said. 'You had a bit of an accident, but you're all right now.'

Inspector Kirby did try to move, but he couldn't.

'You lost a couple of fingers,' said Billy's mum. 'I've bandaged up the rest, so they should be OK for now.'

Inspector Kirby tried to speak. But he couldn't do that either.

'I've taped your jaw up,' said Billy's mum. 'Don't want you making any noise now, do we?'

Inspector Kirby strained and struggled but to no avail. Billy's mum stroked his forehead. 'Now don't go getting yourself all upset. I did warn you not to touch the handbag, didn't I? But you did touch it, so you only have yourself to blame. You see the handbag has to be fed every week and it was Billy's job to feed it. And Billy always fed it with bits of Granny. But Billy's taken Granny with him and the handbag's been getting really hungry. It needs fresh meat, you see. Fresh human meat.'

Inspector Kirby's eyes were starting from their sockets.

'It's lucky you happened by, really,' continued Billy's mum. 'And most fortuitous that the telephone rang. It was one of your superiors asking after you. I told them that you'd just left and I'd seen you getting into an old VW Camper van. So I don't think they'll come bothering us again.'

Inspector Kirby shook and shivered.

Billy's mum covered him up with an old dog blanket. 'I've put you inside this portmanteau,' she said, 'because Billy took Granny's suitcase, but you probably would have found it a bit cramped in there. There's air holes in the lid, so it's not cruel or anything. And I've taken the liberty of injecting you with a special drug from the Amazon. It slows down the metabolism so you'll only need feeding about once a week. So I can do that when I come for another finger. So that's perfect, isn't it?'

And so saying Mrs Barnes closed the lid of the portmanteau, locked it and pushed it under her bed.

And then she went down for her supper.

Lunchtime with the Piper

The piper with the auld grey beard
Who spoke as soon as he appeared,
Both soon wore out his welcome and the new seat of
    his kilt.
The Campbells (whom the others hate)
Thought out their schemes, both small and great,
And made a living diving for the silver-coloured silt.

The piper got off in a huff.
He said, 'They think I'm Peter Brough,'*
Who speaks without a tremble or a flicker of his lips.
But I am more like Elvis P,
Whose Rock 'n' Roll is ecstasy,
And who could pull more crumpet with a flicker of his
    hips.

The piper spoke of ages past,
And men who sailed before the mast,
And when the 6.5 Special ran on time,
And of Don Lang and Hayley Bill
Who gave his boyhood days a thrill,
When men drank ale as men should do, not alcoholic
    lime.

The Campbells listened to his tale,
And watched the piper turning pale,
And some wept in their sporrans (though I saw a
    couple smirk),

*The popular 1950s BBC Radio ventriloquist

And when the talk had turned to frogs,
And sassy knacks and English dogs,
The piper said, 'Well stuff all that, I must be back at
   work.'

11

Accept anything. Then explain it your way.
CHARLES FORT

I walked into the Jolly Gardeners just as the piper was walking out. Which suited me fine, as I could never stand the bloke. Not that I have anything against the Scots you understand, after all I'm one myself, a direct descendant of William Wallace. But that piper really got up my nose. And anyway, I had some pretty heavy-duty thinking that needed to be done and where better to do it than here?

I was anonymous here. The folk in this sleepy rural hamlet knew nothing of my Lazlo Woodbine persona or my world-saving escapades. Here they knew me as Mr Rupert Tractor, a route planner for the local foxhunt.

Now, as it was a Friday lunchtime, the last person I expected to see serving behind the bar was the lead singer of the now legendary 1960s garage-psyche band The 13th Floor Elevators. So I was doubly surprised to see instead that it was Paul.

'Paul,' I said. 'I thought you were dead.'

Paul looked up slowly from his crossword. 'If I

can come up with a snappy rejoinder to that, I'll let you know,' said he.

'But you were reading the book. The Johnny Quinn book.'

'Johnny *who*?' asked Paul.

'Don't give me that. Johnny Quinn. *Snuff Fiction*, you had a copy.'

'Oh, Johnny Quinn. Funny you should mention him. After you left that Tuesday evening, I got to thinking about Johnny Quinn, and the more I thought about him, the less I seemed to remember.'

'Don't try that on me,' I told him. 'You had the book, I saw it with my own two eyes.'

'What, *this* book?' Paul pulled the book from beneath the counter. White card cover. Publisher's proof copy. He handed it to me and I examined it.

The Sniff Function by Jimmy Quonn.

'Easy mistake,' said Paul. 'It had me going for a while.'

'Huh!' I said.

'Pint of the usual, was it?'

'Whatever the usual might happen to be, yes.'

'I'll see if I can find a suitable glass.'

I stood and waited patiently, and at length my patience was rewarded and Paul pulled me a pint of something or other.

'Thanks,' I said, paying for and bearing it away. I plonked myself down in my favourite corner and muttered under my breath.

'Easy mistake, my arse,' I muttered.

'Not too sold on that explanation, then, chief?'

'It's all a bloody conspiracy.'

'Ain't that the truth. So tell me, chief, now that

154

you have the voodoo handbag, what are you going to do with it? Give it back to Mrs Barnes?'

'Are you kidding, Barry? That woman is a stone bonker. Think of that poor Inspector Kirby boxed up under the bed.'

'Yeah, I've been wondering about that for the last ten years, chief. How come when she whispered to you in your shed about what she'd done to the Inspector, and you threw up everywhere and everything. How come you didn't just go to the police and tell them?'

'What? Breach of confidentiality of a client? I have my standards to maintain. I'm a professional, Barry.'

'You certainly are, chief. So what *are* you going to do with the handbag?'

'I am going to use it to destroy Billy Barnes and close down the Necronet.'

'You do have a real downer on Mr Barnes, don't you, chief?'

'A *real downer*? I spent ten years trapped in the Necronet because of that maniac. And another three months in the loony bin.'

'You can't actually prove it was his fault, chief.'

'He's to blame, Barry. Billy Barnes is a serial killer and if he's not stopped he'll bring the world as we know it to an end.'

'Billy Barnes *is* the World Leader, chief.'

'Oh yeah? And how did he get to be the World Leader?'

'Hard work? Dedication? Natural aptitude?'

'Bullshit!'

'No doubt there was a certain amount of bullshit involved, but isn't there always?'

'I hate him and I will destroy him!'

'Not so loud, chief, folk are beginning to stare.'

'He's a murdering bastard,' I whispered. 'And he'll kill us all.'

'You're not perhaps, just a tad jealous, by any chance?'

'*Jealous?!*'

'Well, the two of you did go to school together, and he has done rather better for himself than you, hasn't he?'

'Better than me? What do you mean?'

'Well, he is the World Leader, chief. And you—'

'And me *what*?'

'Well, chief, there are some who might suggest that you are nothing more than a paranoid schizophrenic with a multiple personality disorder and a persecution complex.'

'Outrageous! And who might suggest such a thing?'

'Well, there was the doctor at the mental institution you've just escaped from.'

'Oh, him.'

'Him, chief.'

'And what about you, Barry? Do you think I'm mad?'

'Me, chief? Absolutely not. But then, what would I know? I'm only a voice in your head.'

'Quite so. And anyway, I can prove I'm not mad. I've got the voodoo handbag.'

'And this would be the handbag that eats people, would it?'

'It certainly would.' I pulled the voodoo handbag from the poacher's pocket of my trench coat and placed it on the table. 'There you go,' I said. 'Disprove that.'

'Would that I could, chief. Although—'

'Although what?'

'Well, it doesn't look all that hungry right now, does it? I mean, it's not exactly gnashing, or anything.'

I gave the handbag a bit of close scrutiny. And I had to confess that it didn't look all that menacing. It just looked like a rather badly cast old plaster handbag. 'Perhaps it's already been fed today,' I said. 'Or it's sleeping.'

'Sleeping, chief. That would probably be it. Let sleeping bags lie, eh?'

'Are you taking the piss?'

'Not me, chief.'

'Well, don't. You know what I went through, Barry. You know I was trapped for ten years inside the Necronet.'

'Now that's not altogether accurate is it, chief? I mean I wasn't actually in there with you, was I?'

'No. But *I* was there, and it was all down to that bastard Barnes.'

'So you keep saying, chief. But remember, I only caught up with you again when you were in the mental hospital. I don't really know exactly what you went through and why you hate Billy Barnes so much.'

'Do I have to go through the entire thing all over again?'

'It might be helpful, chief.'

'All right. So where was I?'

'Well, chief, Billy Barnes had just got himself a

job as information gatherer at Necrosoft and his mum had just come around to your shed, told you the horrible tale about Inspector Kirby, and asked you to find the voodoo handbag.'

'Ah, yes.'

'But she hadn't explained how the handbag came to be missing.'

'And she never did. I had to find that out for myself.'

'And you followed Billy Barnes to Brentford, did you?'

'Kill two birds with one stone, Barry. I figured that Billy probably *did* have the handbag, so I went in search of him.'

'And what happened when you found him?'

'Well, let's not get ahead of ourselves here. It took me a while to find him, and before that, other things happened. Shall I continue with the story?'

'Please do.'

'OK.'

The estate agent showed Billy around the penthouse flat.

'This is very much top of the range,' she said. 'This suite offers the most wonderful views of Brentford there are to be had. From here you can see the water tower.' She pointed with a long slim finger. 'And the famous gasometer. And beyond there the river bridge to Kew and the Royal Gardens.'

Billy's gaze followed the direction of the pointing finger, and then returned along the hand arm shoulder and neck to the attractive face of the elegant young woman. 'Very nice,' said Billy.

The estate agent smiled up at him, turned and strode across the black marble floor upon long slender legs. 'You have your fully fitted kitchen,' she said. 'Very hi-tech, very chic. Your lounge here, all mirror tiles and Bauhaus furniture, and the bathroom, with a Jacuzzi, of course.'

'Of course,' said Billy.

'And will you be living here alone, Mr Barnes?'

'I haven't made my mind up yet.'

'Well, it certainly suits you. You look right at home here, as if it was built for you.'

'Why, thank you very much. And what is through that door over there?'

'That is the master bedroom, would you like to see it?'

'All in good time.'

'Well I'm sure that you'll like it. And the suite is all ready for anyone to move in. Fridge fully stocked, champagne on ice.'

'Perhaps we might enjoy a glass or two now.'

The estate agent laughed a pretty laugh. 'Not until the contracts are completed, I'm afraid.'

'Oh, don't be afraid.' Billy took something from his pocket; it was wrapped in silver foil. 'Something for you,' he said. 'A present.'

'A present for me?'

'Just for you.'

The estate agent took the present and unwrapped it. It was a brightly coloured plastic something. 'What is it?' she asked, as she gave it a squeeze.

'It's called a pleaser,' said Billy. 'Now let's get that champagne open, and then we can explore the master bedroom.'

Smart Hat

That's a smart hat, Billy,
A fine and bonny lid,
A tasteful piece of headwear,
You're sporting there, our kid.

You look like Humpty Gocart,
With all that canny brim,
And it's a rare old compliment
To say you look like him.

It really really suits you,
You know I wouldn't lie,
You cut a dashing figure, lad,
They'll cheer as you go by.

I only wish I had one
So I could wear it too,
And all the folk would say I looked
As half as good as you.

From an ingratiating follower of natty headgear

12

Hang on by your fingernails and never look down
RORSCHACH
(inventor of the ink blot)

The hat looked good on Billy, and so did the coat. They suited him and he suited them. The chap at the tailor's remarked upon this and so did his assistant. They helped Billy carry his purchases out to his car. His new car, the one driven by the lady chauffeur.

The lady chauffeur who had, until recently, been an estate agent. They loaded Billy's buys into the boot and waved as the chauffeur drove him away.

'He really suits that car,' said the tailor chap, and his assistant agreed.

Billy sat in the back seat, tinkering with the CD player. In his opinion this car suited him very well. It was a definite cut above that belonging to the now defunct young man. It wasn't top of the range, but it was the best his lady chauffeur could afford. The car phone rang and Billy answered it.

'Barnes,' he said.

'Billy,' said the voice of Mr Dyke. 'Settling in all

161

right? Got yourself all sorted with a place to stay, I hear.'

'I'm fine,' said Billy.

'Splendid. Then it's time for you to go to work.'

Billy's mother sat a long time in the shed talking to the lad who would be Woodbine. But she communicated no further details regarding the mysterious disappearance of the voodoo handbag. Evidently glad to have got the whispering side of it out of the way, she made a great deal of noise. Rattling flowerpots about and banging the walls of the shed with a shovel.

Eventually several neighbours came to complain, there was some unpleasantness and Billy's mum was forcibly evicted.

The lad who would be Woodbine sat and pondered. He had been offered a weekly retainer – a sum coincidentally equal to that of Granny's old age pension – to locate and return the handbag. And, he concluded, as he would remind his Holy Guardian Sprout some ten years later, the best way to go about this was to kill the two birdies with the single stone and seek out Billy Barnes.

And this he set about doing.

Now it has to be admitted (although not yet by him) that he was not exactly in the Billy Barnes league when it came to the matter of mental agility.

Here was a lad of good intention, hell bent on becoming a famous Private Eye, but not exactly, how shall we put it, *gifted*. He had read Hugo Rune and his Law of Obviosity, but he had not fully grasped all the principles.

When he left the shed, a month later, somewhat grey and sallow of face due to the restricted diet of uncooked potatoes, he had at least reached the conclusion that although the shed seemed a very likely candidate for the least most obvious of all least most obvious places for Billy Barnes to turn up handbag in hand (and therefore the most obvious place that he would), he obviously wasn't going to yet!

And so, perhaps, rather than risk starvation, it might be as well to begin the search elsewhere.

And as Brentford was as much of an elsewhere as anywhere else, and the lad had an uncle called Brian who lived there, then Brentford seemed as good a place as any to begin.

And so he, which is to say *I*, arrived upon my Uncle Brian's doorstep with a smiling face and a change of underwear. The year was 1977 and the date was 27 July. It was a Sunday and a sunny one at that.

Uncle Brian opened the door. He was a short man, Uncle Brian, positively dwarf-like. He wasn't Welsh, but then who ever thought that he was?

'Who is it?' asked Uncle Brian.

'It's me,' I said.

'Well, you never can be too careful, come in.'

And I went in.

I had to squeeze past a lot of cardboard boxes that were blocking up the hall. 'What do you have in these?' I asked my uncle.

'Rubber gloves. Would you care for a cup of something?'

'Tea would be nice.'

163

'Yes, wouldn't it?'

Uncle Brian led me into his front room. It had been stripped of all furniture and the floor was covered in cushions. 'Having a party?' I asked.

'Sleeping,' said my uncle. 'I sleep as much as I can, wherever I can. To sort out all the world's problems.'

'Top man,' I said. 'If the people in power spent more time sleeping and less time trying to sort out all the world's problems, the world's problems would probably sort themselves out.'

'Have you been drinking?' my uncle asked.

'No,' I said.

'Well you should try it. I do, it helps me to sleep.'

'I see,' I said. But I didn't.

'You don't,' said my uncle. 'But sit down, I'll explain.'

So I did, and he did.

'Dreams,' said my uncle. 'The power of dreams. Where do you think ideas come from?'

'You think them up,' I said.

'Yes, but where do they come from?'

'You think them up,' I said again.

'No, no, no,' said my uncle. 'They have to come from somewhere. They don't just spontaneously appear in your head.'

'I think they sort of do. I think an idea is actually composed of lots of different other ideas that sort of give birth to it.'

'Cobblers,' said my uncle. 'When you ask someone how they came up with a really amazing idea, they'll say "it just popped into my head" or "it came to me all at once" or "I had a dream" or "I had a vision", or something similar.'

'So you're saying that ideas come from outside your head.'

'No, they come from inside. But from a different world inside, the world of dreams.'

'I don't think it's a different world,' I said. 'I think that when you're asleep, your mind is sort of idling, and dreams are just jumbled-up information.'

Uncle Brian shook his head. 'It's a different world, we enter it when we are asleep and dreaming. It seems weird to us because we are strangers there, we don't understand the laws that govern it. It's a world of pure idea, you see. Thought only, with no physical substance. Pure idea. Sometimes we bring a little of that back with us into the waking world. And pow, we have a new idea.'

'And that's what you're trying for?'

'Exactly. A big idea. Hence the dream surfing.'

'What is that, exactly?'

'When you go to bed at night you set your alarm, you need a digital one, you set it to go off at random times in the night to wake you up. Wake you up while you're dreaming. Break in on your dreams, see? Because normally, in the natural way of things, you only wake up when a dream is over, and so you don't remember any of it. This way you'll hit a few dreams in the night, you wake up with a start and hastily write down whatever you can remember.'

'Does it work?' I asked.

My uncle made a grumpy face. It was the kind of grumpy face that people who haven't been sleeping too well often make. 'Speaking of work,' said my uncle. 'What have you been doing with yourself?'

'I have become a private detective,' I said, preening at the lapels of my trench coat.

'I thought you were in show business. Carlos the Chaos Cockroach, wasn't it?'

'I don't do that any more.'

'But wasn't it something to do with the butterfly of chaos theory? Didn't you claim to be able to cause great events to occur by moving biros about and sticking paperclips on your ear?'

'I'm over that now.'

'The tablets are helping, are they?'

'Tablets always help, that's what tablets are for, isn't it?'

'My sleeping tablets definitely help,' my uncle yawned.

'Do you want to get your head down for half an hour?' I asked.

'No, I'll be fine. But if I doze off in the middle of a conversation, don't take it personally, it's not because you're dull, or anything.'

'I understand,' I said.

'So tell me about this private detective work of yours. It must be very interesting.'

'It is,' I said. 'This case I'm on now for instance—'

'Zzzzzzzzzzz,' went my uncle.

About an hour later an alarm went off and my uncle awoke. He snatched up a notebook and wrote frantically with a biro.

'Come up with a good'n?' I asked, when he'd finished.

My uncle examined his writings. 'Very bloody odd,' he said. 'But I suppose it must mean something.'

'What have you written?'

'Well, I had this dream that I was in a fishing port somewhere. There were all those whaling boats, very old-fashioned, and I went into this bar on the quay and got into conversation with this ancient mariner.'

'And he gave you an albatross?'

'He gave me a message to give to you.'

'What?'

'He said you were in a great danger and that you should beware of a Billy Barnes.'

'*What?*'

'Billy Barnes. Do you know a Billy Barnes, then?'

'I used to go to school with him. It's Billy Barnes I'm searching for.'

'Well, perhaps you'd better jack it in.'

'Bugger me,' I said.

'No thanks,' said my uncle.

'But it's quite incredible. You dreaming his name. Did the ancient mariner say anything else?'

Uncle Brian consulted his notes (which rang a future bell somewhere). 'I have the word CHEESE written down in big letters and underlined.'

'So what does that mean? That I should beware of cheese?'

Uncle Brian shook his head. 'It's probably a symbol. You get lots of symbolism in dreams. Cheese probably doesn't mean cheese, it means something else.'

'Like what?'

'Well, what do you associate with cheese?'

'Mousetraps?' I said.

'Mousetraps, good. And where would you find a mousetrap?'

'In the larder?'

'The larder, right. And a *Lada* is a kind of car, isn't it?'

'Not a very good one, I'd prefer a BMW.'

'Then that's probably what it means, you'd better be careful when you drive your BMW.'

'I don't own a BMW.'

'All right. Let's try another tack. What else do you associate with cheese?'

'Onions.'

'Why onions?'

'Cheese and onion crisps.'

'Yeah, that's a good one.'

'It is?'

'Well, an onion is a vegetable and crisps are made out of vegetables. So where do you get vegetables?'

'Out of the larder?'

'Hm,' said my uncle. 'So what does cheese rhyme with?'

'Peas?' I said.

'Anything else?'

'Keys?'

'Ah yes,' said my uncle. 'Keys, you have something there.'

'I do?'

'The Green Carnation Club,' said my uncle. 'It must mean that.'

'What, you have the keys to the place or something?'

'No, it's simple world association. Keys. Keys go in locks. Locks rhymes with box. Cricketers wear protective boxes. Cricketers bowl "overs", over rhymes with Rover, Rover is a dog, dogs chase cats, cats have nine lives and Oscar Wilde lived at nine Chesham Place, London.'

'And Oscar Wilde wore a green carnation.'

'Exactly. And the Green Carnation Club is in Moby Dick Terrace, just round the corner.'

'And Moby Dick was a whale and you dreamed about whaling boats.'

'There you go, then,' said my uncle. 'And I'll bet Billy Barnes drives a BMW.'

I shook my head. 'Incredible,' I said, and I meant it.

And my uncle smiled. 'A piece of cake,' he said.

'*Cheese cake?*'

Oh how he laughed.

'But I'll tell you one thing,' said my uncle. 'If you do go to the Green Carnation, watch out for yourself.'

'You mean it's a gay bar, I'm not worried about that.'

'No, its *the* bar. The one in all the jokes. You know "a man walks into a bar". Those jokes. The Green Carnation is the bar where all those jokes originate from.'

'You're kidding.'

'Everything has to come from somewhere,' said my uncle.

And he was right, of course.

★

I shouldn't have gone to the Green Carnation that night. I should have gone straight home when I left Uncle Brian's. If I'd gone straight home, then I'd never have got involved in any of the horror. I'd have been safe. And perhaps, years later, I might even have asked Billy Barnes for a job. But then, if I hadn't gone to the Green Carnation, I wouldn't be telling you this story now, or perhaps I would, but you wouldn't be there to read it. Or perhaps you would, but I wouldn't, or I would, or maybe I wouldn't.

I'm not completely certain.

But I did go along to the Green Carnation.

And there was a BMW parked out the front.

It didn't belong to Billy Barnes though, it belonged to Johnny Ringpeace, the nightclub owner. Johnny hailed from the North, where real men hail from. Real men with button-up flies and spittle on their boots. Johnny was well hard. He had a tattooed todger, a guard dog named Ganesha and a boil called Norris on the back of his neck.

As I wandered into the bar Johnny was arguing with a customer.

'And I'm telling *you*!' shouted Johnny. 'You can't bring that dog in here.'

'Oh, come on,' said the customer. 'Just a swift half and I'll be on my way.'

'Not with that dog, you'll have to leave him outside.'

'Why?' asked the customer.

'Because if my dog sees him, he'll kill him, that's why.'

'I'm sure he won't,' said the customer.

'He bloody will. He's a Rottweiler, he'll make mincemeat of him.'

'Oh, I bet he won't.'

'Bet? *Bet*? You wanna bet, do you?' Johnny dug into the back pocket of his leather trousers. 'Well, here's a ton, says he will.'

'A hundred pounds?' The customer looked a little worried.

'Take the bet or piss off.'

'OK!' The customer dipped into his pocket and counted one hundred pounds onto the bar. 'This is ridiculous,' he said.

'We'll see about that, *Ganesha!*'

A very large Rottweiler came bounding around the bar counter. 'Kill boy!' shouted Johnny. And the Rottweiler moved in for the kill.

It was all over in moments. But terrible moments they were. The howling, the ripping, the blood.

Johnny stared over the bar counter. All that remained of Ganesha were a few bits of gory fur and a tail.

'Bloody hell,' said Johnny. 'Bloody hell.'

'Sorry,' said the customer, quickly pocketing his winnings.

'I don't believe it. I *do not* believe it.' Johnny had a sweat on now. 'It ate my bloody dog. *It ate him!*'

'Sorry,' said the customer.

'I don't care about sorry. I want one of those dogs like yours. I've gotta have one of those dogs like yours. What's it called?'

'Well,' said the customer. 'I call it a short-eared, long-nosed, bald-haired, bow-legged spaniel. But my wife calls it a crocodile.'

Oh how we laughed.

I ordered a Death by Cider, was called a 'country twat' and settled for a lager. I took myself over to a darkened corner and sat myself down. Johnny's barmaid got a mop and bucket and cleaned up Ganesha's remains. The bloke with the crocodile drank his half and left the bar.

I gave the place a good looking over. It defied description so I do not attempt to give it any. I sipped at my lager instead.

Presently the bar door swung open, and in walked three young business types. I suppose it should really have been an Englishman, an Irishman and a Scotsman, but it wasn't. It was just three young business types. They were your standard business types. Those horrible dark suits that seem never to have been in fashion. Those portable phones they carry like symbols of power. The pink sweaty faces, the premature balding. You always have the feeling that they probably do really unpleasant things to the women they get into bed. And they do talk so *very* loudly. And always about their holidays.

'Bring me something long and cold with plenty of gin in it,' one said to Johnny. Johnny brought out his wife.

'I'm off for three weeks' seal-culling this year,' said one of the business types.

'Done that,' said another. 'I'm off hunting snow leopard. New seat covers for the Porsche.'

'White tiger are better for that,' said the third. 'Bagged three last year. Two in a game reserve and one in a zoo.'

172

Bastards! I thought. People with money have all the fun.

'I was surfing the net the other day,' said business type one. 'And I came across this web site called Murder Inc. They advertise the ultimate sporting holiday for the weapons enthusiast. Fly you out to a trouble spot somewhere and let you take pot shots at the natives. You can't bring back trophies, obviously – you won't get them through customs. But they video it all for you, so you can relive the fun.'

'I've heard of that,' said business type number two. 'Apparently they've been in business for more than one hundred years. They claim that all the major assassinations of the twentieth century were actually booked through them.'

'What, do you mean JFK, people like that?'

'Chap from a gun club in Leeds took him out on a two-week package.'

'Do you have their number?' asked business type three, priming up his portable phone.

'Not on me, sorry. I have it back at my business, though.'

'And where is your business, exactly?'

'Elsewhere.'

Elsewhere? I squinted at the business types and then I saw him. It was Billy Barnes. I hadn't recognized him at first. He looked so like the other two. Just like them. But it was definitely him. Well, as definitely as it could be, anyway.

I rose to say hello, and then thought better of it. My uncle's dream had been pretty specific. *Beware of Billy Barnes*, and here he was, right here in the Green Carnation.

I would play things safely, listen to his conversation, follow him and see what he was up to.

'Of course,' said Billy. 'The real thing in holidays this year is to take the supreme trip.'

'Supreme trip?' said number two.

'Virtual tours,' said Billy. 'Go anywhere, do anything and experience *everything*, without ever leaving your armchair.'

'What, a computer simulation?' asked number three.

Billy nodded. 'That's what I've heard.'

'It's not perfected yet,' said number two.

'You know about it, then?' Billy asked.

'My company are working on something similar. It's very hush hush, the commercial potential is vast. I'm in crypto-encodement, top secret stuff, I can't talk about it.'

'You're full of shit,' said number three.

'I'm not,' said number two.

'Tell me more,' said Billy.

'Can't,' said number two. 'You might be a spy from Necrosoft for all I know.'

'Necrosoft?' said Billy. 'What's Necrosoft?'

'The opposition. They'd give a lot to get their hands on what I know.'

'Sell it to them, then.'

Number two laughed. 'No way. I copyright everything I do. I'll be onto big wonga when it all goes on-line.'

'Good luck to you, then,' said Billy. 'Let me get another round in.'

★

And I watched him all through the evening. He got plenty more rounds in, but he only drank fruit juice himself. The bar filled up with Englishmen, Irishmen and Scotsmen, Grenadier Guards, blokes with parrots on their shoulders, a man with a twelve-inch pianist and a chap with a head the size of an orange. But I ignored the gags and kept my eye upon Billy. Business type number three staggered off around ten, but Billy kept number two talking and kept on buying him drinks. At closing time Billy offered him a lift home.

I followed them outside. Billy said something about his car being just around the corner, put his arm about the young man's shoulder and led him away.

I followed, stealthily.

They wandered down Moby Dick Terrace, crossed the High Street and then turned into Horseferry Lane.

And I followed with further stealth.

They were almost at the lock gates, where the Grand Union Canal meets the River Thames, when the young man began to express his doubts. I ducked down behind a dustbin and watched. There was something of a struggle, though rather one-sided, and then Billy hit him. The young man went down and I watched from hiding as Billy began to assemble some kind of electronic apparatus from pieces he'd been carrying in various pockets. It looked almost like a 1950s ray gun to me. Billy held the thing to the temple of the young man and squeezed the trigger. The young man twitched horribly and then went limp. Billy dismantled his ray gun and placed the parts back in his pockets. And then he lifted the young man's body, carried it to the river bank and dropped it into the water. And then he turned, grinned and called, 'Come out, then, I know you're there.'

I was all crouched down behind a dustbin and kept very still.

'I know you're there,' said Billy. 'I know you followed us.'

I rose as silently as I could amongst the shadows and prepared to take my leave at the hurry up. And then something hit me very hard on top of the head.

I turned and staggered and took in the image of a beautiful woman with haunted eyes, dressed in a chauffeur's uniform. And then I found myself tumbling down once more into that deep dark whirling pit of oblivion so beloved of the 1950s American genre Private Eye.

And it didn't half hurt.

Sundown on Jim the Wooller

Jim the Wooller leaned a leather arm upon the bar.
'One more for the road?' said Musty Fuller.
'I'll take one, if one there be,
For there's no-one alive but me,
And I'm the last of all men,
Jim the Wooller.'

Jim the Wooller drained his road one to the dregs.
'I thank you for that drink, my Musty Fuller,
It likes me fine, this Auckland Rum,
I drank some watching *Things to Come*,
And realized that I'm the last of all men,
Jim the Wooller.'

Jim the Wooller spat with haste into the cuspidor.
'I must be going now, my Musty Fuller,
For I've no time to sleep,
Shearing thirty million sheep,
And it's no fun at all to be
The last man,
Jim the Wooller.'

13

The way to a man's belief is through
confusion and absurdity.

JACQUES VALLEE

I awoke in some confusion, feeling most absurd.
It wasn't the bopping on the head I objected to,
it was the manner of the bopping. Bopped by a
dame! Woodbine would never have let himself get
bopped by a dame! Tricked by one, maybe, deceived
by one, done wrong by one, but never actually
bopped on the head by one. The ignominy, the
shame.

But then *I* wasn't Woodbine.

In fact, when it came right down to it, I had to
confess I was really crap at being Woodbine. I hadn't
been in character at all when I got bopped on the
head. And I hadn't been indulging in the usual
banter with Barry either. I'd really fouled up and I'd
got my just deserts. I had no-one to blame but
myself.

But enough of self pity.

'That was your bloody fault, Barry,' I said. 'You
could have warned me she was coming. Call yourself a Holy Guardian Sprout?'

But Barry did not reply.

'Don't sulk,' I told him. 'Just admit that it was all your fault, and we'll say no more about it.'

But Barry still did not reply.

'All right, then,' I said, 'it wasn't *all* your fault. Most, but not *all*.'

But Barry—

'Barry,' I said. 'Are you there?'

I shook my head, and tapped at my temples. 'Barry? Barry?' But he wasn't there. I could feel he wasn't there. My head felt, well, empty, really.

'Bloody typical,' I said. 'Just like God, never around when you need him.'

I struggled to my feet and rubbed at my head. But my head didn't hurt. Inside or outside. There was no bruising. I felt fine.

'She must have hit me with something really soft. Now where exactly am I?' I had a good old look around. I wasn't in an alleyway, which I would have been had I been playing Woodbine, but wherever I was, it looked far from familiar.

Because it looked far from anywhere.

Absolutely anywhere.

I was standing upon an utterly flat surface. Like sheet ice, or clear plastic, or something. And it just went off in every direction. And the sky—

'Oh, shit!' I said. 'The sky.'

The sky was white. Paper white. I'd never seen a sky like that before. But then, was it actually the sky? The harder I looked, the more uncertain I became. Perhaps it wasn't the sky, at all. Perhaps it was a ceiling. Perhaps I was inside some vast modern building, with a white ceiling and a plastic floor. That had to be it. But whatever it was, I had to be off.

For one thing I had to call the police. I may have indulged in client confidentiality with Billy's mum regarding the boxed-up Inspector Kirby, but this was different. I wasn't in Billy's pay, and that bastard had murdered someone. I'd actually witnessed a real-life murder. And that was no laughing matter.

'Where is the exit?' I asked myself.

'I do not know,' I replied.

But I set off to find out.

Now, I don't know what exactly was wrong with my wristwatch, but it had stopped working.

I was most upset by this, because it was a really expensive wristwatch. A *Piaget*. An image thing, I don't want to dwell on it. But I will say this, you can always tell a man by the quality of his wristwatch. The same way you can judge a woman's morals by her shoes. My dad could tell a woman's age just by looking at her knees. But sadly that was a skill he never passed on to me.

But I digress. My watch had ceased to function, and although my legs were working fine, they didn't seem to be getting me anywhere. How far had I walked? And, when it came to that, was I walking *into* this place, or *out* of it?

I was lost all right, and that was a fact.

I remembered being lost before. Once before. A long time before, when I was a small boy. My dad had taken me to the British Museum to show me the shrunken heads. We'd been walking through the Egyptian gallery, and I'd stopped to look at a sarcophagus in a glass case. I was fascinated by all the hieroglyphics. Row after vertical row. What did they mean and who had drawn them? Who were these people who had once been living but now were so long dead? I asked my dad, but he wasn't there. I was all on my own in that long gallery. All alone amongst the dead. And right there and right then I understood, for the first time, the loneliness of death. It just hit me out of the blue and it hit me very hard. The young are far from death, the young consider themselves immortal. Aged aunties or grandparents die, but not the young, their time is now. And my time was now. But I was here. Alone amongst the dead whose times were very long ago.

And I grew afraid and I wept.

Wept as I was weeping now.

Weeping now? I wiped tears from my cheeks. I *was* weeping now. Why was I weeping?

And where—?

I looked all about me. I was no longer all alone in the middle of nowhere. I was all alone in—

The Egyptian gallery of the British Museum.

And it was all exactly as I remembered it. I was standing by the very case. The one with the sarcophagus with the hieroglyphics. And the smell of the place and that certain light, it was *exactly* how I remembered it.

And at this I became *very* afraid.

'Are you all right, son? Lost your dad have you?'

I looked up. And I remembered this man. He was the curator of the Egyptian antiquities. It was he who had found me when I was a child. He who had taken me by the hand and led me around until we found my dad.

'Come on,' said the curator. 'Let's see where he is.'

And he reached out his hand.

'No,' I said, backing away. 'I'm not a child any more. I'm not here.'

And he faded away. Right in front of my eyes. He faded away and was gone.

And so too the Egyptian gallery.

And I was all alone once more. All alone in the very middle of nowhere. And then it dawned upon me. Because it was then that the loneliness of death closed in all about me and then spread out in every direction.

And I knew what had happened.

And why I was here.

And I knew why Barry wasn't with me any more.

Because his job was over. Because he only guarded the living.

And I was no longer one of the living.

Billy Barnes had killed me.

I was dead.

Wandering in Deserts

Out of water,
Out of luck,
Curse the sun,
And curse the truck.
Curse the fabled pharaoh's gold,
Curse that gearbox, ten years old,
Curse the greed of mortal man,
Curse the drive-shaft full of sand,
Curse the Fates that brought me here,
Curse the sodding second gear,
Wish I was home drinking beer.

Not wandering in deserts.

14

If you flick the words, the ideas will come
into being.
JIM CAMPBELL

I was dead.

And I was angry.

Angry at being dead. Furious at being dead and angry with the living. I remember as a child having chickenpox. And that made me angry. Not angry about the pain or the discomfort, but angry with everybody else. The well people, the people who didn't have chicken-pox. I would sit at my bedroom window and glare down at them as they walked along the street. How dare they be well when I was ill. It wasn't fair and it made me angry.

As you get older you get used to life not being fair. You take for granted that life isn't fair, and so you just do your best and try to get whatever you can out of it. But you're still angry, deep down inside, even if you can't admit it to yourself. You're still angry.

Or at least *I* was, anyway.

But now I was dead I was really angry.

This wasn't just a view from a bedroom window,

this was an overview of every living person in the world. No matter how rich or how wretched. I was jealous and angry with every single one of them. Because they were still living and I was not.

But none more so than Billy Barnes.

He was responsible for my death. And he was the one who would pay.

'I'll find him!' I shouted. 'And I'll haunt him. I'll haunt him until he dies, and then I'll meet with him face to face and kick his head in.'

The thought of eternal revenge cheered me slightly, but then another thought entered my head. If I *was* dead, then where was I? I wasn't in hell, but this sure as hell wasn't heaven.

The third and most obvious option had to be limbo. And if I was in limbo then it meant that God hadn't yet made up his mind about which way to send me. And if that was the case, then it might be a wise move to dispel all thoughts of anger and revenge and concentrate more upon peace and tranquillity and things of that nature.

Then I could get up amongst the choirs celestial with the all but certain knowledge that Billy Barnes would be getting his comeuppance in the furnaces below.

And that thought cheered me up no end at all.

But I hastily struck it from my mind. That was gloating over another's impending misfortune wasn't it? And that was sinful, surely? God wouldn't go for that kind of thing. God only went for purity of thought.

'Shit!' I said. 'That's a tricky one. How can you have purity of thought, when you know deep down inside that having purity of thought is something that will get you into heaven? That makes purity of thought a motive in itself rather than purity of thought for its own sake. And therefore it's *not* purity of thought. It's *im*purity of thought.'

'That's your basic human dilemma when it comes to matters spiritual,' said the wandering mendicant.

I looked across at him and nodded.

'I'll have another pint of best bitter, if you please,' he said and I got up to get in the round.

And then I looked all around myself. And then I sat back down. 'I'm in the Jolly Gardeners,' I said. 'What the f—'

'It's a cushion,' said the mendicant. 'You need someone you can trust.'

'I what?'

'You trust Andy, don't you? Ask him.'

'I *do* trust Andy. How did you know that?'

'*I* don't. *I* only know what *you* know. Ask Andy. Ask Andy what's going on.'

'I will.' I stumbled over to the bar. 'What the fuck's going on?' I asked Andy. 'What the fuck am I doing here? I'm dead.'

'You're not dead,' said the barman, shaking his head. 'Dismiss such thoughts from your mind.'

'How can I do that? What's going on?'

'You've been downloaded,' said Andy. 'Into the Necronet.'

'The Necronet? What's that?'

'It's a virtual world. A computer simulation.'

'You mean I'm inside a computer game?'

'It's not a game,' said Andy. 'But that's what

186

you're in. You're experiencing a holographic representation of reality. The reality is your reality, created from your memories and experiences. You're thinking this.'

'You mean I'm dreaming it? I'm asleep and dreaming?'

'It's not a dream. You won't wake up.'

'I don't understand any of this.'

'Have a drink,' said Andy. 'You'll feel better once you've had a drink.'

'Yes,' I said. 'Yes. All right. Give me a pint of Death by Cider. *No!* Strike that. Give me one of those Long Life beers.'

'Coming right up.' Andy pulled me a pint and passed it across. 'Taste it,' he said. 'Tell me if it isn't the best lager you've ever tasted in your life.'

I raised the glass to my lips. 'It won't be,' I told him. 'The best lager I ever had in my life was in India when I was doing the Hippy Trail back in the Sixties. I remember it as if it was only yesterday. Well, today actually.' I took a sip. 'And this is just what it tasted like,' I said very slowly.

'Digital memory,' said Andy. 'Think about it for a moment. You have total recall, don't you? Of everything you've ever done or seen. You remembered being in the Egyptian gallery and so you relived it exactly as it happened. Just think for a moment, try it.'

I thought for a moment. And I tried to imagine being able to recall everything I'd ever seen and everything I'd ever done all at once. And it hit me like a tidal wave.

I staggered back from the bar.

'Systems overload,' said Andy. 'Reboot and start again.'

I shook my head. I stamped at the floor. 'This floor is real,' I told Andy. 'This is no computer simulation.'

'Then it's not being dead either, is it?'

'No,' I said. 'I suppose not.'

'So can you get a grip of that? You're *not* dead. Keep telling yourself you're *not* dead.'

'I'm not dead,' I said. And I liked the sound of it. 'I'm not dead. I'm not dead. Hey, everybody! *I'm not dead!*'

'*What's all this?*' asked Sean O'Reilly, breezing in. 'Did you say you weren't dead?'

'I'm not dead, Sean,' I said. 'I thought I was, but I'm not. Isn't that brilliant?'

'Brilliant,' said Sean. 'Have you read any good books lately? I've just read this one by Johnny Qu—'

'Hang about,' I said, turning back to Andy. 'I still don't get any of this. This is real, this place. I can feel it, smell it. It's solid.'

'That's how you remember it,' said Andy.

'You mean it's built from my memories?'

'Thought has substance here.'

'I don't understand. But, wait, no, hang about. If I'm inside a computer simulation, how do I turn it off? How do I get out again? Have I got some kind of virtual reality headset on or something? Where are the controls?'

'I'm not programmed to provide that information.'

'Programmed? Who programmed you?'

'I am a product of Necrosoft Industries. I am here to provide you with all the information you require to make your stay here a pleasant one.'

'I don't want to stay here,' I said. 'I want to get out. Tell me how to get out.'

'I am not programmed to provide that information.'

'Then tell me who is.'

'Access denied,' said Andy.

'Oh yeah?'

'Oh yeah,' said Andy. 'But listen, just think about it. Why would you want to get out? Here you have total recall. A digital memory. You can call to mind anything wonderful that's ever happened to you and relive it, whenever you choose, again and again, as often as you want. You can explore this world, travel to any part of it. It's not just composed of your memories, there are thousands of others, a world-wide database. Limitless scope for experience and development. For ever and ever.'

'Bollocks,' I said. 'Outside in the real world, I'm going to have to go to the toilet sooner or later. I'll have to take the headset off.'

'Don't think about that,' said Andy. 'Think only of the possibilities. No harm can come to you here. There's no sickness, no death, only the exchange of experience and information. So much to see, so much to learn. So much to enjoy.'

'You sound like a bloody travel commercial.'

'How dare you,' said Andy. 'I'm an information package.'

'You can stuff your information. I want out.'

189

'You can't get out,' said Andy. 'Put such thoughts from your mind, or—'

'Or what?'

'Or it may be necessary to initiate a programme of corrective therapy.'

'And what is that supposed to mean?'

'I am not programmed to provide that information.'

'I'll just bet you're not.' I took my perfect pint and returned to my favourite corner. I was angry. Not quite so angry as I had been. But still pretty angry.

But then was it *real* anger?

After all, I was sitting in a virtual pub, drinking virtual beer, so perhaps it was only virtual anger.

'No,' I said to myself. 'It's real anger all right. And I'll get out of here somehow. I'm not spending the rest of my life inside a computer simulation, no matter how good the beer tastes. I can't be bought off with a digital memory and a limitless scope for experience. So what if I can live out again the most wonderful moments of my life in perfect detail?'

So what—

And I sat there and looked at her across the table. In that restaurant in Lewes, on that Saturday in March. She with her passionate amber eyes and fascinating mouth. And we were so in love then we could hardly eat. And I could smell her hair and touch her and—

'No!' I shouted, and I jumped from my chair in the Jolly Gardeners. 'I loved her and lost her, and it isn't pleasure to relive the happiest moments of your life. It's torment. Utter torment.'

'Easy there,' said Andy. 'You'll get the hang of it. Selective thinking is your man. Take it a little at a time. And calmly.'

'No!' I cried. 'I bloody won't. I want out of this. The real world may suck, but this sucks worse. To remember everything in perfect detail. Every mistake you've ever made. Every bit of pain you've caused to others. I am in hell. Let me out of here. Help me! Help me!'

And then somebody hit me. Or blanked me out or something. And everything diminished to a tiny dot upon a screen, then vanished. Into black.

And then returned in dazzling white.

And I was sitting in the doctor's office, staring at the ceiling.

The doctor said I was a paranoid schizophrenic.

Well, he didn't actually *say* it, but—

'Tell me about the Necronet,' the doctor said.

'The Necronet?' I shook my head.

'The place where you say you were trapped. This virtual world inside a computer somewhere.'

'I don't understand.' I shook my head again.

The doctor consulted his notes. 'You said that it was impossible to tell it from the real world, but you knew that it was simulation composed from your memories and experiences.'

'Andy told me.'

'Andy.' The doctor leafed through further notes. 'The landlord of the Jolly Gardeners.'

'Yes, that's him.'

'You were drinking at the time?'

'I had one drink.'

'Just the one.'

'Only one drink, yes.'

'Virtual beer, you say?'

'Yes, it wasn't real. None of it was real.'

'But it felt real. It was solid. But you knew it wasn't real.' The doctor adjusted his monocle. I'd once had a monocle like that. Although mine had plain glass. An image thing, I don't want to dwell on it.

'Do you still believe yourself to be in a virtual world?' the doctor asked.

'I don't know, I—'

'You don't know.'

'I mean, I—'

'This world was, you say, composed of *your* memories. Do you ever remember seeing me before? Have you ever been in this room before?'

'I can't remember.' I jerked my head from side to side. 'Why am I all trussed up like this? Take off this straitjacket.'

'All in good time.' The doctor rooted about amongst his notes. 'Digital memory,' he said.

'Yes?' I said.

'Total recall. You were downloaded into this Necronet and you had total recall. You could relive any memory. Access any previous thought.'

'That's right.'

'And can you do that now?'

I thought about this. 'No,' I said. 'I can't.'

'And so what do you conclude from this?'

'That I'm no longer in the Necronet?'

'Very good. Very good. We're making progress. Now what do you remember? About the night of July the twenty-seventh, for instance?'

'I was in Brentford.'

'Good.'

'I followed Billy Barnes.'

'Yes,' the doctor paused. 'Billy Barnes. This name crops up again and again in your notes. Why were you following him?'

'I was searching for the voodoo handbag.'

'Ah yes. We have a great many notes about that. Let's just stick with Billy Barnes for a moment. You followed him down Horseferry Lane.'

'And he murdered a young businessman. I saw him do it.'

'This man?' The doctor displayed a post-mortem photo. The same young man, pale and bloated on a slab.

'Yes,' I said, as I turned away my face.

'And you didn't know this man. You'd never seen him before.'

'Only in that pub with Billy Barnes.'

'So you had no motive. This was an act of random violence.'

'What?'

'You approached this man. Argued with him. Struck him down and threw him into the Thames.'

'I did no such thing. What are you saying?'

'Look at this.' The doctor drew my attention to a small TV set on his desk. He slotted in a video, thumbed a remote control and turned the screen in my direction.

An image flickered. A night view, looking down on Horseferry Lane, obviously from some security camera. Two men appeared, walking together, laughing and joking. Billy Barnes and the young business type. They seemed the very best of friends. And then from the shadows a third man appeared. Lurching drunkenly, a length of timber in his hand.

I blinked at the screen; this third man was me.

I watched as I swung the length of timber. Knocking Billy Barnes aside, then striking the young man again and again. Then dragging his body to the riverside and heaving it in. And then there was a further struggle with Billy, now risen. A struggle I lost as he laid me out with a perfect right to the chin.

The screen blanked and the doctor tut-tut-tutted. 'And there it is,' he said. 'And all in full colour. There is talk of Mr Barnes being awarded a commendation for good citizenship.'

'No!' I shouted. 'No. No. No. That's a fake. That's been doctored. It isn't real.'

'A computer simulation, perhaps?'

'Yes, that's it. Billy Barnes must have done it to implicate me.'

'It does far more than implicate you,' said the doctor. 'It tries and convicts you also.'

'But it's a fake. Barnes must have done it. While I was in the Necronet. He set me up. I was there and I saw him. Some woman hit me. His accomplice. I'm innocent. I didn't do this. You have to believe me.'

'I think that's enough for now,' said the doctor. 'I think we'll have you returned to your room.'

'You're in this!' I shouted. 'It's a conspiracy. You're in the pay of that murdering bastard Barnes.'

The doctor pressed a little button on his desk and

the door swung open to reveal a very large male nurse.

'Nurse Cecil,' said the doctor. 'Please take the gentleman back to his room.'

'No!' I cried, struggling to no avail. 'There's something going on here. Something big.'

'Shall I administer the gentleman's medication?' asked male nurse Cecil.

'Yes,' said the doctor. 'And use the big syringe.'

'The really big one with the extra-long needle?'

'I think that will do the trick,' said the doctor.

'No!' I shouted. 'No! No! No!'

But it was yes. And I was hauled away kicking and screaming, effing and blinding, to pain and further oblivion.

I stood in line for breakfast clutching my regulation steel tray. I was in pretty poor shape both mentally and physically. All that stuff about a drowning man clutching at straws is as true as it gets. But I didn't even seem to have straws to clutch at.

The big ugly son-of-a-bitch dolloped porridge onto a chipped enamel plate and poked it in my direction. I plucked a spoon from the bucket, took up my tucker and sought out an empty table. 'Barry,' I kept whispering. 'Barry, where are you? Barry?'

But Barry wasn't there. I was all alone, fearing for my sanity, without even a voice in my head for comfort.

'Anybody sitting here?'

I looked up to find a young man looking down at

me. He had a narrow face, a pointy nose and a gingery moustache. He looked pretty normal but that was no guarantee here.

'You tell me,' I said.

He raised a quizzical ginger eyebrow. 'The chair's empty,' he said.

'Then if it's empty for you it's empty for me.'

The young man sat down and placed his tray upon the table. I stared at his plate. Mushrooms, sausage, fried egg, toast. The young man caught my stare. 'I can't be having with porridge,' he said. 'Sits in my guts like a stone gnome in a tart's window box. Can't be having with it.'

'Nor me, but how—'

'Management services,' he said, flashing a badge on his lapel.

'You're not an inmate, then?'

The young man put a long thin finger to his lips. 'I am. Look again.'

I squinted at the badge. It was a bottle top secured by Sellotape. 'But how?' I asked.

The young man winked. 'They think they're smart, but they're not. They're thicker than a donkey's dick. I come and go as I please. That porridge looks really crap, would you like my sausage?'

'Yes please.'

The young man forked his sausage onto my plate.

'Thanks very much,' I said.

'The name's Roger,' said the young man.

'Rob,' I said.

'Please to meet you, Rob. Still angry?'

'Damn right!'

'Great stuff.' Roger tucked into his tucker. 'I've been watching you,' he said as he tucked. 'Muttering away. Observing you for weeks, I have. You're not like the rest, you've still got it.'

'Got what?'

'A sense of self, you still know who you are.'

'Not for much longer I reckon.'

'Then we'll have to get you out of here quick, won't we?'

'What?'

'Are you in the computer industry, Rob?'

I shook my head. 'Absolutely *not*.'

'Thought not. But the rest of them. Everyone here. They're all something in the computer industry. Research scientists, systems analysts, programme writers. All of them.'

'All of them?'

'Makes you think, doesn't it?'

I glanced around at the other inmates. They sat, staring dumbly ahead of them, slowly munching porridge.

'Zombies,' said Roger. 'Automatons. Utterly conditioned. Blank as Frank and banjo-brained.'

'I have to get out of here,' I said.

'I know you do and I'll help. Have they been giving you these?'

He opened his hand to reveal several capsules on his palm.

'Tablets,' I said. 'Same as the ones I'm taking. I used to be under the impression that tablets always helped. I'm not so certain now.'

'But have you been taking them?'

'Of course. Just because I've lost faith in them doesn't mean they're *not* helping.'

'Look.' Roger plucked one of the capsules from his palm and carefully pulled it apart. 'What do you make of that?'

I examined the contents. 'It's a micro-circuit. A silicone chip, or something.'

'Not what you'd expect to find in a tablet, eh?'

'Absolutely not. Listen, what's going on here? Do you know?'

'I've got a pretty good idea. It's something really big and it all has to do with a company called Necrosoft.'

'Billy bloody Barnes,' I whispered.

'Yeah, that bastard,' said Roger.

'You know him?'

'It was him who got me banged up in here. Simple misunderstanding. I met him in a pub, tried to put a bit of business his way. He thought I'd ripped him off and bosh, I'm nicked.'

'And did you rip him off?'

'Only a bit.'

'How much of a bit?'

'By about seventy thousand.'

'Quid?'

'No,' said Roger. 'Right-handed rubber gloves.'

How He Talked

Oh, our Roger was here last night,
You know Roger,
Roger by nature,
Roger by dodger,
Friend to the poor,
And a crutch to his mother,
Who lost all her coinage,
One way or another.

He stayed for an hour,
He drew and he chalked,
Made maps out of flour,
How he talked,
How he talked.

I said, nice to see you,
He said, he was glad,
Roger by nature,
Roger the lad.
The king of the gypsies,
A rogue with a rug,
A gay desperado,
A penitent thug.

He tipped me the wink,
He smiled as he walked,
We went for a drink,
How he talked,
How he talked.

15

Lex Talionis – The Law of Retaliation

'Yeah, all right,' said Roger. 'So I'm a stealth fox/dog/horse/human hybrid, but we don't choose our parents, do we?'

'No,' I said, 'I suppose we don't.'

'I'm quite a rarity as it happens. You won't find many blokes like me about.'

'That's hardly surprising. Bestiality is not exactly an everyday thing.'

'Come off it,' said Roger.

'What?'

'Haven't you ever wondered why so many dogs look like their owners?'

'You're not saying—'

'There's a lot of splashing about going on in the gene pool nowadays. They're breeding pigs with human genes in them to use for heart transplants. So a bloke is transplanted with one of these hearts, he's got some pig in him then, hasn't he? And who's to say where that will lead in a generation or two?'

'So you reckon that eventually all the species on earth could intermingle.'

'Every one that can. It will be the next step up the evolutionary ladder.'

'What a load of old toot.'

'Please yourself. But I'm telling you the truth. Surely you've noticed how people's attitudes have changed towards animals? And I don't mean just their fondness for dogs and cats. What about all those protests about live sheep exports? And all that "Save the whale and protect endangered species"? Mankind never cared about anything like that before. But every year that goes by, people become closer and closer to animals. Shit, they even have CDs of singing dolphins. And more and more people are turning vegetarian, why do you think that is?'

I shrugged.

'Perhaps they've already got a bit of sheep in them.' Roger ran a long and pointy tongue about his lips. 'Makes you think,' he said. 'But listen, do you want me to help get you out of here, or what?'

'Yes, please,' I said.

'OK. I'll do it, but in return you must do something for me.'

'What's that?'

'I need a mate.'

'Fair enough,' I said. 'I'll be your mate.'

'Not that kind of mate, you twat. I need a mate to mate with. One of my own.'

'I thought you considered all humanity fair game, as it were.'

Roger shook his head. 'I don't want to join. I'm an outsider and I intend to remain one. I'm not joining any pack, I want to mate with one of my own, and that's that.'

'Well, how would I know where to look?'

'You're a detective, aren't you?'

'Yeah, but—'

'I've got a photo. Of my mate.'

'You have?'

Roger fished it from his pocket and handed it to me. 'She's an estate agent. Most of my kind go into professions like that, used-car selling, the law, she was great at what she did, but then she went missing.'

I examined the photo. 'Bugger me,' I said.

'If you think it will help,' said Roger.

'No, I mean, I've seen this woman. She was dressed in a chauffeur's uniform. She walloped me. I think she's in the pay of Billy Barnes.'

'Right.' Roger snatched back the photo and tucked it away. 'Then we're in this thing together. Are you up to escaping?'

'Yes I am.'

'Then let's do it.'

I was very impressed by the way Roger did it. I didn't see quite how he did it, but did it he did.

'How did you do that?' I asked, once we were out in the car park.

'It's what I do best,' Roger said. 'That and eating chickens, of course. Can't seem to break loose of that habit. Show me a hen house and I just go berserk. Rush in there, ripping and chewing, feathers everywhere and—'

'Quite,' I said. 'But I'd rather not know.'

'Sorry. So, which car do you fancy?'

'You're thinking of stealing a car?'

Roger shrugged. 'Unless you have a better idea.'

'No, it's fine with me, after all I'm a convicted murderer. What's a bit of grand auto theft?'

'Small change,' said Roger. 'So which one do you fancy?'

I pointed. 'That one,' I said. 'The electric blue 1958 Cadillac Eldorado, with the big fins.'

'Just the jobbie.'

Again I didn't see quite how he did it, but Roger got the engine running and the soft top down. He sat at the wheel and I sat down beside him.

'So,' he said, 'which way?'

'Brentford, I suppose. That's where I last saw Billy Barnes and your foxy lady.'

'So which way's Brentford?'

'I don't know, which town are we in?'

Roger shrugged once more. 'I've no idea,' he said.

'Well just drive out of the car park and we'll find out.'

'Fair enough.'

Roger drove us out of the car park and we found ourselves travelling through a modern-looking town that could have been anywhere. A branch of Next, a branch of Gap, a branch of the Body Shop. Roger followed the one-way system . . .

And soon . . .

'We're back in the car park,' I said.

'Should I try another way?'

'I think so, yes.'

Roger drove us out once more. He took a left

turn this time, and soon we were passing a branch of Next, a branch of Gap and a branch of the Body Shop. And then we were back on the one-way system and back in the car park.

'You prat,' I said to Roger. 'Let me drive.'

And so I drove. Out of the car park, second turn on the right, past the branch of Next, past the branch of Gap . . .

'What the fuck is this?' I asked as I drove back into the car park.

'Always the same,' said Roger. 'I was hoping you might have been different.'

'*I* might?'

'Well, I've tried all the other inmates. But no sod seems to know how to get out of this town.'

'We'll walk,' I said.

'Tried it.'

'You've tried walking?'

'Dozens of times, but it's always the same, no matter how far I walk, I always end up here. That's why they're so lax on security I suppose, no-one can go anywhere.'

'That is bloody absurd. If you keep on walking you must get *somewhere*.'

'Not from here,' said Roger. 'I think it's like some kind of Möbius strip. No matter which way you go you always end up in the same place.'

'We'll walk,' I said.

And we did.

We walked for hours, this way and that way and round about. But no matter where we walked or how far we walked, we always ended up right back at the hospital.

It must have been around the twelfth time when we returned to find Nurse Cecil waiting for us.

'Your lunch is getting cold,' he said.

So we went in for lunch.

'Will you be having another go later?' Nurse Cecil asked. 'I could make you up some sandwiches and a flask of coffee if you want.'

'Most amusing,' I said, but I wasn't amused.

'Feathered wings,' said Roger, 'we might try feathered wings.'

After lunch (mine was porridge, Roger's was T-bone steak and chips), I sat in the recreation room pondering my lot. Certain thoughts entered my head and I kept them there. The morning had been like one of those terrible dreams where you're desperately trying to get somewhere but you can't. You miss the bus and the train and your feet don't work properly and you wake up in a right old state flapping your hands about and going 'No, no, no.'

There obviously had to be some way of escaping from this hospital and this nightmare town. But obviously it wasn't the obvious way.

Which left . . .

My behaviour all the next week was exemplary. I mopped floors and smiled politely at the male nurses and the doctors, I even shared a joke or two with Cecil. I watched Roger as he came and went, but I never ventured out again into the car park.

★

The doctor said I was making progress.

Well, he didn't actually say it, but—

'Tell me about the Necronet,' the doctor said.

'What can I tell you?' I asked. 'In theory it is a virtual world created by computer technology. The personalities and memories of people can be downloaded into it. The world in there would appear as real to them as the world out here.'

'And you believe that you entered this virtual world?'

'The way to a man's belief is through confusion and absurdity,' I said. 'Jacques Vallée said that. I've been giving it a lot of thought over the last week.'

'And what conclusions have you come to?'

I shrugged in my straitjacket. 'Well, take the security video for instance. That would appear to show me murdering the young businessman. I could argue that there are numerous ways it might have been faked, but it is doubtful that anyone would believe me.'

'The question is surely what *you* believe.'

'I should believe the evidence of my own eyes. Even if it conflicts with what I remember.'

'Or think you remember.'

'Exactly. And there we have the problem. Is my memory accurate? Perhaps I did kill the young man, but I've blanked it from my memory. It's possible.'

'More than possible,' said the doctor.

'Indeed. My problem appears to be in establishing what is actually real and what isn't. You see within the Necronet I had a digital memory, I could call up any past experience and instantly replay it, be right in the place it happened. Solid and real. I no longer have a digital memory, therefore I must conclude that I am back in reality. That this hospital is in the real world.'

'Very good.'

'And yet, when I tried to escape from the hospital last week I found that no matter where I went I came right round in a circle and ended up here.'

'This town is a planner's nightmare,' said the doctor.

I nodded. 'Nightmare,' I said. 'My thoughts entirely. Or like one of those computer games where you're in a maze and unless you can work out the secret passwords, and get the energy and stuff, you just go round and round in circles for ever.'

'A rather unfortunate analogy,' said the doctor. 'Considering your circumstances.'

'I agree, because if I was still inside the computer simulation, I *would* have the digital memory.'

'Exactly,' said the doctor.

'Unless . . .'

'Unless what?'

'Unless my digital memory was being suppressed.'

'Oh dear,' said the doctor, reaching towards the little button on his desk.

'No please, bear with me just one minute. Imagine this scenario. Imagine that I never left the Necronet. That this is not the real world and not a real hospital.'

'What a pity,' said the doctor. 'And you have been behaving yourself so well. I thought the tablets were really beginning to help.'

'I stopped taking the tablets,' I said. 'I haven't taken them for the last week.'

The doctor shook his head sadly, and his finger pressed upon the button.

'I believe that the tablets are memory suppressants,' I continued. 'Little silicone chips with programmes that deny me access to my own memories. I believe that if I had my digital memory back, all I would have to do to escape from this place would be to think my way out of it. Imagine myself somewhere else, somewhere I used to be, and I'd be out. Gone. In the twinkling of an eye.'

The office door opened and Nurse Cecil loomed.

'Kindly take the gentleman back to his room,' said the doctor. 'And double his dosage from now on.'

Nurse Cecil stood with an idiot grin on his face.

'What gentleman?' he asked.

Run of the Place

They'd given Old Arthur the run of the place,
And you should have seen the smile on his face,
As he walked in his dressing gown, staring in space,
As he whistled the Warsaw Concerto.

They'd given Old Arthur a new woollen hat,
He looked pleased as Punch as he went out in that,
With his book of the prophets and raggedy cat,
That he knew as Louisa Alberto.

They'd given Old Arthur a picture of Bog,
Which he kept on the shelf with his seed catalogue,
Some small paper mice and a nice china dog,
That would snuffle your ankles and smell you.

They'd given Old Arthur the key to the gate,
Which was not all that shrewd, as I'll tell if you'll wait.
For he wandered outside and was killed by a truck,
Which quite spoiled his day, I can tell you.

16

Be reasonable. Demand the impossible.
SITUATIONIST GRAFFITO

The followers of the John Frum Cargo Cult sat upon their homemade airstrip and stared into the azure sky.

'John Frum, he come,' said one. 'Bring cargo, all be rich.'

'Soon, now,' said another. 'Real soon, now.'

'I've been expecting him for quite some time,' said a native with a hat.

'Expecting who?' asked a fourth, a surly fellow with a human finger bone through his nose.

The first three natives looked up at him in awe.

'John Frum,' they said. 'John Frum.'

'Oh, him. He'll be along. Just you wait.'

And so they waited.

And the next day they waited again.

As they did for the next two days.

And the next.

★

One native said, 'It won't be long now.'

Another said, 'I shouldn't think so.'

Another one said, 'Where's the bloke with the hat gone?'

About a week later one of them said, 'I wouldn't be surprised if John Frum came at any time now.'

'Nor would I,' said another. 'Has anyone seen the bloke with the bone lately?'

About three weeks after that, on a fine sunny morning, John Frum did come back. But, disappointed that there was no-one around to welcome him, he went away again, leaving a note which said that he would definitely return at a later date.

'There,' said a native. 'I told you he'd come back.'

'And he could come back again at any time now,' said another.

A native with a bald head pointed to the sky. 'Isn't that him?' he said.

But it wasn't.

And so they decided to wait.

I came ashore on the east side of the island. The sea was as warm and blue as I had imagined it to be.

I remembered, as a child, having read Arthur Thickett's book on the Melanesian cargo cults *John Frum He Come: An Anthropological Study of Cargo Culture*, and enjoying it very much. In fact I could now recall every single word of that book, as I could with all the others I had read in my life. Over fifteen thousand books. Fifteen thousand four hundred and thirty-seven, to be precise. And not a Johnny Quinn among them.

I wasn't angry any more, but I was determined. Determined to escape from the Necronet and bring Billy Barnes to justice.

'Anger is one of the sinews of the soul,' wrote Thomas Fuller in his book *The Holy State and the Profane State*. On page fifty-three actually, which was the last page I got up to, before getting bored and turning instead to *The Beano*. But I'm sure he was right, it was one of them. My father once said, 'If you're not angry, you're not alive,' and I can remember exactly when he said it. So I was a little bit angry, but not so much as to let it cloud my judgement.

True, I was still trapped in the Necronet, but here I was not quite the twat I had been outside in the real world. Here I could recall the consequences of every action I had ever taken. So, surely, here I could never make the same mistake twice.

I sloshed up the beach, took off my shirt and spread it on the sand to dry. And then I took off the rest of my clothes and sat naked, soaking up the sun.

It was pretty blissful.

But was it safe?

I had taken considerable care with my choice of destination before I thought my way out of the hospital. I wanted somewhere really obscure, the least most obvious of all the least most obvious, least most obvious places they'd expect me to choose. Somewhere they couldn't track me to. I decided upon this island because although I'd read the book about it and taken in all the detail and description of the place, I didn't actually know exactly where it was. I couldn't have found it on a map, because I'd never seen it on a map. I had to be safe here. For a while at least. And from here I could plot my escape.

In comfort.

Arthur Thickett's book had been written in 1961 when the John Frum cargo cult had a great many followers. The cargo cults began in earnest during the Second World War, which was the first time white men had arrived on the islands in any large numbers. The natives watched the airstrips being built, and the conning towers constructed. They looked on as the white men landed their aircraft, opened up the cargo bays and brought out cargo. Cargo, marvellous things, things that the natives had never seen before. And the natives simply sat down and reasoned it out. And their reasoning was impeccable. Clearly the white men were, if not gods themselves, certainly in cahoots with the gods. And so if they did as the white men had done, they could get some of this God-given cargo for themselves. And so they constructed pretend airstrips and conning towers and dressed themselves in pretend uniforms, and marched about saying things like 'Roger Wilko' as they'd heard the white men say.

But the cargo didn't come.

The white men, seeing what the natives were up to, tried to reason with them. But the natives weren't having any. They *knew* what the white men were up to, and they weren't going to be tricked out of their share of cargo.

I remember (perfectly) seeing a TV documentary about it in the early Sixties. Armand Denis said to one of the elders of the cult, 'But you have been waiting nearly twenty-five years, don't you understand? Your god John Frum is not coming back.'

The old native looked him squarely in the eyes. 'You've been waiting nearly two thousand years for your god to return,' he said. 'So what makes you think that mine won't get here first?'

'He will,' I said and I rose from the sand. The book had described John as wearing a white suit and carrying an umbrella. I thought about this. And then, straightening my white lapels and swinging my umbrella, I marched off along the beach towards the village.

Blazer Dyke stared off towards the gasometer. The weather was far from tropical in Brentford and the rain spat curses at his office window. Blazer turned and re-seated himself at his cedar desk, glared across it and said, 'I'm not impressed.'

'Excuse me, please,' said Billy Barnes.

'I'm not impressed at all. In fact I am furious.'

'I don't understand,' said Billy.

'You have exceeded your authority. You have downloaded subjects into the Necronet without permission.'

'Only one or two,' said Billy.

'Only one or two? You fail to see the gravity of this.'

'I do,' said Billy.

'Subject one, Roger Vulpes.'

'Con man,' said Billy. 'He tried to rip me off.'

'Your chauffeur's fiancé.'

'He might have been.'

'And you disposed of his body?'

'Splosh!' said Billy.

'And subject two?'

'He witnessed the disposal of the crypto-encoder. I was being careful.'

'But not careful enough. And what did you do with his body? Splosh! too?'

'I have it nice and safe,' said Billy, 'in a suitcase under my bed. I have a use for it.'

'You have no idea what you've done, do you?'

'No,' said Billy. 'What have I done?'

'Possibly jeopardized the success of the entire project.'

'I don't see how—'

'Well, I'll tell you. Subject two has escaped.'

'From the Necronet? That's impossible.'

'Not from the Necronet. No-one can escape from the Necronet. Once you're in, you stay in. Unless someone here chooses to upload you back into your body. He has escaped from our jurisdiction. His whereabouts are presently unknown.'

'Delete his file,' said Billy. 'Close him down, pull the plug on him.'

'Can't be done if we can't locate his whereabouts.'

'Why?' asked Billy.

'Because the Necronet is not fully on-line. It is not globally linked. The subjects chosen to be downloaded into it are chosen with great care for the information they can give us.'

'The grannies aren't.'

'The grannies are harmless. They mostly think they've died and gone to heaven.'

'So why isn't this chap harmless? I went to school with the twat, they don't come much more harmless.'

Blazer Dyke sighed. 'We have certain programmes written into the system. Carrot and stick programmes. The subject behaves well, then he enjoys his heaven on earth, his world of fantasy sex and high living. If he behaves badly, then he is sent for rehabilitation in the virtual hospital. It's automatic, no-one has to press any buttons at this end.'

'I still don't see what the problem is.'

'He escaped. He didn't take his virtual medication.'

'Then you should thank me,' said Billy.

'Thank you?'

'For exposing a flaw in the system.'

'This flaw in the system could cost us everything.'

'I still don't see how. You haven't explained to me how.'

'Ever heard of the term "computer virus"? This chap is buzzing around in there at the speed of thought. He can be anywhere and everywhere if he puts his mind to it. We could access valuable information and he could supply us with garbage and we wouldn't know the difference.'

'You're over-reacting,' said Billy. 'It won't happen.'

'Oh, won't it though?'

'No, it won't. If I know anything about him, he's

probably set himself up as a god to some cult on a tropical island.'

'You really think so, do you?'

'That's what I'd do, if I were him.'

'Absurd,' said Blazer Dyke.

'It's anything but. Your standard adolescent fantasy: white god on a tropical island with dusky maidens pandering to your every need. An obvious choice.'

'Do you realize what it would take to scan through every possible tropical island? And every date?'

'Not necessary,' said Billy.

'And why not?'

'Because he will go on doing the most obvious thing. Where was he thinking about when his bad attitude got him automatically zapped straight into the virtual hospital?'

'A pub,' said Blazer Dyke. 'His local, the Jolly Gardeners. The information package to ease him into his new situation was the landlord. It's all automatic, it works upon the subject's trust.'

'Well, there you have it,' said Billy. 'And he'll go back there, you wait and see. By which time you will have tightened up your virtual hospital programme, turning it perhaps into a virtual gas chamber.'

'And what makes you think he'll go back to the Jolly Gardeners?'

Billy sighed. 'Because it's so obvious. What do all those criminals who escape to foreign parts say? "I really miss being home drinking a good old pint of English beer." He'll go back when he gets bored with paradise. Trust me, he will.'

Blazer Dyke nodded slowly. 'You're a very clever boy, Billy,' he said. 'But don't be too clever. I shall watch your progress carefully. Do not let me down again.'

Billy smiled. 'I won't,' he said.

I was pretty hot by the time I reached the village, and was just thinking how much I'd enjoy a pint of good old English beer, when I saw something that struck the thought from my mind. In the middle of the village square was a large throne-like chair, constructed from used car parts and bamboo, and sitting on this, surrounded by bowing natives, was a chap in a white suit. He had an umbrella resting upon his lap.

I marched speedily in his direction. 'Oi!' I shouted. 'Oi! You! What do you think you're up to?'

The figure on the throne made a startled face. 'Who are you?' he asked.

'I'm John Frum, of course.'

'You certainly aren't.'

'I certainly am!'

'You're *not*,' he said. '*I'm* John Frum.'

I glared at him eye to eye. Well, almost eye to eye, he was up a bit from me. 'You're bloody not,' I said. 'But I know who you are, you're—'

'Hold it right there.' The chap put up his hands and climbed down from his throne. Waving his rising subjects aside he pushed me before him.

'Stop pushing,' I said.

'Just a quiet word or two.'

218

'I'm not interested in any quiet words. You're an impostor.'

'So are you.'

'But I got here first.'

'Look,' I said. 'I know who you are. You're Arthur Thickett.'

'Sssh,' said Arthur Thickett. 'You'll spoil everything.'

'Spoil everything? You're deceiving these poor natives. It's outrageous.'

'It's perfectly harmless. And how do you know who I am?'

'I read your book. Your photo's on the dust jacket.'

'Well, at least somebody remembers me.'

'It was a great book. But what are you doing here?'

'I'd have thought that was patently obvious. But what are *you* doing here? You shouldn't be here. This isn't your dream.'

'My dream?'

'It's my dream,' said Arthur. 'I'm dreaming this and you shouldn't be here. So piss off, will you?'

'I certainly will not. But hang about, your dream? Do you mean that you're not in the Necronet?'

'What's a Necronet?'

'Never mind. But are you actually telling me that you're dreaming this?'

'It's called lucid dreaming. I'm in an altered state.'

'Go on.'

Arthur sighed. 'Look,' he said, 'after the book failed I fell upon hard times. Took to drink, it's a common enough thing with writers; they might have some talent and they've all got big egos, but most of them are weak underneath. They can't function in the everyday world, they can't get relationships together. They're fantasists, they inhabit their own fantasy worlds.'

'And are you saying that this is one of those?'

'In a way. It's lucid dreaming. It's the only thing that keeps me sane. Lets me escape from the real world. You take this special drug that comes from the Amazon and you go into an altered state. You can take control of whatever you dream. Being on this island was the happiest time of my life. So I dream that I'm here and I dream that I'm John Frum.'

'Incredible. So you're dreaming now? Dreaming this?'

'Exactly. And that's why you shouldn't be here.'

'But I am here.'

'Yes, you are. So I'd better have my natives chop off your head.'

'I wouldn't try it, if I were you.'

'Oh no?'

'Oh no!' I thought about what it would be like to be fifty feet tall and looking down on Arthur Thickett. And then I thought myself normal again, and helped him onto his feet.

'You fainted,' I said.

'I can't do that,' said Arthur.

'What, faint? You just did.'

'No, make myself grow like that. What drug are you on?'

'I'm not on any drug. And I'm sorry I frightened you. But listen. I want you to do something for me.

220

If you do it for me I will get out of your dream and never bother you again. How does that sound?'

'It sounds wonderful,' said Arthur. 'All my natives have run away.'

'They'll be back. Now this is what I want you to do. When you wake up I want you to go to the police and tell them . . .' And I explained to Arthur about Billy Barnes and the murder I'd witnessed. And about Necrosoft and the Necronet. And when I'd finished, I said to Arthur, 'So, will you do that for me?'

Arthur took off his Panama hat and scratched his head. 'I do foresee one or two problems,' he said.

'Like what?'

'Well, I'm dreaming, aren't I? And if I go to the police and make these accusations, and they ask me for proof, well . . .'

'Hm,' I said. 'I see what you mean. You could lie of course, you could say that you overheard a bloke in a pub talking about it. And think of this, when Billy Barnes is arrested and brought to justice, you'll be a hero. You can write a book about it.'

'Oh yes,' said Arthur. 'I do like the sound of that.'

'And don't forget, you must tell them all about Necrosoft and the Necronet. They're going to have to get someone who knows all about computers to release me from here.'

'Computers,' said Arthur. 'It all sounds so terribly futuristic.'

'Cutting edge of Nineties' technology.'

'Did you say *Nineties*' technology?'

'Of course, what did you think?'

'So you're saying that this crime was committed in the 1990s.'

'Of course.'

'And so you're from the 1990s?'

'Arthur,' I said, 'what are you trying to say?'

'Only this,' said Arthur. 'I'm not dreaming this in the 1990s. I'm dreaming this in nineteen sixty-five.'

Agamemnon's Beard

So much for the cat that won't stand up,
Or the dog that won't lie down.
Derek dug and dug and dug,
In the backstreets of the town.

He upped the cobbles in his yard,
And sunk some sample bores.
Then channel-grooved towards the north,
Along the lowland shores.

When questioned of his diggings,
He said, though people jeered,
That he was searching ceaselessly
For Agamemnon's beard.

'A worthy prize,' said brother Mike,
He hoping for a share,
'I'll lend you my new mountain bike,
With saddle bags to spare.'

So Derek rode to Canterbury,
Parked his bike and spade,
And asked the bishop his advice.
'I dunno, son,' he said.

But if you keep searching hard enough for something,
There's a good chance you'll eventually find it.

17

Never go to bed mad. Stay up and fight.
PHYLLIS DILLER

I didn't get too angry with Arthur Thickett. After all, it really wasn't his fault that he was in 1965 and I was in 1997. So I didn't get too angry. Violent, yes. I *did* get violent.

But he took it like the English gent he was. And after the natives returned and patched up his bruises, he introduced me to them as his brother Derek. We got along very well, Arthur and I. He was an interesting fellow, and I think he quite enjoyed having me for company. I told him all about the Hippy Trail and Woodstock, and he said he'd probably give them a go. And he told me all about the mysterious drug from the Amazon and lucid dreaming.

It did come as quite a revelation to learn that the world of so-called cyberspace, which I now inhabited, was the same world that we visit in our dreams, or when we do hallucinogenic drugs or have a mystical experience. Arthur referred to it as the *weird space*, the *mundus magicus*. Not a physical place, but real none the less.

Little did I know that ten years from now I would be shouting these truths at a doctor in the Conspiracy Theorists' Correctional Facility. And that this doctor would not believe a word.

'What do you know about voodoo?' I asked Arthur, as we sat upon a rock diddling our toes in the ocean.

'I spent three years in Haiti,' said Mr Thickett, 'back in the late Forties. I learned what I could, but a white face isn't welcome at the ceremonies.'

'What do you know about Maîtresse Ezilée?'

'Enough to avoid rummaging in her handbag.'

'Go on.'

'Well, firstly voodoo is not a cult like John Frum. John Frum is based on a misconception. Voodoo is a full-blown religion with a pantheon of gods. What is fascinating about voodoo is that it did not stem from Africa. It was not imported, it sprang into being in a complete form on Haiti. But each voodoo god echoes a previous god in another religion. Maîtresse Ezilée is a good example. She echoes the Virgin Mary. But the Virgin Mary of course is an echo of previous female divinities.'

'You think all religions share a common origin?'

'That's a popularly held belief, but I don't subscribe to it. What if Maîtresse Ezilée is the Virgin Mary in her latest incarnation? What if all the voodoo gods were previously other gods known by other names?'

'What would be the point? Why would gods do that?'

'Ah,' said Arthur, 'the point is this. The voodoo

225

gods are living gods. They're right here and now on earth. The voodoo priests and priestesses commune with them daily. You don't do that in other religions. Christians may talk about being "filled with the spirit", but Jesus doesn't come into their living rooms for a cup of tea and a chat. Christians know where Jesus is, he's in heaven.'

'But not with his mum, if she's in Haiti.'

'Perhaps they take it in turns,' said Arthur. 'What is also interesting is to trace the roots of each religion. Some, as we all know, are spread on the "conquer and convert" principle. But each religion has an exact point of origin where it sprang into being. You can mark them on a map of the world. And I don't think there's anything random about it. It's as if the gods choose a particular place for a particular reason. But, before you ask, I have no idea what this reason might be.'

'You've clearly given it a lot of thought,' I said. 'Tell me some more about Maîtresse Ezilée.'

'She's an odd one. On the one hand she's your standard mother goddess, her followers are her children, she rewards the righteous and punishes the unrighteous. But then you have all this business about her bag.'

'The voodoo handbag.'

'She is supposed to carry this bag made from skulls. In the centre of it is a human skull, but all around are other skulls which are not human.'

'Animal skulls.'

'Not animal. Beings from the spirit world. The bag has a cult following of its own. It is venerated as something apart.'

'Isn't it supposed to be able to transport you into the spirit world?'

'On a one-way trip, I'd have thought. It's rumoured that human sacrifices are made to the bag.'

'I've heard such rumours. But the handbag is a real thing, it's physical, you could walk up and touch it?'

'I wouldn't recommend that. But it is real. It's not some legend. It's an actual artefact. I've never seen it myself, but I have a friend who told me that a friend of his once saw it.'

'Well, you don't argue with evidence like that.'

'So what is your interest in Maîtresse Ezilée and her voodoo handbag?'

'It's all part of the Billy Barnes business. Billy's mother claims that the handbag has been held in protection by her family for several generations. Billy went missing, and then the handbag, shortly afterwards.'

'And you think that this Billy Barnes might have it?'

'He'd apparently been feeding it with bits of his granny. And he took her when he went. For all I know he's got some other poor bugger boxed up under his bed being fed to the handbag a finger at a time.'

'Horrible,' said Arthur. 'But listen, I have to go now, the drug's beginning to wear off. Is there anything you'd like me to do for you back in nineteen sixty-five?'

I shook my head. 'Nineteen sixty-five was a pretty unmemorable year, really. It's a bit early to go warning Elvis that he should diet or trying to persuade John Lennon not to move to America. But listen, the summer after next, make sure you're in San Francisco. That will be *the* place to be. The Summer of Love, it will be called. Be there or be square.'

'Thanks very much,' said Arthur.

'And Arthur—'

'What's that?'

'If you bump into a chap called Charlie Manson in San Francisco, turn around quietly and walk the other way.'

'Charlie Manson. All right, I'll remember that.'

'I'll see you some time, then.'

'Don't be a stranger,' said Arthur, and he vanished.

I sat awhile on the rock and skipped pebbles over the ocean. It was tempting just to stay here, enjoy the dusky maidens, the coconut wine and all the other benefits of godhood. Or maybe I should dream up a neighbouring island and establish my own personal cult there. One of those Free Love jobbies with me as Lord High Muckamuck and a bevy of nubile porno actresses for acolytes. All right, I know it's your bog standard male fantasy fodder, but come on, imagine if you could really do it.

And I *could* really do it.

And one part of me wanted to.

One part in particular.

But I knew it was a bad idea. After all I *was* a fugitive. And the point was that I *was* here. And here wasn't *real*. Not here in the Necronet. It seemed real and it was tempting, but it wasn't real and all the pleasures here were synthetic. I wanted out and I wanted back into the real world. And so I really couldn't lounge about here wasting time.

The sun shone down on the beach and I got to thinking how nice it might be to enjoy a good old pint of English beer to refresh the senses and aid cogitation.

And so, with a kind of theatrical puff (which is not to be confused with a theatrical poof), I vanished too.

POOF!

Just like that.

Poof indeed! As a matter of interest, have you ever wondered about the kind of noise the Big Bang made? And whether, in fact, it was the *first* noise? If it *was* the first noise, then it was undoubtedly the biggest and the loudest, and all later noises are a terrible let down in comparison. But *was* it the first noise?

I remember being taught at school that sound cannot travel through a vacuum. And if that's the case, then the Big Bang couldn't make any sound at all in the infinite vacuum of space. Which would mean that it wasn't really a Big Bang at all, was it?

It was more of a Big Poof!

It always tickles me when a scientist comes up with a new theory about how the universe began. And especially how he always has a string of equations to support this theory. What on earth (or off it) do mathematical equations have to do with the creation of the universe? Mankind invented mathematics, the universe invented itself.

It seems to me that the string of equations says a great deal more about the scientist's inflated opinion of his own intelligence than anything else. To actually believe that he can reduce anything as irreducible as universal creation to a string of equations! What a bloody cheek!

Who do these people think they're kidding?

However, that said, there is one man who figured it all out. But you won't find him in the bestseller's list alongside Stephen Hawking. Because this man doesn't own a pocket calculator, and this man's attitude is that 'If it can't be worked out on the back of a cigarette packet, then it can't be worked out at all'.

This man's name is Hugo Rune, and Rune's Universal Creation Solution,* of which Rune's Law of Obviosity is an offshoot, stands alone for its simplicity and elegance.

Rune's Universal Creation Solution states:

The birth of the universe was the most impossible thing that could ever happen: and that's why it happened.

It might take you a little time to get your head around that one. But it's worth it in the end, because it has to be the solution. Emphasis must be

*It is important to note that Rune uses the word *solution* here rather than *theory*. Rune's currency was Ultimate Truths. One of his many maxims was: 'Once I have conclusively solved a problem, I do not refer to my solution as a theory.'

put upon certain words. The word *most* for instance. The birth of the universe was the *most* impossible thing that could ever happen. Think about that. In an eternity of timelessness many other impossible things *could* happen. But the birth of the universe was the *most* impossible. And that's why it happened.

Naturally the grey beards of the scientific community, outraged that Rune should have solved it all with such ease and no equations, demanded that he explain his solution more fully. It wasn't enough that he had given an explanation that actually explained things, they wanted to know *how* it explained things. And by what route he had arrived at this explanation.

Rune gave a lecture, where he patiently explained to the grey beards how it all worked.

In essence it was this:

Order out of chaos. Before order you had randomness. Randomness down to a molecular level. Universal randomness – endless, endless, randomness. And then you had a coincidence. The first ever coincidence. A seemingly impossible thing to happen. Two bits of randomness doing the same thing at the same moment. The first coincidence, a new event in the history of the universe. Something altogether new. This new thing couldn't have happened had not the coincidence occurred. This new thing was in itself a new piece of randomness, utterly unique. Until it bumped into another thing, identical to itself, that had occurred due to similar coincidence elsewhere. When the two met, something new again happened, because this coincidence was another new event. And so on and so forth, but all this simultaneously in an infinitesimal moment. Bang!

Big Bang!

Rune did explain that we had the wrong idea about the universe. The physical universe, which is composed of matter, is not incredibly large. It is infinitesimally small. Space is endless, but there isn't that much matter in it. The Big Bang was really a very small bang. No big deal at all in fact. Something that happened on a microscopic level. A tiny event.

The grey beards stroked their grey beards. It did appear to explain everything. But they asked Rune whether it could be simplified. Reduced in fact to a few letters. If Randomness was called R, and coincidence was C, and creation of the universe was B (for Big Bang), how did it work?

Was it $R + R = C$, $C^2 = B$, or was it $B = R^2 \times C^2$?

Rune explained that you'd have to break the Rs up: R① would be original randomness, also known as R^0; R② would be the second act of randomness, post-coincidence, but prior to R③, when two post-coincidence events coincided simultaneously to create a third (R④). B itself was a combination of $R①^2 \times R②^2 \times R③^2 \times R④^2$. Recurring.

What were the catalysts that sparked the original random events? asked the grey beards. And how did these fit into the equation? Could these be called ORs?

Rune took up a piece of chalk and went over to the blackboard.

He never gave another lecture on the subject.

And he never worked out the equation.

Some say that he spent the rest of his life trying. But others, who are better informed and were present at the lecture, state that Rune laid about the grey beards with his stout stick before adjourning to the pub for a pint.

A pint of good old English beer, probably.

I gave the Jolly Gardeners a miss. I mean, come on now, did you really think I was going to make my way back there and walk straight into a trap?

You did? Then shame on you.

I dreamed up a pub of my own. I called it Rob's Bar, placed myself behind the counter, and peopled it with all the folk I'd ever wanted to meet.

There was Captain Beefheart playing dominoes with Salvador Dalí, Aleister Crowley chatting up Madonna, Hugo Rune arguing with Einstein, Oscar Wilde coming out of the Gents, and Long John Holmes going into the Ladies.

I sipped my good old English beer, served a pint of Death by Cider to Jimi Hendrix, and smiled upon the congregation. They were all chatting happily away, in fact they all seemed to be on first-name terms. It's typical that, isn't it, the way the rich and famous chum up together. I was about to serve Bob Dylan (the young version, not the present-day plonker) when I had to leave the bar for a moment to eject David Bowie whom I hadn't invited.

I returned to the bar, served Bob and then bashed my knobkerry down upon the counter. 'Ladies and gentlemen,' I said. 'If I might just have your attention for a moment.'

The hubbub continued and I was ignored.

'Ladies and gentlemen, please.'

More hubbub.

I bashed my knobkerry down with some force. 'Ladies and gentlemen, *please*.'

Further hubbub.

'Please! Please! Please!' and Bash! Bash! Bash!

The hubbub ceased and heads turned in my direction.

'Thank you,' I said. 'Now you are probably wondering why I brought you all here.'

I gazed at them and they gazed at me.

'Well, in case you *were* wondering, it's this—'

And they all started hubbubbing all over again.

'Now stop that!' I bashed with considerable vigour. 'I have asked you here because I have admired your work in the past and I would value your—'

Chris Eubank came forward and handed me something.

'What's that?' I asked.

'Autographed photo,' said Chris.

'Well, thank you very much, but that's not what I want.'

Chris snatched it back. 'Just watch it!' he said. 'Twat.'

'I would value your opinions,' I continued. 'You see, each one of you has in some way helped to shape my life. A record here, a painting there, some show or event I went to.'

'Excuse me,' said Hugo Rune, 'but who exactly are you?'

'I'm Rob,' I said. 'And this is my bar. My dream bar actually.'

'And are you famous?'

'No.'

'Then what possible interest would you be to us?'

'Now stop all that,' I said. 'I'm well aware of how you rich and famous chum up, that's only to be expected. But if it wasn't for the little people like me to buy your records and so forth, you wouldn't be rich and famous.'

'I think you miss the point,' said Rune. 'We are rich and famous because we are different. We are the herd leaders, we change society, alter the direction of the herd.'

'And that's why I'd value your opinions, you see, I'm in a lot of trouble. I'm trapped here and I need all the help I can get so—'

'Have to stop you there,' said Rune. 'You really are missing the point. Do you recall Margaret Thatcher saying "There is no such thing as society, only groups of individuals"?'

'Yes,' I said.

'Well, she was talking out of her handbag. What she should have said was "There is a group of individuals. And there's the rest. And the rest equals society." '

'You pompous prat,' I said.

'It is the privilege of the dwarf to insult the giant.'

'The dwarf on the giant's shoulders sees the furthest of the two.'

'Not if he doesn't get a leg-up.'

235

'And you're not going to give me that leg-up. Is that it?'

'You're a statistic,' said Rune. 'A sales figure. Those at the top do not view you as an individual. Only as a percentage.'

'You callous bastard.'

'Callousness does not enter into it.'

'Come on,' I said. 'Anyone here. I've supported you. The least you can do is help me out when I'm in trouble.'

'Help you out?' Rune raised a startling eyebrow. 'And where were you when *we* needed helping out? Take Mr Keith Richards here.' Keith waved and I waved back. 'Where were you when he was going through his heroin addiction? Did you turn up at the hospital offering to change his bed pan?'

'Some fans did.'

'But not *you*.'

'Well, not me personally.'

'In fact you're probably one of those bastards who secretly enjoys it when someone famous goes off the rails. Gets involved in some scandal, loses all their money. You get a vicarious thrill from that. The tabloids wouldn't sell any copies if it wasn't for people like you who glory in the problems of the famous.'

'We don't—'

'Aha!' said Rune. '*We*, that's what you said, *we*. You're not an individual. You're one of the herd that buys the tabloids.'

'I *am* an individual. But come on, give me a break.'

'No,' said Rune, 'we won't. Take Ms Madonna

here.' Madonna waved and I waved back. 'She has millions of fans. Imagine if every single one wrote to her asking her for advice. She might well want to give it, and indeed she is a very caring person, but she wouldn't have time. She couldn't possibly answer all those letters. So she does what she does. She entertains, and that makes millions of people happy all at once.'

'So you won't help me out? That's what you're saying?'

'We can't,' said Rune. 'We have already helped you out. You said it yourself. Each one of us here has in some way helped to shape your life. That is what *we* do. Through our music, our books, our paintings. It's not callous that we cannot deal with you personally. It's just not how it works. Do you understand what I'm saying?'

'Yes,' I said, and nodded gloomily.

'We're not bad people,' said Rune.

'No, I understand that.'

'It's simply how it is.'

'Yes, OK.'

'You must do your thing and we must do ours.'

'All right, I get the message.'

'It's the way of the world, it's—'

'I said *all right*! Don't labour the point. You're not going to help me, but it's not your fault that you can't.'

'Precisely,' said Rune.

'Then you might as well all piss off.'

'What?' said Rune.

'Piss off, you're no use to me.'

'We're having a drink and a chat,' said Rune.

237

'Yeah well, there's no point in it now.'

'That's hardly for you to say, is it?'

'It *is* for me to say, now piss off the lot of you.'

'You ill-mannered little twat,' said Hugo Rune.

'Don't call me a twat, you fat bastard.'

And then Hugo Rune swung his stout stick and hit me in the face, and I swung my knobkerry and hit Chris Eubank, and Chris Eubank chinned Max Miller and John Steinbeck head-butted Edith Sitwell and Andy Warhol kicked Tod Browning in the knackers, and everything sort of fell to pieces all around me.

I sighed as Lawrence of Arabia punched my lights out.

'That's showbiz,' said Lawrence.

Faster Dad Faster
(The shoulder-carrier's revenge)

Faster Dad faster,
The little one cried,
To his wretched dad with the acne.
Faster Dad, gee up,
Hurry on, me up,
We must be home,
In time for our tea up.

Poor Dad persisted
This pitiless toil
For his sly ungrateful offspring.
Blast, curse and blow it,
Hold on and stow it.
He wished he could rip off,
His son's head and throw it.

Faster Dad faster,
The little one shouted.
His father struggled on manfully.
Hurry Dad, do Dad,
Am I worrying you Dad?
Here, was that *my head*
You ripped off and threw Dad?

18

It's all true, or ought to be; and
more and better besides.
SIR WINSTON CHURCHILL
(of King Arthur)

I wasn't angry. I was upset. I was hurt. I was sore
from the hammering Lawrence gave me. But I
wasn't actually angry. I suppose I should have expected it. But you don't, do you? It was yet another
revelation.

I was learning all the time.

I sat all alone in Rob's Bar sipping good old English
beer and listening to the screams, as the private
militia I had created in my head took the famous
people I'd dreamed up and fed them one by one
into a big leaf-shredder of my own imagination. It
was clear that I was going to have to do this thing on
my own. I might meet up with others on the way
who could help me out a bit, but for the most part
this would be a one-man operation.

The work of an individual with a mission.

But where to start? That was the problem.

And I really wasn't all that keen on going it alone.

There had to be someone I could turn to. And then it dawned on me that there was. There was one individual who would help me out. Someone who had already tried to help me out.

The ancient mariner in my Uncle Brian's dream.

He'd warned me to stay clear of Billy Barnes, so he'd known the danger I was in. But who was he and where was he?

'Right,' I said. 'Find the ancient mariner. So how might I go about this?'

And then a thought hit me, so I went with it.

Billy Barnes had been thinking. High in his penthouse, comfy in his chair, television on, glass of something tasty and feet up on the chauffeur.

'I'm not paid enough,' said Billy. 'I am worth a great deal more to Necrosoft than I'm being paid.'

The chauffeur, kneeling, naked but for her gloves, which Billy had lined with pleaser, said nothing. She had learned when it was acceptable to speak and when it was not.

'You agree, don't you?' said Billy.

'I do,' said the naked woman.

Billy took a sleek remote controller and angled it towards the TV screen. 'I've been six months with Necrosoft now,' he continued. 'And in my capacity as information gatherer, I have gathered twenty-three subjects at Dyke's request. I enjoy my work, but I do not feel appreciated. Do you know what I mean?'

The naked woman turned her haunted eyes upon Billy. She knew exactly what he meant. And a great deal more.

'Now, here.' Billy thumbed the controller and the TV screen displayed a wealth of facts and figures. 'Here we see projections for the expansion of the Necronet. Nationwide advertising, interfacing with financial bodies, involvement with government departments. This is top secret stuff by the way, I gathered it whilst unobserved. Necrosoft has a finger in almost every profitable pie there is. Look at that, and that.'

The chauffeur did as she was told.

'Fast food, name brand sportswear, the music industry. Six more hospitals acquired for the downloading of elderly relatives. Ten thousand legitimate downloadings at one thousand pounds a time. Expansion, expansion. The public can't get enough of Necrosoft. This is big. Bigger than anything I could ever have imagined. And I think big. Don't I?' Billy gave the kneeling woman a nudge in the ribs.

'You do think big,' she replied.

'Information gatherer will not do,' said Billy. 'Company director might do. Company chairman would definitely do. But information gatherer will *not* do.'

Billy watched the figures moving on the screen. 'Toys and games. Military hardware, military software, the urban and rural pacification programmes. Oh, look, dairy farming, Necrosoft have just acquired a string of dairy farms. Why do you think that might be?'

'Milk,' said the kneeling woman.

'Milk,' said Billy. 'Genetically modified, no doubt. Further pacification and control. It's all so beautiful. So ordered. So organized. But who is behind it, eh? Who runs Necrosoft? Who owns it? Who invented the Necronet?'

'I don't know,' said the kneeling woman.

'And neither do I. But I mean to find out. And I can't do that when I'm only a humble information gatherer. I need to move up, acquire a more senior position in the company. I think it's time for Blazer Dyke to meet with a tragic accident. Once he is downloaded I will be able to access all the information I require to further my career.'

Billy lifted his feet from the kneeling woman's shoulders, rose and gazed down at her beautiful naked body. And then he unzipped his trousers and knelt down behind her. 'Let us celebrate in a special way,' said Billy as he ran the remote controller down the chauffeur's trembling back.

Blazer Dyke shook his head and tut-tut-tutted. He sat behind his cedar desk, surrounded by his phones. In the middle of the desk stood a portable TV monitor.

On the screen Billy Barnes performed acts of cruelty upon his chauffeur.

'You're a very wicked boy,' said Blazer Dyke. 'I can see that I was wise to have installed micro cameras in every room of your penthouse. You have become a liability.'

And Blazer Dyke lifted one of his many phones and tapped out a code.

In the rear of a chauffeur-driven car not unlike Billy's, a mobile phone began to ring.

*

My telephone was silent. Silent as the unhewn marble of some great sculpture yet to be. Silent as the unravished bride of quietness. Silent. Still.

And speechless.

Yet.

Are not the most precious things in speech the pauses?

Soft breaths? Wherein saying nothing, we say all?

I think it so.

I do declare that words, those sweet thoughts brought to tongue and winged to ear, be fine things in themselves, be pretty birds, that careless freely flutter; yea, but—

KNOCK KNOCK KNOCK

'Careless freely flutter; yea, but—'

KNOCK KNOCK KNOCK

'Barelegs, beery butter; yer butt—'

KNOCK KNOCK KNOCK

I pushed my Remington aside and glared at my partition door. Here was I, seated in my office, trying to compose a sonnet about a silent telephone for my new book *Snuff Poetry: The Verse of Lazlo Woodbine*, when some insensitive philistine cock-smoker comes KNOCK KNOCK goddamn KNOCKING! at my door.

'Go the fuck away!' I shouted in a tone of some authority.

KNOCK KNOCK KNOCK

I opened up my desk drawer and drew out the trusty Smith and Wesson.

KNOCK KNOCK KNOCK

I glared at my partition door. Beyond the frosted

glass etched with the words LAZLO WOODBINE INVESTIGATIONS in Caslon Old Face (and only decipherable from this side, due to its being installed by a dyslexic glazier), I spied a shadow.

It was the shadow of a man.

A man of five feet eleven. Twelve stone one pound. Clipped beard, slightly broken nose, receding hairline, rounded shoulders. A man wearing a trench coat and a snap-brimmed fedora.

I didn't know the man. But I knew that kind of shadow.

In my business knowing that kind of shadow can mean the difference between walking the dog and spanking the monkey. If you know what I mean. And I'm sure that you do.

'Come,' I called, in a voice as suave as a tailor's turnup.

The handle turned and my door swung like Sinatra. Framed in the portal stood a man six feet two in height, thirteen stone in weight, beardless in beard, long-nosed, hirsute and broad-shouldered. He wore an evening suit, Wellington boots and a bowler hat.

'I must get that glass door fixed,' I said.

'Mr Woodbine?' I said. 'Mr Lazlo Woodbine?'

'That's my name, buddy,' I replied. 'But who are you to use it?'

'I'm in trouble,' I said, 'and I've come to you because you are the world's most famous fictional detective. I've read every one of your books and if anyone can help me, you can.'

I nodded slowly and coolly. Nothing fancy, nothing showy. Just a slow nod and a cool one, too. A nod that said all that needed to be said. Without actually having to say it.

'What does that nod mean?' I asked.

'Just hold on,' I said. 'Is this me, or is this you?'

'Sorry?' I said.

'We're both working in the first person. We can't both do that, it won't make sense.'

'Sorry,' I said, once more. 'It's my fault. I was working as a private detective. I called myself Lazlo Woodbine and everything. But I'm in real trouble, and only the real Woodbine can help me.'

'I'm sorry, fella,' I said. 'But one of us is going to have to drop out of the first person. And that one of us isn't going to be me.'

'All right,' said the guy. 'I'll do it. How's that?'

I offered him a steely gaze. 'Say it again.'

'All right,' he said once more. 'I'll do it. How's that?'

'That's just dandy.' I fished a bottle of Bourbon from the drawer of my desk, two glasses, a pair of lace coasters, a couple of napkins, a round of chicken sandwiches, knives, forks, spoons, a condiment set shaped like a little chromium liner with the salt and pepper pots for funnels, a note pad, pencils, pencil sharpener in case the pencils got blunt, rubber in case I made a mistake, yellow highlighter pen in case I had to highlight anything in yellow, street maps, maps of the country, a miniature globe of the world, passport, traveller's cheques, seasick tablets, a small box containing Elastoplast dressings, needle and thread, compass, three clips of bullets, a change of underwear, book on Esperanto—

'Fags,' I said. 'Now where did I put those fags?'

'They're on your desk,' said the guy.

'Oh yeah, thanks.' I swept all the junk back into my drawer. 'Care for an oily?'

'Oily?'

'Oily rag, fag.'

'No thanks, I'll just smoke my pipe if that's OK.'

'Sure,' I said. 'What kind of pipe do you have there?'

'A Meerschaum, like Sherlock Holmes used to smoke.'

'Holmes never smoked a Meerschaum,' I said. 'He smoked "a greasy clay pipe". Read the books if you don't believe me.'

The guy re-ran the entire works of Sir Arthur Conan Doyle through his head. Not that I knew he was doing it. Although I might well have guessed. 'You're right,' he said. 'He only smokes a Meerschaum in the Sidney Padget drawings.'

'There you go then, fella. If you're going to smoke a pipe, then get yourself something individual, something that says *you*.'

'What kind do you think?'

'Well,' I said, 'what about a corncob?'

'Too "backwoods America".'

'Church warden?'

'Too "middle America".'

'Peace pipe?'

'Too "Native America".'

'Something more exotic then. Hubble-bubble, hookah, opium pipe, narghile—'

'Isn't that the same as a hookah?'

'OK. Dudeen?'

'That's the same as a clay pipe.'

'Calumet?'

'Peace pipe.'

'Buddy,' I said, 'you sure know your pipes.'

'Listen,' said the guy, 'in my trade, knowing your pipes can mean the difference between swinging the lead or swallowing the—'

'Hold it!' I shouted. 'Now hold it right there. I can put up with you knocking at the door and interrupting my muse. I can put up with you talking in the first person—'

'Which I've now stopped,' he said.

'Which you've now stopped. But I will *not*, repeat *not*, have you ripping off my catch-phrases. Do I make myself clear?'

'Clearer than an author's conscience.'

'Was that one of mine?'

'I don't think so.'

'OK. So let us sit here, drink Bourbon, smoke Camel cigarettes. You tell me your problem, and I will solve it for you without even leaving my chair.'

'How?' asked the guy.

'By using my powers of deduction. I have become a consulting detective along the lines of Sherlock Holmes.'

'But that's hardly your style. What about the trail of corpses and the dame who does you wrong? What about the other three locations, the alley, the bar (where you talk the load of old toot), and the rooftop?'

'I've finished with all that stuff,' I said. 'Since I retired I mostly write poetry and edit literary journals.'

'Retire? You can't retire. Holmes retired to the Sussex Downs but Woodbine never retired.'

'I would have done, if my author hadn't been killed in a freak accident involving a Jaffa orange and female undergarments. He was going to have me pull off my biggest ever case then retire in a blaze of glory. Unfortunately he croaked before completing the novel.'

'Consider yourself as being ghost-written,' said the guy. 'This will definitely be your biggest case.'

I stroked the chiselled chin of my lantern jaw. There was something I didn't like about this guy. Something that made me uneasy. Something shifty about the way he carried himself. Something unwholesome, ungodly even, sinister in fact. Something verging on the satanic, something—

'Turn it in,' said the guy.

'Sorry,' I said, 'I was just thinking aloud.'

'You want to watch that,' he said.

Et cetera.

'Go on, then,' I said, 'tell me what you got and I'll tell you what it gets.'

And the guy spilled his guts. He told me about how he'd tried to be a Private Eye. And about Billy Barnes and his mum and the case of the voodoo handbag. And about trying to track Barnes, and the warning in Uncle Brian's dream. And about Necrosoft and being trapped in the Necronet, and thinking his way onto a Melanesian island, and meeting Arthur Thickett, and learning of the dream space, and dreaming up a bar full of heroes, and then finally dreaming up me.

And when he had finished, I sat back in my chair and whistled.

'Why the whistle?' he asked.

'Because,' I said, 'that is the biggest load of old toot I've ever heard in my life.'

'What?' went the guy. 'But it's true. All true.'

'It might be true, or it might be toot. Either way it's all the same to me.'

'So what are you saying?'

'I'm saying, kid, that I wouldn't touch this case. Wrong genre. This is science fiction you're talking about. I wouldn't take on a sci-fi case, it's more than my reputation's worth. I'm strictly "life on the mean streets a man must walk". That's what my readers want. They can empathize with me. Sure, I have the eccentric catch-phrases and the running gags, but each case has a beginning, a middle, and an end that everyone can understand. Baddies who are baddies and goodies who are goodies. And a subtext running through it saying that the American way is best. This stuff of yours is all over the place. Characters coming and going, no proper continuity. Where's it all leading? Where's it all going to end?'

'Does this mean you won't take the case?'

'I didn't say that.'

'Then you will take the case?'

'I didn't say that either. Listen, what you want me to do is locate this ancient mariner guy, right?'

'That's why I thought of you, you're the best.'

'And you think this ancient mariner guy will show you how to get out of the Necronet and back into your body, wherever that might be, and then you will deal with this Billy Barnes.'

'Bring him to justice, right.'

'Right, but from what you've been telling me, Billy Barnes is a pretty smart cookie.'

The guy shrugged. 'Not that smart,' he said.

The telephone began to ring.

But it was not the one on Lazlo's desk.

It was one of the many on that of Blazer Dyke.

'Mr Dyke,' said Mr Dyke.

'It's me, sir,' came the voice of a young man. 'I'm outside Barnes' penthouse.'

'Good,' said Blazer Dyke. 'You will find a duplicate key beneath the potted palm to the right of the door.'

There was a pause, then –

'Found it, sir.'

'Good, then enter the apartment cautiously. I have Barnes on the monitor, he is still in the lounge doing unspeakable things to his chauffeur.'

'He's a bastard, sir.'

'He is. Now just make sure he's a dead bastard. You'd better shoot the chauffeur, too. She's seen and heard far too much.'

'Do you want me to download Barnes before I kill him, sir?'

'Absolutely not. I do *not* want Billy Barnes at loose in the Necronet.'

'As you say, sir. A bullet through each. Quick and clean.'

'I'll stay on the line, keep me informed. I'll watch you on the monitor.'

'I'm going in then, sir.'

'Good.'

Pause. Then –

'I'm in the hall.'

'Good. He's still busy at the chauffeur. Go into the lounge and take him by surprise.'

Pause.

Then greater pause, then –

'There's nobody here, sir.'

'Go into the lounge, they're in there.'

'I *am* in the lounge, sir.'

'You're not in the lounge, I can't see you on the screen.'

'Perhaps he *is* in the lounge,' said the voice of Billy Barnes. 'But perhaps you can't see him.'

Blazer Dyke looked up in horror. Billy Barnes stood before his desk. He was holding a gun. 'Hand me the phone,' whispered Billy. 'Don't say another word.'

'How—'

'Not one word.' Billy took the receiver and covered the mouthpiece.

'But you're—' Blazer pointed to the monitor screen where the image of Billy Barnes continued with his dirty work.

'The wonders of science,' said Billy. 'A little something I prepared earlier. Remember, you did tell me to be careful, and I have been careful. Very careful. I kept a wary eye open for any more of those little micro cameras that caught me out the first time. And what did I find? You'd installed some in my penthouse. So I hacked into your security system. My would-be assassin is standing in an empty lounge while you watch a performance I recorded yesterday and began playing through your

252

system an hour ago. My would-be assassin is there, and your would-be assassin is here.'

'No,' said Blazer. 'Wait—'

'Sir,' came the voice of the young man down the phone. 'There's no-one here, sir. I've searched the entire place.'

Billy kept the mouthpiece covered. He held the phone towards Blazer Dyke. 'Tell him to look in the big cupboard in the lounge. Tell him to bring all the files he finds there.'

'Files? I don't understand.'

'Just tell him, and I will be merciful with you.'

Blazer Dyke took the telephone. 'Go to the big cupboard in the lounge,' he said. 'Bring me all the files you find there.'

'OK, sir,' said the young man.

Billy replaced the receiver, then he fished a rather gory-looking remote controller from his pocket and pointed it at the monitor screen. 'Why don't we see how he gets on?' Billy said.

Blazer Dyke watched the young man cross the lounge. Saw him open the big cupboard. Heard his voice as he spoke into his mobile phone, relayed to the monitor by bugs in the apartment. 'I'm at the cupboard, sir, opening it, looking inside. It's dark in here, sir, there's no light.'

Blazer looked on as the young man stepped into the cupboard and was lost to view on the screen.

'I can't see any files, sir. There's an odd smell. Rotten, it is. Hang on, there's something here. Something white. It's a . . . no . . . wait. What is this, it's moving. It's—'

And then, 'Aaaaaaaaaaaaagh!'

And then silence.

'Oh dear,' said Billy. 'He seems to have met with a tragic accident.'

Blazer Dyke's hand moved slowly beneath his desk.

'No,' said Billy. 'Hands up. No touching of alarm buttons.'

'Can't we talk about this?' Blazer Dyke had a sweat on now. 'Promotion, a rise in salary—'

'No,' said Billy. 'I do believe that you cannot be trusted. I tried out your chair six months ago. It suited me then, it will suit me now.'

'Are you going to' – Blazer Dyke's voice was a whisper – 'download me?'

'You must have heard me say that.'

'I did,' said Blazer Dyke. 'You said it to your chauffeur, before you—' He glanced at the remote control.

'I'm a control freak,' said Billy. 'And I just can't be trusted, either. It's the Necronet for you, yes.'

'Thanks at least for that,' said Blazer Dyke.

'I hardly think thanks are in order. You will be despatched directly to the hospital facility.'

'No!' Blazer shook his head. 'I altered the programme. It's a gas chamber now.'

'Bummer,' said Billy, as he clubbed down Blazer Dyke. 'But he that liveth by the sword of technology, shall die by that very sword.'

Poets On Holiday

Where the beach meets the sea,
And the family tree,
Gets a little bit wet about the roots,
The poets skip round,
And lie on the ground,
Spoiling their sensible suits.

Where the pierhead flag,
Is beginning to drag,
And winter is coming to town,
The poets in flats,
Sit huddled with cats,
Their jaws going up and down.

Where the old Channel ferry,
In shades of white and cherry,
And its funnels in a dirty coloured green,
Comes sailing into port,
With the rations running short.
And the poets on the decks,
With the lifebelts round their necks,
Moaning about facilities,
There's no paper in the utilities,
While the meat was under-cooked,
And the cabins over-booked,
And generally making a bloody nuisance of
    themselves.

Poets being just a bloody nuisance.
Then it's time to set sail on your own,
Go forth,
Strike out,
And so on.

19

A violent man will respond poorly to
a gift of flowers.
REG MOMBASSA

Lazlo Woodbine replaced his telephone receiver, made final notes upon a sheet of paper, then pushed it across his desk to the young man in the bowler hat.

'What's this?' the young man asked.

'I've called in a lot of favours for you, kid,' said the great detective. 'These are the directions to your ancient mariner. He lives in a seaport called Arkham.'

The young man read the directions aloud.

'Go through office door. Turn left, down stairway into street. Turn right. Turn right again into alleyway beside Fangio's bar. At end of alleyway enter the Desert of No Return, cross desert until you reach the Mountains of Madness, go through the Cave of Ultimate Horrors to the Land of the Screaming Skulls. Then ask directions from there.'

There was a pause.

Brief, but pregnant.

'What is this crap?' the young man asked.

Lazlo Woodbine smiled a certain smile. 'It's your genre, kid, not mine. Like I say, I'm strictly "mean streets". I wouldn't go in for all that Mountains of Madness fol-de-rol.'

'Nor me. Arkham, did you say? I'll think my way there at once.'

Lazlo put up a hand. 'It won't work.'

'Why not?'

'Because you've never been to Arkham. You have no memory to call up in order to create the place. In order to get to Arkham you'll just have to travel through all those ludicrous places. There's no way round it, kid.'

'There has to be some way round it.'

'Kid, consider what you've already learned. This Necronet of yours occupies the same hypothetical space occupied by dreams, right? The dream space, the weird space, the *mundus magicus*. This is the place where ideas come from, where they originate. I'm a fictitious detective, I came from the dreaming mind of an author. That's the world I inhabit. And I enter the world of my reader's imagination. Each reader sees me a little differently, visualizes my surroundings a little differently, creates a slightly different world for me to inhabit. But all in here,' Lazlo tapped his temple. 'And it's all one world, really.'

'I don't understand what you're trying to say.'

'I'm trying to say that you shouldn't be here, kid. What Billy Barnes and Necrosoft are doing is wrong. I'm not saying that technology is wrong. But to bridge the two worlds, the outside world and the inner, the physical and the metaphysical, that's gonna blow all the circuits.'

'I still don't get it.'

'OK. I'll say it once more, and I'll say it plain. You got downloaded, right? You're no longer inside your own head, right?'

'Right.'

'So whose head do you think you're in now?'

'I'm not in anybody's head. I'm in cyberspace. Inside the Necronet.'

'And where *is* that, *exactly*?'

'I don't know, *exactly*.'

'Then I'll tell you where it is.'

'Go on.'

'Buddy, you're now inside God's head.'

I must confess that I was rattled. Severely rattled. When I bade farewell to Lazlo, left his office, turned left, went down the stairway, turned right into the street and right again into the alleyway by Fangio's bar, I was severely rattled.

Sure, I knew, as we all know, that without our dreams and our imaginings, mankind wouldn't be mankind. But to think that when we dream, we actually enter the mind of God, that was a new one on me. And that was one *big* number.

So what was I doing now? I looked down at my feet. Walking around inside God's head?

And for that matter, why was I wearing welling-ton boots?

I plucked at my apparel.

And an evening suit!

I felt at my head.

And a bowler hat!

259

I'd never thought that lot up.

'Oh dear,' I said, 'perhaps I'm beginning to lose it. Perhaps I'm going mad. That won't do, a mad thought inside God's head.'

And then it hit me. As it would. About what Lazlo had meant when he talked about blowing all the circuits. If Billy and his cohorts at Necrosoft were downloading people into the Necronet, they were unwittingly downloading them into the mind of God. It would be like God having multiple personality disorder, or being possessed by demons. God would become a paranoid schizophrenic.

God would eventually go mad.

I looked up the alleyway and down it. Behind me, the streets of Manhattan, before me the Desert of No Return. There was no-one around, so I dropped to my knees.

'Dear God,' I said, putting my hands together. 'Now I know in the past it's always been me asking you for things. But I've been learning a lot of lessons recently, about give and take, and stuff like that. So I don't want to ask you for anything now. The reason I'm praying like this is to tell you that Mr Woodbine has put me in the picture, about me being in your mind, and everything. And I just wanted to say that I'm going to get out. And when I do, I'll get everyone else out as well and leave your mind at peace. Peace of mind, right? Well, that's all I'm saying, I'm not asking for anything, I'm just volunteering my services. I'll do my best. OK?

Love Robert.
Amen.'

I crossed myself, stood up and dusted down the trousers of my evening suit. 'Right,' I said. 'If it has to be the Desert of No Return, then it has to be. But watch out, Billy Barnes, because I'm coming to get you.'

If Billy Barnes was worried by the prospect of a man in a bowler hat, evening suit and wellington boots attempting a crossing of the Desert of No Return inside the mind of God in order to come and get him, he was hiding it well.

Billy sat in the office of Blazer Dyke. The office that now had the name of Billy Barnes on the door. The intercom buzzed and Billy said, 'Yes?'

'The Secretary of State to see you, sir.'

'The Secretary of State? I thought the Prime Minister was coming in person.'

'Some pressing business of an international nature has come up.'

'Business elsewhere,' said Billy.

'Pardon, sir?'

'Never mind, send in the Secretary of State.'

'Certainly, sir.'

The office door opened and Billy's new secretary, a woman of remarkable beauty but for the haunted look in her eyes, ushered in a man of unremarkable character.

'Giles Grimpin,' said the Secretary of State, extending his hand. 'Very pleased to meet you.'

Billy Barnes shook the proffered hand. Its palm was sweaty. He smiled at the Secretary of State. A very sweaty individual. He was plump and

261

somewhat shabby. He had dandruff on the shoulders of his ill-fitting suit.

'Be seated,' said Billy, and the Secretary sat.

'Coffee?' asked Billy. 'Or would you prefer something stronger?'

'Well, the sun is over the yard arm. Perhaps a small Scotch.'

'Indeed.' Billy crossed to the drinks cabinet. Poured a large Scotch and a Perrier water for himself.

'Thank you,' said Giles Grimpin, accepting his glass.

Billy reseated himself. 'I assume that your department have read through all the documentation I sent them.'

Giles Grimpin nodded. 'All the technical stuff, yes.'

'And does my proposal meet with your approval?'

Giles Grimpin turned his glass between his podgy fingers. 'It's all somewhat radical,' he said.

'Radical, yes, but you see the economic benefits. These are very large.'

'They are,' said Giles. 'Very profitable, in fact, but—'

'But?' said Billy.

'But compulsory downloading at the age of sixty-five: that in essence is what you're suggesting.'

'We have all the technology in place. Thousands have already been downloaded voluntarily.'

'Ah,' said Giles Grimpin. 'You use the word *voluntarily*. This is not altogether accurate, is it? In essence people have been paying you one thousand

pounds a head to download their unwanted depen-
dants.'

'In essence,' said Billy. 'Do you have any objec-
tion to that?'

'None at all, in fact—'

'In fact,' said Billy, 'we downloaded your aunt
just last week.'

'The poor creature,' said Giles Grimpin. 'She was
beyond medical help. It was an act of human kindness.'

'Exactly,' said Billy. 'Although whether being a
grumpy old woman who kept turning up at your
house unannounced to complain about the bypass
going through next to her garden actually qualifies
as "beyond medical help" . . .'

'She was very ill,' said Giles Grimpin. 'Mentally.'

'An act of human kindness,' said Billy. 'As they
are all acts of human kindness. Sending the dear
ones off to paradise; what greater act of kindness
could there be?'

'None,' said Giles. 'Might I have another Scotch?'

'Indeed you might.'

'So,' said Giles, his glass refreshed, 'all this said,
compulsory downloading at sixty-five, we'd never
swing that through the House of Commons.'

'You are in government with a very large
majority. Surely it is only a matter of the PM giving
it the go-ahead.'

'Wheels within wheels,' said Giles. 'I suppose if
the PM's advisors were to stress the economic
advantages.'

'Which are great,' said Billy. 'No more paying out
of old-age pensions, no more care for the elderly.

More housing made available to the young.'

'It's very tempting,' said Giles. 'Very tempting indeed. But the public, the man in the street—'

'The herd,' said Billy. 'You mean the herd.'

'The general population.'

'The herd.'

'Not an expression we in government like to use. But nevertheless, in essence—'

'In essence,' said Billy. 'They will do what you tell them to do. As long as it's made to look as if you're *not* telling them. As long as it's something to aspire to, rather than something compulsory. I have an advertising campaign already worked out.'

'You're very thorough.'

'I have to be. And so, can I rely on your support?'

'I don't know.' Giles Grimpin mopped at his brow with an oversized red gingham handkerchief. 'Something doesn't gel. Something makes me feel uneasy.'

'In essence,' said Billy, 'the Necronet offers eternal life. No death, no pain, only everlasting pleasure. Your fantasies brought to life. Do whatever you want for as long as you want. Heaven on earth. Who could want more than that?'

'Not me,' said Giles. 'But all the same, it amounts to euthanasia on a national scale.'

'Britain leads the way,' said Billy. 'Today Britain, tomorrow the world.'

'I really don't know.'

Billy shook his head. 'I do wish I could count on your support.'

'I'll have to think about it. Weigh up the pros and cons.'

'Of course,' said Billy. 'But if you did agree, do you think you could persuade the PM?'

'Absolutely. I hold his ear. If I advised him to go for it, he would.'

'That's fine, then.' Billy turned up his palms. 'What more could I ask?'

'Good,' said Giles. 'Well, I have to be off.'

Billy rose to shake his hand. 'Oh, just one more thing,' he said.

'What's that?'

'I have something for you. A gift.'

'A gift? For me?'

'For you,' said Billy. 'I'm sure you'll like it. It's called a pleaser.'

There was nothing too pleasing about the Desert of No Return. It looked hot and dry and forbidding. How far can a man walk into a desert? That was a famous question. How far can a man walk into a desert of no return? That was another.

'Well,' I said to myself. 'What I need here is a guide. Who is good with deserts? Lawrence of Arabia?' No, I'd had him fed into a leaf shredder. I could think him up again, but he probably wouldn't be too good with a desert like this. How about Conan the Barbarian, he'd done a lot of desert work. And places like the Swamp of Eternal Doom were right up his street. No, stuff Conan, what I really needed was some transportation. A halftrack, or a Land Rover. Yeah, that was it, a Land Rover. One of those trans-continental exploration jobbies with all the extras. I pictured one that I'd seen in the May 1963 edition of *National Geographic* while sitting in the dentist's waiting room.

And then I stood back from it and smiled.

It was a beauty. Exactly as I remembered it.

This would get me across any desert.

I put my foot on the running board and opened the driver's door.

And found myself staring in at nothing.

Now what did the interior of a Land Rover look like? I'd never been in one.

And—

I stepped down and upped the bonnet.

I'd never seen the engine either. And for that matter I didn't actually know how the internal combustion engine functioned. I don't know how that one slipped by me. I probably hadn't been paying attention when it was explained.

I sighed as I perused the empty bonnet space.

Mind you, I did know how a leaf shredder worked. I wondered whether I could convert one to run this Land Rover. They were plug-in, so it would need a few miles of cable.

'Oh, sod it,' I said. 'I'll just have to walk.'

And so I did.

It was dull in that desert. Hot and dry and dull. And the thought that I was actually walking about inside God's head did nothing to alleviate this dullness. I couldn't imagine why God would have a place like this inside his head anyway. But then I suppose that if God is everywhere and everywhen he has everything in his head. I made a mental note to look up Hugo Rune at some future time and put him right about his Universal Creation Solution. It seemed probable that the entire universe was nothing more than a thought in God's head. Possibly even a passing thought. Could that be right?

I shook my head. 'God knows,' I said.

I don't know how far I walked into the desert before I found myself walking out of it again. Half way would be my guess. But it certainly didn't take too long, so half way couldn't have been that far.

I stood amongst the foothills of a lofty mountain range. 'That was a very small desert,' I said to myself. 'I wonder why it's called the Desert of No Return? Probably because I have no intention of returning through it.'

And I perked right up at this. The places I had to pass through might have silly fantasy names, but that didn't mean they had to be a problem.

They were probably just symbols, or metaphors, or something. Freudian stuff to do with rites of passage and exploring the inner self. A journey into me, perhaps.

'A piece of cake,' I said. 'I'll breeze through this.'

It's remarkable just how wrong you can be sometimes, isn't it?

The Bill to authorize compulsory downloading at sixty-five passed through the House of Lords un-opposed.

There could possibly have been some opposition from certain elder statesmen, but there wasn't. For these elder statesmen had already been downloaded by their relatives.

Certain clauses were written into the Bill: that

compulsory downloading did not apply to members of the government being one; a tax upon the pension funds of the downloaded being another; the nationalization of Necrosoft Industries being a third.

'Nationalization!' Billy stormed up and down on the plush carpeting of his new office. It was a big office right at the top of the building. It had been unoccupied, as if just waiting for him. And it had to be said, he looked *right* in it.

'Nationalization?'

The Prime Minister, who had called by en route to business elsewhere, shot Billy a quizzical glance. 'You seem most upset,' he observed. 'Almost as if *you* own Necrosoft.'

'Not yet,' muttered Billy under his breath. 'But soon.'

'You must surely understand that it had to happen. Necrosoft is simply too large, too important to remain in private hands.'

'Governments don't nationalize any more.' Billy threw up his hands in protest. 'They privatize. They sell off utilities. Bung profitable institutions into the private sector to line their own pockets and those of their friends. Directorships, productivity bonuses, windfalls. We all know how it works.'

'Happily the *we* you speak of do not all know how it works.'

'Well, *I* do,' said Billy.

The Prime Minister smiled. 'Mr Barnes,' he said, 'do you know who owns Necrosoft?'

Billy shook his head. 'Actually, I don't,' he confessed.

'Well, *I* do,' said the Prime Minister.

'You do?'

'I do. A gentleman named Henry Doors. A recluse whose whereabouts are presently unknown.'

'I know that name,' Billy scratched at his head. 'It rings a bell somewhere. Didn't Henry Doors invent a car engine that ran on tap water, or something? And he wrote a book, what was it called? Endless something, wasn't it?'

'*Endless Journey*,' said the PM.

'That's right. I'm sure I've got a copy of that somewhere.'

'I thought I had,' said the PM. 'But I must have lent it to someone. I tried to order it again from Waterstone's but it must be out of print.'

'I act directly for Mr Doors,' said Billy, shameless in the lie. 'I make all major decisions regarding policy and development. Nationalization is out of the question. Necrosoft must remain an independent private company.'

'Really?' asked the PM. 'And why might that be?'

'Because I say so,' said Billy.

The PM smiled again. What a nice smile he had. 'Billy,' he said. 'May I call you Billy? Yes, of course I may. Billy, Necrosoft was originally funded by the US government to develop weaponry.'

'I know that. It was to sidestep the Freedom of Information Act.'

'Of course. But such funding ended years ago. Necrosoft is independent. It supplies urban pacification systems on a worldwide basis. The revenues from that are vast. The revenues from downloading fees are equally vast. The revenues from software to link Internet users to the Necronet are equally vast. Have you any idea what this company is worth?'

'Some,' said Billy.

'Henry Doors is the richest man in the world.'

'I wonder where he lives,' said Billy.

'Don't we both? So far we have been unable to locate him. Tracing his financial interests leads us around in circles. The forced nationalization of his company may just draw him out.'

'And that's the point, is it? To draw him out?'

'We must negotiate with him face to face. Necrosoft's technology must not fall into foreign hands. The hand that controls Necrosoft will one day control the world.'

'Indeed,' said Billy. 'I somehow thought it might.'

'The government and Necrosoft must become one,' said the PM. 'And then you will see Britain rise as a world power once again. Oh yes.'

Billy nodded thoughtfully. 'You're so right,' he said. 'It makes perfect sense. I wonder how I didn't think of it before.'

The PM smiled his winning smile. 'Then we're agreed,' he said.

'We are,' said Billy, smiling too. 'And I've a little gift for you.'

Weep No More for Uncle Albert

Weep no more for Uncle Albert,
Somewhere in the Necronet.
Out here all his fond relations
Divvy up what they can get.

To young Tim I leave my motor,
Toby gets my scarf,
Tom Boy, you can have my muffler,
And my book of *Garth*.

Not a chair left there to sit on,
Not a sofa you can get on,
Picture patches on the wall,
Rolled-up lino in the hall,
Hinges taken from the butt,
Turfs are raised and flowers cut.

And Auntie looks a little queer,
She comes up sixty-five this year.

But weep no more for Uncle Albert,
He's above it now.

20

Science without conscience is the death of the soul.
FRANÇOIS RABELAIS (*c.* 1494–1553)

The doctor said I was a paranoid schizophrenic.

Well, he didn't actually say it, but we knew he was thinking it.

'Tell me more about your work,' the doctor said.

'My work? You mean my detective work?'

'That's what you do then, is it? Detective work?' The doctor viewed me through his pince-nez. I'd had a pair of those once. But mine had tinted glass. An image thing, I don't want to dwell on it.

'I did do detective work,' I said carefully. 'But I wasn't very good at it. I never managed to find anything I was supposed to be searching for.'

'Such as the' – the doctor consulted his case notes – 'handbag? The voodoo handbag? What exactly is that?'

'It all got terribly complicated. I sort of lost track of what I was doing.'

'You were confused.'

'Very.'

'But you're not so confused now.'

'Not so much. No.'

'The tablets are helping then, are they?'

'Tablets always help. That's what tablets are for, isn't it?'

The doctor rose from his chair and drifted over to the window. I noticed the way his toecaps lightly brushed the top of the wastepaper bin.

'Am I boring you?' the doctor asked. 'You keep nodding off. Are you tired?'

'Me? No, no. I never sleep.'

'Never? Not at all?'

'I don't dare to fall asleep. If I fall asleep I might dream, and if I dream I'll be back in there. Back in the Necronet. I'm not going back in there. Not me. Not ever.'

'Quite,' said the doctor. 'So you never sleep at all.'

'Maybe a minute or two. But no dreams. If dreams come, Barry wakes me up.'

'Your Holy Guardian, Barry?'

'He's a sprout. From God's garden. God has a very big garden. Very big. It goes on and on for ever. I've been there, it's very beautiful.'

'Inside the mind of God?'

'That's where we all go when we dream. I think that's also where we all go when we die. Because you can meet dead people in your dreams, can't you? And they're not dead when you meet them.'

'And you met dead people?'

'Only the one.'

'Do you want to talk about that?'

'No, I don't.'

'Careful on that chair,' said the doctor. 'You might fall over the mountain.'

I edged my chair away from the precipice. Four legs safely on the ground and two feet flat. 'You shouldn't drift about,' I told the doctor. 'You could get blown away. They'd never find you, you'd blow out into the desert.'

'I have special tablets,' said the doctor. 'They keep my feet heavy. They're gravitational.'

'*Wake up, chief!*'

'Thanks, Barry.'

'Did you drift off again?'

'Only for a moment.' I took a deep breath. 'Barry woke me.'

'So you're still here?'

'Yes. Those glasses are new.'

'I think they make me look a bit like Clark Kent,' said the doctor, removing his black-framed spectacles. 'But didn't you once have a pair like these? An image thing, wasn't it?'

'I can't remember clearly any more. I know too many things.'

'But couldn't you remember everything?' The doctor returned to his desk and went through a bit more case note consultation. 'Digital memory. Total recall. Positively photographic.'

'It's how magic works.'

'Magic? Where does magic come into this?'

'It's most of this.'

'Voodoo magic?'

'Some of it, yes.'

'Superstition,' said the doctor. 'Science is the new magic. Would you mind if I kissed you on the mouth?'

'*Wake up, chief!*'

'Thanks, Barry.'

'Enforced wakefulness leading to psychosis,' the doctor said as he wrote further case notes. 'Recommend that the patient be placed on a course of—'

'No,' I shouted. 'No sleeping tablets, I mustn't dream, don't you understand? I mustn't dream.'

The doctor reached forward and pressed that little button on his desk.

'No dreams! No!' I pushed back on my chair. 'I'll go over the edge. I will.'

'You'll be fine,' the doctor smiled. No teeth. The doctor had no teeth. The back legs of my chair squeaked on the lino as I pushed towards the cliff edge.

'Don't try to stop me. I'm going to jump.'

'You'll wake up if you jump.'

'I'm not asleep. I'm awake now.'

'Wake up—'

And I jumped.

And I fell.

And I woke up in some confusion.

'Barry, you bastard. You let me jump that time.'

The wind shuffled sand around my wellington boots.

I looked up at the Mountains of Madness.

'Barry. Barry? *Barry?*'

But I was all on my own again.

Before the Cave of Ultimate Horrors.

And frankly I was well pissed off.

'I'm well pissed off,' said Billy Barnes. 'You mean that you found no trace at all?'

The beautiful secretary turned down her haunted

275

eyes. 'At first all the shopkeepers I talked to thought they remembered Henry Doors and had read his book. But the more they thought about it, the less they seemed to remember. And eventually they all said that they probably didn't remember him at all.'

'And the library?'

'The library, and the posh companies that trace rare books. I've asked all of them. Are you absolutely certain there is a Henry Doors, sir?'

Billy swung around in his expensive chair. 'Absolutely certain. Carry on searching. Don't eat. Don't sleep. Search the company records, trace the name through Somerset House. Use every means at your disposal. Find Henry Doors.'

Tears welled in the haunted eyes. 'Yes, sir,' said the secretary. 'Whatever you say.'

When the door had closed upon her, Billy swept expensive objects from his desk, rose and kicked his chair over.

Henry Doors was the man. Target number one. The big trophy. If he could insinuate himself into the service of Henry Doors, it would not take too long for Billy to become Henry Doors. And then the wealth. The power. It could all be his.

A telephone began to ring.

Billy snatched it up. 'What is it?' he shouted.

'There's a Mr Henry Doors on the line,' said the voice of Billy's secretary.

My hands were trembling and my knees knocking, too. And it wasn't because of the prospect of a stroll in the Cave of Ultimate Horrors. It was all that stuff. That stuff in the doctor's office. Am I awake?

Am I asleep? Was that madness, or was that something else? Am I dreaming this? Are you dreaming me? Am I dreaming you? Who's actually awake and who isn't?

I made fists. I'm sure I had to be learning something. I just wished I knew what it was supposed to be.

I took deep breaths. Right. Cave of Ultimate Horrors. If the Mountains of Madness had played on my paranoia, were still playing on it, actually, then *was* I asleep? What would the cave play on? What were my ultimate horrors?

I dreaded to think.

'I hope you don't think this too forward of me,' said the voice of Henry Doors. 'And I know you're a very busy man, but I was wondering if we might get together for a bit of a chat.'

'A bit of a chat,' said Billy.

'If that's all right with you.'

'Certainly, when—'

'My car is waiting in the car park. Perhaps you might cancel all further appointments for the day.'

'Indeed,' said Billy. 'I will.'

The car was all Billy might have expected. A white stretch-Merc with blacked-out windows. As Billy approached, a rear door swung open. Electric door, nice touch.

Billy peered into the car. A young man in a white designer suit and Ray Bans beckoned him inside. Billy climbed in and the door closed upon him.

The young man comfied himself upon the tan

leather seating. 'Henry Doors,' he said. 'Excuse me if I don't shake your hand.'

'Excuse me if I don't shake yours,' said Billy.

Henry Doors grinned wolfishly. He had the look of a male model, or one of those brat pack film lads who used to be so popular. Killer cheekbones, floppy hair, beach tan.

'You expected someone older,' said Henry.

'Yes I did.'

'Then let me tell you a little bit about myself. I was born in San Francisco in nineteen sixty-seven, the Summer of Love. My mother was a Carmelite nun, my father – well, who can say, women are habitual liars. I was brought up on a farm in Wisconsin, under the supervision of agents of the American government. They protected me from harm. I have a way with computers, an empathy you might say, and I was writing my own programmes by the time I was nine. By the age of fifteen I had founded Necrosoft and was already a multimillionaire. Any questions?'

'Many,' said Billy.

'Well, keep them to yourself. I have been watching your progress, Billy, right from the start. Your every move has been closely observed. Your rise through the company ranks. Your conversation last week with the PM.'

'You overheard my conversation?'

'Watched you on screen. The entire Necrosoft building is under camera surveillance. It's built into the very walls. Very subtle stuff. I hear all and I see all.'

'Where does this leave me?' Billy asked.

'With your trousers round your ankles and your bare arse in the air.'

'Indeed,' said Billy.

'The question is, do I pat your bottom kindly, or ram my—'

'I get the picture.'

'You are the picture, Billy. Because you are in the frame. Tell me this, and answer honestly because I will know if you lie. If you could gain control, how much control would you want?'

'All,' said Billy, without hesitation.

'All seems very fair to me.'

'It does?'

'I need someone to assume control. Someone ruthlessly ambitious. Someone who will let nothing and no-one stand in their way. Someone such as you.'

'But why should you offer this to me? This company is yours.'

'I don't want the company, Billy. I want you to have the company. Ownership of the company means nothing to me. It's what the company does that matters.'

'The Necronet.'

'Exactly. The PM wants to nationalize Necrosoft. He wants the government and Necrosoft to become one. That is my wish too. Let both become one, but with you at the helm.'

'That was my intention,' said Billy, 'should I have failed to locate you.'

'Well, go for it, my boy. Spread the Necronet around the world. Encompass the globe with it. Download millions and millions and millions—'

'To what ultimate end?'

'Call me an ecologist. Call me one who cares about the planet. All this overcrowding, all this pollution. We have it in our power to save the world.'

'Or destroy it,' said Billy.

'I hope I don't detect a twinge of conscience there.'

'Not a bit of it. I have no concern for the herd, drive them all to the abattoir, I don't care.'

'Not all,' said Henry. 'The prime stock you keep for breeding purposes.'

'I see,' said Billy, who didn't.

'You don't,' said Henry, who did. 'There are too many people, Billy. Too many little people. Too many nonentities. And they jabber away, don't they? In their banal little voices. Jabbering and jabbering. It drives you mad, doesn't it? All that jabbering. Imagine if they were all inside your head, all of them, jabbering at once. It would drive you insane.'

'It would,' said Billy.

'So let's clear them all away to somewhere, so we don't have to hear their jabbering.'

'Into the Necronet.'

'Exactly. And then the world is a better place for us, isn't it?'

'Much better,' said Billy. 'And so you'll let me control Necrosoft, and ultimately—'

'You'll control the world, Billy. You will become the World Leader.'

'And you will remain in the background?'

'I always remain in the background. That is what *I* do best.'

'Who are you?' asked Billy. 'Who are you, really?'

'Come on,' said Henry Doors, 'you've worked it out by now, surely?'

Billy shook his head.

'Where's that flyer I sent you?'

'Flyer?'

'It came with the pleaser. In the package that led you to Brentford. I know you still carry it with you as a keepsake.'

'This?' Billy produced a sheet of crumpled paper from his pocket.

'Read it out again, Billy.'

And Billy read it out.

'Surfing the web?
Anyone can do that! Why not
Try something *really* radical?
Access the dear departed by body-boarding the
Necronet.

Never has it been more
Easy. All you have to do is
Enter the Soul
Database, by taking a left-hand turn off the
Information Superhighway and

You're there. In the Land
Of the Virtual Dead.
U know it makes sense'

'It says it all, Billy, doesn't it? The soul database, all those millions of souls, no more heaven, no more hell, but endless paradise in cyberspace. Wish

281

fulfilment, fantasy fulfilment. The virtual dead, happy in their virtual wonderland.'

'It says more than that,' said Billy.

'What, the acrostic? I couldn't resist it, Billy, it made me laugh.'

'The acrostic, yes. I spotted it right away. Read the first letters down and you have SATAN NEEDS YOU. A bit of a giveaway, perhaps.'

'Just my little joke. Something for the heavy metal fans.'

'Tell me, I need to know.'

'Who I am? What I am? Am I a man? Am I a god? Are you dreaming me or am I dreaming you?'

'You're not a god,' said Billy. 'But—'

'I might be the Devil? Satan? The Anti-Christ? Well, I might be. But if science is the new religion, Billy, then surely I am its god.'

'God,' I said. 'It's dark in here. No chance of a light, I suppose?' I felt my way along. It was black. Black as night. Black as the grave. Black as death?

Death was the ultimate horror, surely?

The walls were smooth, featureless. I had no idea how far I'd come or how far I had to go. How far can a man walk into a mountain? Perhaps the cave just went on and on and on. Like that Möbius strip of a town surrounding the virtual hospital. No matter how far you went, you never went anywhere. Was that an ultimate horror? Worse than death?

Or was it madness? Or isolation? Or just being lost?

Or was it to be powerless? Utterly powerless.

Utterly without control.

While something dreadful happened.

And you couldn't do a thing to stop it.

The elevation of Billy Barnes to the exalted position of World Leader was timed to coincide with the millennial celebrations. The plain people of Brentford watched it on TV. They'd had their celebrations a couple of years earlier to avoid the rush, and were looking forward to a period of peace and love and a night in with the telly.

The fireworks and the motor cavalcades, the speeches and the swearing in, the fly-pasts, and the raising of the one-world flag with its Necrosoft logo, all made for an exciting watch. But not *that* exciting.

The camera panned over the hundreds that lined the route of the motor cavalcade. And it was hundreds now, not thousands. The population of America had been almost halved. As had that of the rest of the world.

Not so that of Brentford, however. The Brentford populace had little truck with computers and Necronets. They'd seen all this kind of stuff before, so they were just keeping their heads down in the hope that it would all blow over and not involve them personally. As it had so often in the past.

Uncle Brian watched the celebrations on TV.

'Billy Barnes,' he said thoughtfully. 'I wonder if that's the same Billy Barnes the ancient mariner in my dream told me to warn my young nephew about. And come to think of it, what ever *did* happen to my nephew?'

★

I stumbled out of the Cave of Ultimate Horrors into a world of bright whiteness. I stopped and I blinked and I took off my bowler hat and scratched at my head. Had I missed something, or what?

I had gone into the *right* Cave of Ultimate Horrors, hadn't I? I hadn't perhaps gone into the Cave of Very Little Horror at all, but Just a Bit of Dark and Dank, by mistake?

I shrugged. And then it struck me that while I'd been wandering about in there, something really dreadful might have happened. Something I might have prevented, but had been utterly powerless to do so.

'Phew,' I said. 'What an ultimate horror that would be. Let's trust that it isn't the case.' And then I rubbed my hands together. 'So,' I continued cheerfully, 'where's this Land of Screaming Skulls, then? Oh, shit!'

> *And I beheld Golgotha. Which is*
> *the place of the skull. And I beheld*
> *the multitude there. They that had*
> *lived and now were dead. And they*
> *cried unto me, saying woe unto*
> *thee that hath deserted us.*

Before me a plain of white beneath a sky of likewise hueless hue. And on that plain were human skulls. They clothed the earth and filled the sky. An endless, endless, endless multitude. And they were not still, these dust-dry bones, these husks of men, they were not still. They murmured and they moaned. They gnashed their teeth and ground their jaws. They howled towards the heavens, screaming out for justice and for life. These bones, these skulls, these angry dead. They screamed and screamed and—

'Er, excuse me,' I said, 'does anyone here know the way to Arkham?'

Two Canny Scotsmen Out with a Kite

Two canny Scotsmen out with a kite,
Out with a kite and a string,
Checking the wind and checking the light,
Saying, 'I'll have a wee pull if I might.
'Look at the fine wee thing in flight.'
(It makes the Scotsmen sing.)

Two canny Scotsmen out for a drink,
Out for a drink and a chat,
Out if the telly's gone on the blink,
Saying 'It's your round I think.'
'Look at them washing the pots in the sink.'
(That's where the Scots are at.)

Two canny Scotsmen down for the day,
Down for the day and the match,
'Aye but it's great to see them play.
'We always win both home and away.
'Hoots the noo, that's what I say.
'And what do you think you're looking
at, you Southern bastard? Take that!' etc.*

*Mr Rankin would like to make it clear that as a Scotsman himself he
does not consider this racial stereotyping.

21

Killing is the ultimate simplification of life.
HUGH MACDIARMID (1892–1978)

There was some unpleasantness.

A skull called Yorick thought he knew the way to Arkham. Well, not actually he himself, as he'd never been there. But a skull friend of his had a friend who had. I was not able to trace this particular friend, but I did encounter several other skulls who were sure they knew Arkham and had even been there at some time in the past.

Now I pride myself upon my patience, I'm an easy going chap, but I was anxious, very anxious, to get to Arkham and I was not in the mood to be trifled with. And I know that throwing human skulls around is not a politically correct activity, and I know that effing and blinding inside the mind of God is to say the least distasteful. But I was anxious.

And I did, eventually, learn the route to Arkham.

It was just as I might have imagined it. A fishing village, snuggled down into a bay. An ancient harbour with old-fashioned whaling boats. Steep cobbled streets with gabled cottages leading down to a quayside with an inn called Philthy Phrank's.

As I approached, the rain began to fall.

And it was coming down in buckets by the time I pushed open the rough-hewn oak door and entered the crowded bar. Oak beams and bottle-glass windows, whisky stench and sawdust floor, burnished copper, pewter tankards. A swordfish saw hung over a counter, constructed from whale's ribs.

I hung my bowler hat upon a peg, shook raindrops from my shoulders, and grateful for my wellington boots, I squeezed through the crush of seafaring men and made my way to the bar.

Philthy Phrank was just as I might have imagined him to be. Short and surly, evil-smelling, dressed in rags and tattered. He glared at the world through his one good eye and called no man his brother.

'A pint of Death by Cider,' I said in a macho kind of a way.

Philthy fixed me with his evil peeper. 'Show me coin or get ye hence,' he remarked.

I thought it might be handy to have a pocket full of gold dubloons, so I reached in a hand and fished out a couple.

Philthy Phrank drew me a tankard of gut rot.

'Cheers,' I said.

'Pox,' said Philthy Phrank.

I squinted about the bar. A grey pall of tobacco smoke cloaked the clientèle. They wore sou'westers and rainproofs, favoured eye patches and timber legs, muttered and mumbled and fidgeted about. In a not too distant corner I spied an ancient mariner.

He was just as I might have imagined him to be.

I eased my way between the mutterers and

mumblers and bade him a big how d'ya do.

The ancient one raised a gnarled appendage that had once been a hand and gestured to a vacant chair with it. I pulled up the chair and sat right down.

The ancient one gazed at me with glittering eyes, opened a mouth that offered a vacancy for teeth, spat a tobacco-coloured gobbet of phlegm into my lap and spoke a single word.

'Twat!'

'Excuse me?' I said.

'Twat!' said the ancient one. 'You, boy, are a twat.'

I smiled bravely and pondered over the phlegm in my lap.

'Twat,' said the ancient one once more. 'Twat, twat, twat.'

'Yeah, all right,' I replied. 'I get the picture.'

'What did I tell your Uncle Brian to tell you? Beware of Billy Barnes. I told him. And did you beware, boy? Did you?'

'Not perhaps as much as I should.'

'You twat.'

'Yes well, all right. I think we have established that I'm a twat.'

'You are a twat. Ask any man here.' The old boy nodded all about the place, the seafaring types nodded back.

'We're only allowed the one.' The old boy rootled about in his nose. 'Only the one and I wasted mine on you.'

'Allowed one what? I don't understand?'

'One message from the other side. We're all allowed one, to aid the living.'

'Aid the living? You mean you're—'

'Dead? Of course I'm frigging dead. Every man Jack here's a dead'n. Drinking away our time, till the flesh drops off our bones and we end up on the big heap up the road.'

'What a bummer,' I said.

The old boy shrugged, his shoulder bones made ghastly cracking sounds. 'Serves us right,' he said.

'That's very philosophical of you.'

'Ain't nothin' philosophical about it. It's the way it is and there ain't no other. Did I mention, by the way, that you're a twat?'

'I believe you did, yes.'

'Well you are. I had such big plans for you, we all did, all of us here. We were all going to use our messages on you. Help you to stop Billy Barnes.'

'All of you? But why me?'

'You'd have done. You were searching for him. Over the years we would have advised you in your dreams. And if we had, and you'd bloody listened, the world out there wouldn't be in the shit state it is now.'

'Well there's still time,' I said. 'I haven't been in here long, a few months at the most. I can still stop him doing whatever monstrous things he's doing.'

'A few months?' The old boy threw back his head, and took to a bout of cackling laughter. And then he clawed at his head, which had fallen over his shoulders, and rammed it back into position. 'A few months, boy? You've been in the Necronet for ten long years.'

'I *what*?'

'Time ain't the same in here as it is out there.'

'Ten years?' My stomach dropped. I shook and I shivered. 'Ten years I've been in here. I don't believe it. That can't be right.'

''Tis right, boy. It'll teach you to be a twat, won't it?'

'But my body, out there. Am I dead too now?'

'No, no, no.' The old boy held onto his head and shook it. 'He's still got your body, that Barnes. Keeps it in a suitcase under his bed. You're still alive, what's left of you.'

'Oh no.' I took to chewing on my fingers. 'He's been feeding me to the voodoo handbag. That bastard's been feeding me—'

'Well, there ain't quite so much of you as there used to be. But I'm told they can do all kinds of miracle stuff with surgery nowadays. Sew on a new pecker and everything.'

'*Pecker?* Oh my God!'

'Easy, boy. Don't go all to pieces.' The old boy set in to further chuckling.

'Oh my God! What am I going to do? What am I going to do?'

'Get out of here and best the bastard. That would be my advice.'

'But how? But how?'

The old boy sucked at his sunken gums.

'Don't spit on me again,' I told him.

'I was cogitating, boy.'

'Oh shit. Oh shit, shit shit.'

'You should have got here quicker. All that pissing about on the desert island and in Rob's Bar, what kind of twattery was that?'

'You knew I was doing those things?'

'Course I knew. I watched you.'

'You bloody watched me? And you knew the years were racing by and you did nothing to help me?'

'I'm not God.' The old boy bashed at his right ear and plucked a bit of lettuce from his left. 'You had to find your way to me.'

'Who are you?'

'Me? I'm just an old sea captain. Who I am doesn't matter.'

'I'll bet it does.'

'It don't! But you, boy. You're special.'

'I'm not special.' I shook my head. 'I'm just the same as everybody else. If there's one thing I've learned since I've been trapped in the Necronet, it's that everyone is special. Everyone. Each individual matters. We're all as special as each other. But no-one, no-one has the right to claim that they're more special than anyone else.'

'Well, you've learned something.'

'But at what bloody cost?'

'Don't give up.'

'Give up? I've been sitting here talking to you for five minutes. For all I know, another six months have passed in the real world and that bastard Barnes has fed me into a mincing machine.'

'Actually, that might well be what he has in mind.'

'Oh shit, shit, shit.'

'Now just calm yourself. We have to get you out of here and you have to put paid to Barnes.'

'I certainly do.'

'Drink up your ale.'

'What?'

'Drink your ale. It'll give you strength.'

'Good God.' I drank my ale. 'Hm,' I said, 'good ale. The last time I tasted beer as good as this was—'

'Don't even think about it. But listen here. You've learned much since you've been in here and you can use what you know to defeat Barnes. You must trap him and force the information out of him.'

'Information?'

'How to get you back into your body.'

'Go on.'

'There's only one way you can get to Barnes and that's in his dreams. If you can get yourself into his dreams, you can make him tell you what you need to know.'

'But I don't know what he dreams about. The Necronet, the mind of God, it's endless, infinite. The only people I've met here are the ones I've dreamed up myself. Apart from Arthur Thickett and he was dreaming back in the 1960s. What chance do I have of getting into one of Billy Barnes' dreams?'

'Not much,' said the old boy.

'Thanks a lot.'

'Just listen to me. Say you knew someone who knew someone who knew Billy Barnes. And you asked that someone to ask the someone they knew to ask Billy Barnes what he dreamed about, then—'

'Hold it,' I said. 'Hold it. Hold it. You are suggesting, I believe, that I engage the help of a friend of a friend.'

'That's what all this is all about, ain't it?'

'Search me,' I said.

'You find out what Billy Barnes dreams about,

and the next time he dreams about it, you're there waiting for him.'

'And what do I do when I meet up with him in his dream?'

'Torture the bastard would be my advice.'

'I do like the sound of that. But I do see a slight flaw in all this.'

'Oh, and what's that?'

'*I do not know someone who knows someone who knows frigging Billy Barnes!*'

'Yes you do.'

'No I . . . what am I saying? Of course I do.'

'Of course you do,' said the old boy. 'Only a matter of applying that digital memory of yours, wasn't it?'

By the year 2007 books were only a memory. In the great Health Purge of 2001 all printed matter, books, magazines, newspapers, anything that constituted printing on a page, was destroyed. The dwindling population of the world knew it was all for the best. The dangers of viral infection were far too great and the cost of rubber gloves too high.

Necrosoft, now the planet's single news network, kept the world informed of all that it needed to know: that everything was on the up and things were getting better. Crime was now a thing of the past. Folk never stole, for why should they? They all dressed the same in their Necrowear sports clothes, ate the same burgers at McNecro's, listened to the top ten tunes on the Necropop channel, and thought what they had learned to think. Babies in their cribs sucked upon their pleasers and just as soon as they could talk they praised the name of Billy Barnes.

Barnes himself looked upon all that he had made and found it pleasant to behold. He was off today to approve the finishing touches that had been put to the newly constructed world capital of Barnes. Millions had toiled to create this super city with its mirror-glass towers and golden cupolas. Millions drawn from around the world. The finest architects, artisans and craftsmen. Because only the very best now remained and all these worked, as all men did, for Billy Barnes alone.

'Turn right here,' ordered Billy.

His chauffeur, a gaunt and grey-faced woman who had once been an estate agent, turned the wheel between her fragile fingers, and the long long limo cruised along Barnes Plaza, bound for the palace of he the world adored.

'I'm going to take a nap,' said Billy. 'So drive slowly and when we get there don't let anyone bother me until I wake up.'

'Yes, sir,' said the chauffeur. 'Whatever pleases you.'

'I'm very pleased to be here,' said Roger Vulpes. 'But how *am* I here? How did you get me out of the hospital?'

'I thought you out,' I said. 'I need your help.'

'Bloody nice of you. Who's this old duffer?'

The old duffer let fly a gob of phlegm, but Roger nimbly ducked it.

'Captain Quinn,' said the ancient mariner.

'Quinn?' I asked.

'Captain Jonathan Quinn, whaler, adventurer and novelist.'

'*Johnny* Quinn?'

'You heard of me then, boy?'

'Of course. I read your stuff back in the Sixties.'

'You lying little twat.'

'Any chance of a beer?' asked Roger. 'I've had a rough day. Thought I'd made it out of the hospital on my feathered wings. But the further I flew, the nearer I got back to the car park. My arms are dead tired, I can tell you.'

'He's a twat too, your mate, ain't he.'

'I quite like him,' I said, and went off to get Roger a beer.

I returned to find him deep in conversation with the captain.

'Did you know,' asked Roger, as I handed him his beer, 'that Captain Quinn here was once lost off the Florida Keys in an open boat? His oars had blown over the side in a hurricane and he thought his end had come. So being the pious man he is he prayed to the Lord and—'

'A swordfish saw burst right up through the bottom of the boat.'

The old boy grinned a toothless grin. 'You liked that one, didn't you?' he said.

I sat down at the table and stared at the old boy. 'Dad?' I said. 'Are you my dad?'

The old boy winked. 'I might just be. Or I might just be telling you a tall story.'

I shook my head. 'I think I'm sick of tall stories,' I said.

'They're not always so tall as you think. Take

your mate Roger here, the stealth fox/dog/horse/human hybrid. Now *could* that really happen, I ask you?'

'Probably not,' I said.

'What do you mean, *probably not*?' Roger plucked at his ginger whiskers. 'Don't tell me I don't exist.'

'Of course you exist, boy. Everything exists. Everything exists and does not exist. Simultaneously. An old whaling pal of mine Hugo Rune used to say, "Everything that can happen will happen, and everything that can't happen will happen too, if you're prepared to wait." But he was pissed at the time and he'd lost the plot.'

'Roger,' I said, 'I have to ask you a favour. Do you think you could get yourself into your girlfriend's dreams?'

Roger pulled some more upon his whiskers. 'Whatever are you on about?' he asked.

'It's a plan to defeat Billy Barnes. A cunning plan. Here, let me whisper.'

And I whispered.

The crowd about the World Leader's car also whispered. They knew better than to cheer without permission. They waited patiently until the glossy black window slid down and the gloved hand waved out at them.

And then they cheered and cheered. And as Billy Barnes stepped from the car they cheered and cheered some more.

He looked so right, did Billy. He fitted those clothes and that car. He suited them and they suited him.

Billy waved without conviction, allowed himself to be lifted into the papal chair (a gift from the grateful Pope), and was carried by four liveried Nubians up the twenty-three gentle steps to the marble plaza before the palace.

His hand went gently wave, wave, wave. His thoughts were all his own.

Up on the plaza, foreign ambassadors, heads of state, movie stars and neophytes bowed respectfully. The papal chair descended, Billy rose and smiled and nodded all around.

A woman, naked but for shoes with six-inch heels, proffered an envelope on a silver salver. Billy took the envelope, tore it open, unfolded a letter and read it.

And then a look of fury appeared on his face, and he pushed through the adoring crowd and swept into the palace.

Naked women stood in attendance. Billy offered them not even a glance as he marched into his private office.

Rich with regal trappings, golden bits and bobs and knickery-knackery: opulence a-go-go.

A dark young woman of unsurpassed beauty and no clothes whatever looked up from her desk.

'What of this?' Billy flung down the letter. 'What of this? Tell me!'

The dark young woman gaped at the letter. Her mouth opened and stayed open.

'A letter,' said Billy. 'Someone has sent me a letter. Printed. Words upon a page. And I touched it. I didn't think. I just took the envelope and opened it and touched the paper. If I hadn't had my gloves on I might have become infected.'

'What is it?' The young woman pointed. But didn't touch. 'What does it say?'

'It says "GOTCHA!" And it's signed "The Children of the Revolution".'

'The Children of the Revolution? What revolution?'

'*What* revolution?' Billy calmed himself. 'No,' he said, 'you would not know. But incredible as it might sound, there are some people left upon this planet who do not love me.'

'No,' said the woman. 'I don't believe that.'

'Well there are. And they would like to assassinate me.'

The woman shook her head. Fiercely. Again and again.

'Stop doing that.'

The woman stopped.

'I'll weed them out,' said Billy. 'I'll find them and I'll weed them out.' He looked the woman up and down. 'You're new here, aren't you?'

The woman nodded a swirl of dark hair.

'You'd like to please me, wouldn't you?'

'Oh yes, sir, I would.'

Billy unzipped his trousers. 'Come pray to me,' he said.

'You dirty bastard!'

Billy turned at the voice. A young man in military fatigues, an Uzi automatic in his hands, stood glaring at him.

Billy hastily refastened his flies. 'Who are you?' he demanded.

'Nobody,' said the young man. 'An absolute no-body.'

'Then get the fuck out of my palace.'

'No way.' The young man shook his head. 'Your time is up, Barnes. The Children of the Revolution demand your head on a salver. We demand the right to be free. Free from your slavery.'

'Bullshit!' said Billy. 'There's no such thing as freedom. No-one is free.'

The young man shook his head once more. 'You haven't brainwashed everyone. There's still a few of us left. And you're looking at the last face you'll ever see. You're a dead man, Barnes.' The young man raised his gun.

'No, wait!' Billy raised his hands. 'No. Let's not be hasty. I'm sure we can discuss matters.'

'What is there to discuss? How you and Necro-soft turned the world's people into zombies? How millions have been downloaded into the Necronet, their bodies disposed of, their records erased? How you've risen to power, climbed to the top of the heap? A heap of human skulls.'

'Emotive talk.' Billy fluttered his fingers, then thrust his hands into his trouser pockets. 'I have done more to make this world a better place than any man before me in history. See how people smile, how happy they are.'

'You're a piece of shit, Barnes.'

The young man squeezed upon his trigger.

Two shots rang out.

The young man clutched at the twin holes in his chest, fell bleeding to the floor, and died.

Billy pulled the smoking Derringer from his

pocket and examined his punctured trouser wear.

'Look at that,' he said. 'My favourite suit ruined. It's a good job I have an identical five in the wardrobe. Get someone to haul away this rubbish and swab the floor. But not right this minute.' And Billy set once more to unzipping his fly.

'You dirty bastard, Barnes.'

'What is this, déjà vu?' Billy turned again.

The young man was on his feet. 'You can't kill freedom,' he said.

'Oh, please,' said Billy. 'Spare me the clichés. But how *did* you do that? I thought I put two bullets in your chest.'

'I'm your Nemesis, Billy. You can't kill me.'

'I'm prepared to give it a try.' Billy's hands were back in his pocket.

The young revolutionary shot Billy's left kneecap off.

Billy Barnes awoke with a start.

In the back of his limo with the crowd gathered quietly around.

The chauffeur glanced at him in the driving mirror. 'Are you all right, sir?' she asked. 'You look a little pale.'

'Just a dream,' said Billy. 'It was just a dream.'

Boastful Morgan

'I've got mushrooms in my shed,' said Boastful
  Morgan,
'That are easily the size of dustbin lids.
'And I cook them in a huge enamel saucepan.'
He told tales like that to all the local kids.

Morgan's brain was full of shipwrecks,
And whalers with harpoons,
With their odd Samoan tattoos,
And their parrots and baboons.

Morgan's ears were full of music,
And of soldiers marching by,
And the sounds of seagulls singing,
From their perches in the sky.

Morgan's eyes were full of diamonds,
And the treasures of Peru,
With the gold of Montezuma,
And the Inca riches too.

Morgan's mouth was full of stories,
Of the many lands he'd seen,
Of the fabled Cyclopeans,
And of Dublin in the green.

'I've got spiders in my loft,' said Boastful Morgan,
'With legs as thick as any fellow's arm,
'I play to them upon my Hammond organ,
'But I'm moving soon to live upon a farm.'

22

You can't be rational about life.

DORIS LESSING

'What happened there?'

'You fucked up,' said Roger.

'*I* fucked up? What do you mean *I* fucked up?'

'You shot him in the kneecap, so he woke up.'

'It was your idea to shoot him in the kneecap, not mine.'

'Look,' said Roger, 'I did my stuff, right? I got into my girlfriend's dream. My poor fiancée's dream, and I asked her what Barnes the bastard dreams about. And she said that he'd told her he always dreams about his glorious palace that's staffed by naked women. She described it to me. I described it to you. He dreamed it and you were waiting for him. It was a great plan.'

'But it didn't work.'

'Just because it didn't work doesn't mean it wasn't a great plan.'

'But if he's going to wake up every time I shoot him, I'll never be able to force him to put me back in my body.'

'There are some small holes in this great plan,' said Roger. 'We will just have to try again.'

That very night Billy Barnes dreamed once more about his palace. This time two revolutionaries threw a sack over his head and belaboured him with stout sticks.

Billy Barnes woke up with a start.

The next night Billy had his palace dream again. On this occasion, one of his naked female staff (who was really a revolutionary in a rubber skin suit) slipped a narcotic into Billy's champagne. Billy passed out and found himself dreaming that he was in his palace where a revolutionary grabbed him and threw a sack over his head and—

Billy Barnes woke up with a start from both dreams.

On the third night Billy Barnes did not dream about his palace.

'I don't think he's coming,' said Roger.

'Nor me,' I said.

'So what shall we do?'

I cast an eye over the naked female staff.

'Well . . .'

On the fourth night Roger said, 'The game's up.'

'What?'

'You've been rumbled.'

'What?'

'I've just come from my fiancée's latest dream. She says that Billy's spent the last two days going through computer files. He's matched your face to the revolutionary in his dreams. He knows who you are.'

'He should have recognized me straight away. He's got my body in a suitcase under his bed.'

'Apparently it's not *that* recognizable,' said Roger.

'Oh my God!'

'But you're rumbled. And apparently he's taking steps.'

'What steps?'

'Quite big ones, according to my fiancée. For one thing, he's called on the services of some old bloke to teach him lucid dreaming.'

'Uncle Brian,' I said. 'I'll bet it's my own Uncle Brian.'

'I finally off-loaded my consignment of right-handed rubber gloves onto a bloke called Brian, you don't suppose—'

'I do. But go on, you said, "For *one* thing . . ." '

'Oh yeah. For another thing he's going to delete your file. Erase you from the Necronet.'

'He'll have to catch me first.'

'Apparently not. It's some new software develop-ment, linked to DNA. From the DNA in your body they get what is called a "signature". It's quite unique, well DNA is, isn't it? They feed this signa-ture into the mother computer and it will be able to trace your whereabouts in the Necronet. And once they've located you, then zap, they press the erase button.'

'Shit!' I said. 'Shit, shit, shit.'

'Difficult times for you,' said Roger. 'Wish there was something I could do to help.'

'Don't worry, I'll find something.'

'Look,' said Roger. 'I'm doing my best. I want this Barnes as much as you do. Oh, there was one other thing my fiancée said.'

'Go on.'

'She said that once you've been located, Billy Barnes is intending temporarily to download himself, come in here and give you a serious kicking.'

'Oh bloody hell.'

'Very vindictive chap, Barnes. Very sadistic. Likes to take care of the serious kicking side of business himself whenever possible.'

'*Shit!*'

'I think you already said shit.'

'Then damn, too. I'm done for. What am I going to do?'

'I don't know the answer to that. But there was one more thing. I hadn't quite finished.'

'There's more?'

'Just a wee bit more. After Necrosoft have located you and the downloaded Billy has given you a serious kicking, they're going to upload you back into your body again.'

'But that's what I want. That's perfect.'

Roger shook his head.

'You're shaking your head,' I said.

'I am, I'm afraid. My fiancée said that Billy intends to make "an example" of you. Something along the lines of a public execution, William Wallace style. Hanging, drawing, disembowelling—'

'SHIT!'

'Shirt,' said Billy, and a nameless woman helped him into it. She was nameless, she was naked, for that's the way Billy liked his staff to be. 'It's strange,' he said to his chauffeur; she was dressed, as Billy found her bruises unappealing in the morning. 'It's strange the way things go. Some might say that my sins have returned to haunt me. I would say that I merely have a bit of unfinished business elsewhere.'

The chauffeur nodded. But she didn't speak.

'The last loose end,' said Billy. 'The last little fly in the ointment. The manner of his death, broadcast live worldwide, should make a point to those few non-conformists that remain. You know, I find it incredible to believe that there can still be some ungrateful scum left on this planet who do not love me. Imagine that. Can you imagine that?'

'I can imagine that,' said the chauffeur. 'If you want me to, I can imagine that.'

'Of course you can. But don't. I forbid you to imagine it. Such thoughts would be far too distress-ful for you. *Underpants!*'

A naked woman knelt to put on the royal Y-fronts.

Billy smiled. 'And while you're down there . . .' he said.

'Blow him up?' said Roger. 'How are you going to blow him up?'

'Well,' I said. 'I've been in the Necronet long enough to know how things work. He'll be a stranger here after all. When he comes to give me the kicking, I *could* blow him up. Nuke him. Blast him to atoms. I could, surely.'

'Wouldn't work,' said Roger. 'He won't just walk

into a trap. He's clever, this Barnes. Cleverer than you.'

'He's not *that* clever.'

'He bloody is.'

'Not!'

'Is!'

'Not!'

Hugo Rune, who is extremely clever, once said that if you turn America on its side, everything that's not screwed down rolls to California. It is thought that he nicked the line from Frank Lloyd Wright, whose views on America are widely recorded.

But the point is well made and the World Headquarters of Necrosoft now occupied fifty acres of land just outside San Francisco. The birthplace of Henry Doors.

Henry was there to greet Billy Barnes and his chauffeur. The chauffeur was dragging a suitcase with airholes in the top.

They all went up to the downloading suite in a very swish glass elevator.

'I would strongly advise against this,' said Henry.

'Why?' Billy asked.

'Because you put yourself at personal risk.'

'No,' said Billy. 'At no risk whatsoever. A virtual facsimile of myself enters a virtual world. No harm can come to the real me out here.'

'Your adversary has been in the Necronet for ten years. He might have developed a trick or two.'

'Indeed,' said Billy. 'He will no doubt try to blow me up. That's what I'd do if I were him.'

'If it's that kind of foolishness,' said Henry Doors, 'then you certainly have no need to worry.'

'I am not worried.' Billy smiled. 'In fact I confess to a thrill of anticipation. I'd quite forgotten what it feels like to be opposed. For someone to say no instead of yes. And it will be great fun to experience the Necronet first-hand. And greater fun to administer the kicking. And even greater fun to supervise the execution when I've returned and uploaded him.'

Henry Doors now smiled. 'So thorough in your work,' he said. 'Always the consummate professional.'

'Thank you,' said Billy. 'I do my best to please.'

The downloading suite was all-over black. Black and macho and miniaturized. It's a male thing, black, when it comes to matters electrical. Your white goods are for women, dishwashers, tumble-dryers, fridges, freezers, toasters, steam-irons, all that kind of business. But black is toys-for-boys. CD players, mobile phones, TVs and videos. Check it out next time you're in a store. And have you ever asked yourself why it is that all the telephone answering machines which have little voices that say things like 'You have six calls' have *women's* voices, rather than men's? Yet the speaking clock is now a man? Something to do with subservience and authority? Hm?

Henry Doors looked upon all that he had made and found it pleasing. There were a number of leather couches (black). 'Settle yourself down on one of those,' said Henry. 'And have your chauffeur dump what's left of your adversary onto another. I'll link you both up to the mother computer and set the controls for fifteen minutes. Time moves differently in there, but I want you out again in fifteen minutes real time.'

Billy grinned that grin of his and settled himself onto a couch. A male technician helped him on with a sleek black headset.

On the couch next to Billy's, his chauffeur struggled to position the living remains of something scarcely human. A second technician placed a similar headset over the twisted tortured face.

Henry Doors seated himself before a control panel of a night-time hue, touched panels and engaged circuitry. 'All set, Billy?' he asked.

'All set,' came a muffled reply from beneath the headset.

'Subject's whereabouts have been located. I shall beam you down, as it were.'

'Beam me up, Scotty,' said Roger.

'What is your problem?' I asked.

'Only the small matter of what we're doing up here.'

'It's a rooftop,' I said. 'For the final rooftop confrontation.'

'Why a rooftop, for pity's sake? Why not a fortress or the middle of a minefield, or something?'

'Because Lazlo Woodbine always bested the villain on a rooftop. He worked just the four locations. His office where his clients came, the bar where he talked a load of old toot, the alley where he got into sticky situations, and the rooftop where he had the final confrontation. In one hundred and

310

fifty-eight thrilling adventures Woodbine never deviated from this award-winning format.'

'But I thought you'd agreed that you were crap at playing Woodbine.'

'I was. But if I have to have a final confrontation with Billy Barnes, this is where I'm going to have it.'

Roger shook his head. 'The trench coat suits you,' he said.

'Thanks, I appreciate that. Now, you've done everything I asked you to do, haven't you? The plan is in place?'

'It is a good plan,' said Roger. 'I will admit that it is a good plan. If it works, of course.'

'It *will* work,' I said, in a tone designed to inspire great confidence.

'You don't sound very convinced,' said Roger.

'Oh.'

'So shall I just sort of mooch off somewhere until you're finished?'

'I think that would probably be for the best. I'll give you a shout if I need you.'

'And I'll come running up with the big gun then, shall I?'

'The General Electric mini-gun, yes.'

'Like the one Blaine used in *Predator*?'

'It's a blinder of a gun, you have to confess.'

Roger nodded. 'I'll leave you to it then,' he said. We shook hands.

'I'll get us out,' I said. 'Don't worry.'

'No,' Roger smiled, 'you just get yourself out. I can't go anywhere, I have no body to go back to. Billy Barnes killed me and dumped me in the river. I have to stay here for ever. But I can be with my fiancée now when she dreams. You've given me that. I'm grateful.'

We shook hands again and Roger walked away.

I took a deep breath, adjusted the brim of my fedora just so, and patted the bulge in my trench coat. The bulge of the trusty Smith and Wesson.

'OK, you bastard!' I shouted at the white sky overhead. 'I'm waiting for you. Come and get me, Barnes, you piece of sh—'

Whatever hit me, hit me like a train.

I didn't see it coming, but I felt it arrive.

I flew back across the rooftop, struck one of those ventilator chimney things with the revolving tops that always look so good in Ridley Scott movies, and came to rest inverted and confused.

'What hit me? Who? Where?'

'Here,' came the voice of Billy Barnes, and my left kneecap took a whacking.

'Here!' and my right knee evened the pain in a most alarming fashion.

'I can't see you, you coward,' I cried (real tears). 'Where are you? Come out and fight like a man.'

'Get real, please.'

I was hauled to my feet by the invisible force and flung once more across the rooftop.

'Better call for the mini-gun,' said Billy. 'Because the predator's here.'

I opened my mouth to do just that and received a kick in the teeth. As Billy turned my face to the rooftop and began to grind it back and forwards, I felt that now might well be the time to engage my digital memory and re-run the closing moments of *Predator*.

And this I did.

The sky clouded over and the rain came down in bathtubs.

Billy lurched up as the electrical circuitry of the alien's invisibility suit began to pop and fizzle. I rolled away to watch his materialization.

Billy appeared and stumbled around in the rain, tearing off bits of smouldering costume and flinging them aside. I thought myself unscathed and re-invigorated, dreamed up an umbrella, climbed to my feet and stood under it.

'Good suit,' I called to Billy. 'I'm impressed that you made it work. I couldn't get a car to go in here. Never learned how the internal combustion engine functioned.'

'That's because you're a twat,' said Billy, now standing, well dressed in a sharp black suit beneath an umbrella that was bigger than mine. 'You are simply not as clever as me.'

'Look out behind you,' I said.

'Don't be absurd!'

I stepped out of the path of the charging rhinoceros. Billy, however, did not.

I thought away the rain and took a stroll over to view the damage. 'You've got a big footprint on your head,' I said.

And then I went, 'Aaaaaaagh!' as the grand piano fell on me.

'Childish, I know,' said Billy, smiling down. 'But after the banana skin, the falling grand piano is the number one cartoon classic.'

And then Billy slipped on the banana skin. And I stuffed the big red stick of dynamite down his trousers.

'You forgot this one,' I said, as I ran for cover.

The explosion was really quite impressive. Colourful it was, with the word BOOM in 3D lettering.

Billy staggered up, his face black and his clothes in tatters.

'Most amusing,' he said. 'But we have somewhat wandered away from the target. I have come here to give you a severe kicking before uploading you into your body for public execution, and I don't have time to waste.'

'Watch out for the falling safe,' I said.

Billy side-stepped it and it plunged through the rooftop.

'No,' said Billy, waggling a finger. 'No, no, no.'

'No?' I said.

'No.' Billy plucked from the pocket of his born-again sharp suit a small black toys-for-boys-type contrivance. 'I brought this,' he said.

'Mobile phone?' I asked.

'Remote control,' said Billy. 'Digital memory eraser.'

Click went the button.

'Oh, shit,' I said.

Billy grinned. 'Go on then,' he said. 'Dream up another safe. Impress me.'

I knitted my brow and thought very hard. I squinted at Billy, and then at the sky. But the big weight with 15 TONS printed on it failed to materialize.

'Fucked,' said Billy. 'You're fucked, matey.'

'Come on, Billy,' I said. 'Let's talk about this.' I raised a calming hand. Well, tried to raise one, but

I couldn't. I gaped down in horror at myself. My feet were now encased in concrete and I was all trussed in a straitjacket.

'Now,' said Billy. 'What shall it be? Power drill in the eyeballs? Red hot poker up the jacksy?'

'No, Billy, no, I . . . umph!' The gaffer tape that suddenly smothered my mouth stifled all further conversation.

'Electric cattle prod,' said Billy, thinking one into his hand. 'Necrosoft used to produce these for the police as part of the urban pacification programme. No longer necessary now, of course, no need for such crude measures.'

'Grmph, mmph,' I said, meaning, 'Please have mercy.'

'What was that you said? "Please stick it down my throat"? OK then, if that's what you fancy.'

Billy advanced upon me.

I couldn't scream. I couldn't move. Something cold and steely clamped my head. He faced me, eye to eye. 'You can't stop me,' he whispered. 'I cannot be stopped.'

And then he tore the gaffer tape away and raised the cattle prod.

'No Billy, don't.'

My eyes were shut and I never saw her appear. I heard her voice and when I looked, there she was.

Billy no longer held the prod to my face. He had dropped it on the rooftop. He stood and stared at her too.

Because she was truly something to stare at.

She must have been more than seven feet in height. Willow slim and ebony black. Her cheekbones seemed carved, her slanted eyes showing only the whites. Her mouth was broad, the lips full and passionate. Her hair was arranged in complicated coils that rose to spires and seemed to vanish into air. Of the clothes that covered her slender frame I had an impression of colour but not of fabric. Darting colours that weaved and moved and flowed and drifted. Her right hand weighed heavy with golden rings.

In her left she held a handbag.

'Maîtresse,' Billy whispered. 'Maîtresse Ezilée.'

'I am displeased with you,' said the goddess.

'No,' said Billy. 'I've not displeased you. I have kept the faith, maintained the vigil. Venerated the icon.'

'My bag?' Maîtresse Ezilée raised the handbag. I saw the skulls and I saw again Golgotha. The thousand million bones of the angry dead. 'You have brought torment to the mind of God,' said Maîtresse Elizée. 'You have brought torment to the world of men. You must be punished for your sins.'

'No,' said Billy. 'You'll not punish me. I serve one who is greater than you. I serve Ogoun Badagris.'

Now I remembered this name, and I did so without the aid of my digital memory. Billy's mother had mentioned this name when she'd spoken to me in my shed of the voodoo pantheon. There was Damballo Oueddo, the wisest and most powerful, whose symbol is the serpent; Agoué, god of the sea; Loco, god of the forest; and Maîtresse Ezilée, incarnation of the Blessed Virgin Mary.

And there was Ogoun Badagris, the dreadful and bloody one.

An ideal choice for Billy, I supposed.

'Ogoun Badagris walks the earth,' said Billy. 'His time is now.'

'*Our* time is always now,' said Maîtresse Ezilée.

'*Our* time?'

'Our time, Billy.' And the goddess opened her handbag.

And they stepped out.

Grew into form.

The gods. A pair of gods.

'Agoué, god of the sea.' And I looked and it was the old boy. The ancient mariner. And it was my father. It really was.

'Loco, god of the forest.' It was Roger Vulpes. Stealth fox/dog/ horse/human hybrid. A god of the forest, indeed.

'And Damballo Oueddo?' asked Billy. 'Where is he?'

'He is all around you, Billy. You are inside the mind of the great one, Damballo Oueddo.'

'A mind now addled,' Billy said. 'Ogoun told me how we should inflict the jabbering masses upon Damballo. Possess his mind and drive him insane.'

Maîtresse Ezilée laughed. 'You fool Billy. Damballo gathers all souls to himself. Here in this world of thought. This world of dreams and inspiration from whence spring all ideas we choose to offer mankind.'

Maîtresse Ezilée turned to me. 'Arthur Thickett told you all about this, didn't he?' she said.

'Yes, I, er, yes. He said that he thought the gods reincarnate. Renew themselves and choose new locations for their renewal.'

'As is written,' said Maîtresse Ezilée. 'The cycles of the gods are shown in the symbol of the serpent with its tail in its mouth.'

'And so Ogoun is—'

'He is Satan. Shaitan. Ebilis. Lucifer. Billy knows him as Henry Doors, god of the new religion: science.'

'I've never got on much with computers,' I said.

'Enough,' said Billy. 'I'm not interested. I shall be out of here in a minute. And when I go I'm taking this twat with me. And you lot, you can go on dreaming. No-one worships you any more. You're yesterday's news.'

'If I might just have a word,' said Agoué.

'Hi, Dad,' I said.

'Hi, son,' said my dad. 'Now, Billy,' he continued, 'I know you're going to be leaving us in . . .' My dad looked at his watch. It was a Rolex. I used to have a watch like that. An image thing, I don't want to dwell on it. Well, actually perhaps I do. I never really had a Rolex at all. I just make this stuff up. I can't help it. I don't know why I do it, but I do. It's the tall-story thing, I know it is. '. . . about thirty seconds. But as Henry Doors told you and my son has learned to his cost, time moves differently here. Usually much faster, but we have the power to shift it about somewhat. We can make your last ten seconds an eternity in hell.'

'You can,' said Billy. 'But remember, I know the secret.'

'What secret?'

'The secret of the voodoo handbag.'

'What secret is that?' I asked.

'That it is the *transitus tessera*, the ticket of passage. That it allows beings to move from one world to the next.'

'I knew that,' I said. 'Your mum told me.'

'But she didn't tell you that the beings were the gods. That it's the only way by which they can physically enter the world of men. Men can meet the gods in dreams and visions, and receive the ideas and prophecies they are offered. But the voodoo handbag is the portal by which the gods can enter the physical world of men. The Virgin Mary never gave birth, she merely opened her handbag.'

'But what about the skulls, all those demonic skulls?'

'Guardians,' said Billy, 'to prevent men reaching this world, the world of the gods. Ogoun Badagris chooses who will guard and places them on the bag. He'll choose you, I think, once I have done with you.'

'Off to hell with this shitbag,' I said.

'It's a fair cop,' said Billy. 'But let me say one more thing before you despatch me.'

'What is that?' asked Maîtresse Ezilée.

'Time's up,' said Billy.

And he vanished, just like that.

Black Projections

He cursed the black projections as they grew,
He knew it wasn't quite the thing to do.
But the natives from the town
Turned their backs upon his gown
That he'd won off some old Hindustan guru.

He cursed the black projections that he found,
He ripped them off and flung them to the ground.
But the natives played at jacks,
With their hands behind their backs,
And sold little bags of white stuff by the pound.

He cursed the black projections on his arm,
When he saw them there he cried out in alarm.
But the natives turned away,
They were not inclined to stay,
And they went and got new jobs upon the farm.

And when the black projections had control,
He found it very difficult to bowl.
But the natives in the slips,
Stood with hands upon their hips,
And dined on cottage tea and Dover sole.

I thank you.

23

Everything has to be somewhere and nothing
can ever be anywhere other than where it is.

HUGO RUNE

The doctor said I was a paranoid schizophrenic.

Well, he didn't actually say it. But we knew he
was thinking it.

'Tell me about the Necronet,' the doctor said.

'It's a paradise. A world of bliss,' I said.

'A world of bliss?' The doctor viewed me through
his bifocals. I had never worn glasses like those. An
image thing. I'm very conscious of my image.

'A world of bliss?' The doctor consulted his
notes. 'And yet in previous interviews you have
railed against it, claiming there were beings inside
who are out to get us.'

'There are beings inside. But they are benign. It's
a paradise, a world of bliss. I have to make a phone
call, please release me.'

'Early days for that,' said the doctor. 'Early days.'

'You have to let me make that phone call.'

'Urgent matter, is it?'

'Very urgent, yes.'

'Sorry, no can do. I know that the condemned

man is entitled to a hearty breakfast and all that. But you refused your breakfast, didn't you?'

'I'm not hungry. But I must make a call. You don't realize what you're doing. You don't. You really don't.'

'My role is quite clear,' said the doctor. 'You are a revolutionary. You are condemned to public execution. It will be broadcast live all over the world. My job is to record your final statement and try to assess your mental state. You're quite a prize, you know. Mental illness is very much a thing of the past.'

'Because mental patients are a thing of the past.'

'What was that you said?'

'Nothing. I said nothing. The phone call. Please let me make it.'

'I don't think so,' said the doctor. 'Let's return to the Necronet.'

'I've said enough to you about that. Get me out of this straitjacket, let me free, you bastard.'

'Easy now,' said the doctor. 'Don't upset yourself.'

'You'll get it,' I said. 'When I get out of here, you'll get it. I'll make you pay. You'll suffer. You'll burn.'

'I don't think the tablets are helping,' said the doctor. 'Your rage is as pronounced as ever.'

'Call Henry Doors, make the call for me.'

'Now, Henry Doors.' The doctor consulted his notes. 'This name's come up before. You say he is the mind behind Necrosoft, is that right?'

I nodded.

'Yet there is no record of such an individual. People seem to recall the name. But the more they try to remember, the more they become convinced that they can't. Henry Doors seems more like some urban myth. How do you account for that?'

'He stays in the background. That's what he does best. He's a god. A god who walks upon the earth. Henry Doors is Ogoun Badagris.'

'Ah, yes,' and the doctor flicked through further notes. 'One of this pantheon of gods you say inhabit the Necronet. Something to do with this handbag you keep talking about. This voodoo handbag. Now this was when you were in your Lazlo Woodbine persona, wasn't it?'

'I was never Lazlo Woodbine. I'm *not* Lazlo Woodbine.'

'Ah, sorry. You're someone else now, are you? Who might that be?' More note-turning. 'Carlos the Chaos Cockroach, is it? Or Barry the Talking Sprout?'

'You know who I am! You know who I am!'

'Let's have a look.' The doctor closed his case-note folder. 'But I don't need to look, do I? Because you shout it out again and again. All night and all day. You shout it out. And what do you shout?'

'*I am Billy Barnes!*' I shouted.

'That's right, "I am Billy Barnes." And yet when I look at you, when I look at this raddled wreck, with its missing limbs and its gnawed-away features, I say to myself, this is definitely *not* Billy Barnes. I saw Billy Barnes on the television only this morning being interviewed about the forthcoming execution. Your execution. Sir, you are *not* Billy Barnes.'

'But I *am*!' I shouted. 'He tricked me. He tricked me.'

'This other self of yours? This Lazlo Woodbine person?'

'Him and Roger Vulpes.'

'Ah yes, Roger Vulpes, the stealth fox/dog/horse/human hybrid who is also a god. He was in on this conspiracy too, was he?'

'You don't understand,' I said. 'Let me explain.'

'Go on then,' said the doctor. 'Explain to me once more. But this must be the very last time. Your execution is scheduled for noon today.'

'All right, let me speak. Let me tell you how he tricked me.'

'Go on then, but hurry it up.'

'All right. Firstly, you must understand that I *am* Billy Barnes. Inside, me, in this head. This body is *not* mine. It's the body of the revolutionary, my adversary, a man whose memories and personality I downloaded into the Necronet ten years ago. He tried to escape. He discovered that the Necronet occupies the same space as the dream world. He entered my dreams, tried to get at me. But I woke up each time, he couldn't touch me.'

'So you entered the Necronet yourself to get him, is that right?'

'That's right. That's what I did. To give him a serious kicking before I uploaded him back into his body for execution.'

'I follow this up to a point,' said the doctor. 'But I can't follow how you say that you, that is, your personality, memories whatever, the you that is Billy Barnes, is now inside the body I see before me.'

'He tricked me, I told you. I underestimated him. He pulled it off in the least most obvious of all least most obvious ways. He never really meant to get me in my dreams, it was all a trick. All a trick so that I would enter the Necronet and walk right into a trap.'

'I don't understand the nature of this trap. This was a trap inside the Necronet.'

'No, it was out here. The least most obvious place for it to be. He had Roger Vulpes contact his fiancée in her dreams. She always dreamed of him, so that part was easy.'

'And Roger Vulpes' fiancée was whom?'

'My chauffeur.'

'Carry on.'

'Roger Vulpes spoke to her in her dreams. And while she was asleep he had her take off her gloves. She couldn't have done that while she was awake, she didn't have my permission.'

'Ah yes,' said the doctor. 'These were the special gloves you'd made for her, the ones with the pleaser linings.'

'Exactly. I never noticed that she'd taken them off. I never noticed.'

'So what did she do?'

'At the downloading suite in the Necrosoft Head-quarters. After I'd been downloaded into the Necronet, she switched the headsets. Mine and this bastard whose body I'm now in. She switched them. When Henry Doors uploaded us, he uploaded me into this body and him into mine.'

'Very cunning,' said the doctor. 'Very clever plan.'

'Just let me make the phone call. Let me call

Henry Doors, he'll know when I tell him, when I speak to him, he'll know it's me.'

'The number you gave us has been disconnected,' said the doctor. 'This Henry Doors of yours seems to have gone to ground, as it were.'

'Let me free, you bastard! Let me free!'

'I think that's enough,' said the doctor. 'You are clearly in a delusional state. We'd best get you some medication to calm you down.'

'No! Don't do that! No!'

The doctor reached for the little button on his desk and pushed it. The office door opened and a large male nurse stood looming.

'Nurse Cecil,' said the doctor. 'Please take Mr, well, Mr Whomever-he-thinks-he-is-today back to his room, and—'

'Administer the medication, sir?'

'Administer the medication, yes.'

'No! No! No! No! No!'

'Shall I use the large needle, sir?'

'The very large one, nurse, yes please.'

I was hauled from the office and out into the corridor, booted along it and back into my room.

Well, I say *my* room.

But of course *I* wasn't *me* any more, was I?

The body might have once been mine.

But the mind that now dwelt within it was not.

It was the mind of Billy Barnes.

And so I gave him a kicking before I administered the medication.

Well, I say *I*.

I mean of course Nurse Cecil.

Except that Nurse Cecil's memory and personality had been temporarily downloaded into the Necronet and mine had been temporarily relocated inside his head. Well, you wouldn't begrudge me that extra little bit of triumph, would you?

'Here, shithead,' I said to Billy Barnes. 'You'll never guess what I intend to do with this electric cattle prod.'

WAKE UP, CHIEF!

'Oh, Barry, thanks, did I doze off again?'

'You did, chief, you were dreaming you were Billy Barnes.'

'Was that a nice dream, Barry, or a nightmare?'

'Probably a nice dream, chief, considering how things really worked out.'

'They didn't work out too well then?'

'Not too well.'

'But I can't remember what happened. I'm all confused, things just keep going round in circles again and again and again.'

'Like a serpent with its tail in its mouth, chief.'

'Just like that, Barry. Why is it so dark in here?'

'The cupboard door's locked.'

'Which cupboard's that?'

'The one where Billy keeps the voodoo handbag.'

'What voodoo handbag?'

'The one in the story.'

'What story?'

'The one that we're in.'

'And who are we?'

'We're skulls on the voodoo handbag, chief.'

'What voodoo handbag?'

'The one in the story.'

'What story?'

'The one that we're in.'

'And who are we?'

'We're skulls on a voodoo handbag.'

'What voodoo handbag?'

'The one in the story.'
'What story?'
'The one that we're in.'
'And who are we?'
'We're—'

WAKE UP, CHIEF!

'Oh, Barry, thanks. Did I doze off again?'

'You did, chief. And you mustn't do that. Not in your important role as World Leader.'

'Oh, yes. We pulled it off, didn't we? And you helped, I know you helped.'

'I might have slipped the occasional bit of inspiration in here and there, chief, made the lady chauffeur doze off at the appropriate moment so Roger could get your message to her, things of that nature.'

'You're a good lad, Barry. A regular Holy Guardian.'

'I aim to please, chief, I aim to please. Although sometimes I wonder.'

'Wonder what, Barry?'

'Wonder what we all sometimes wonder, I suppose, chief—'

WHETHER I'M DREAMING YOU,

OR YOU'RE DREAMING
ME.

NECROSOFT WORLDWIDE NEWSFLASH

In an act of supreme mercy and humanitarianism, World Leader Billy Barnes ordered an eleventh-hour stay of execution for the revolutionary variously known as Lazlo Woodbine, Carlos the Chaos Cockroach et al. The World Leader said that he had no wish to take the life of a being so sadly deluded and utterly harmless. The death penalty would never again be used, he said. And the revolutionary would receive treatment at a secure institution.

In a move that stunned the world, Mr Barnes also chose this moment to announce that he is stepping down from office. In future, he said, democratically elected representatives of the people will rule in his place.

He also announced that, as of today, Necrosoft Industries would cease trading.

The world awaits further news.

'Nice one, chief.'
'Thanks, Barry.'